Return to Paradise

Other books by Barbara Cameron

The Quilts of Lancaster County Series

A Time to Love
A Time to Heal
A Time for Peace
Annie's Christmas Wish

The Stitches in Time Series

Her Restless Heart
The Heart's Journey
Heart in Hand

The Quilts of Love Series

Scraps of Evidence

The Amish Road Series

A Road Unknown
Crossroads
One True Path

Twice Blessed: Two Amish Christmas Stories

Barbara Cameron

Abingdon Press
Nashville

Return to Paradise

Macro Editor: Teri Wilhelms

Published in association with Books & Such Literary Agency

Library of Congress Cataloging-in-Publication Data has been requested.

ISBN: 978-1-4267-7088-3

Manufactured in the United States of America

1 2 3 4 5 6 7 8 9 10 / 20 19 18 17 16

For Monica

For cheering me on. Wishing you bestsellerdom!

A Note to the Reader

What does home mean to you? Family? The place you live?

I began thinking about this in the last year or so after losing two members of my birth family within a few months of each other. It became more important to me to be physically closer to my grown children, so with the help of friends, I sold my home of twelve years in a small town and moved to a big city about an hour and a half farther north where I would be closer to my daughter and her little son.

While my little yellow house hadn't been my dream home, it had become a nice, quiet sanctuary for me, and a place to own and also foster a number of dogs. I didn't realize how wrenching it would be to leave it, even though we found a small house that was brighter and located just fifteen minutes from my daughter.

Jennifer, a woman who had started as someone helping me organize and take care of my home, became a good friend and she got me through alternating and unexpected bouts of crying as we packed. I veered between happiness when the house sold quickly—and anxiety about the process of leaving my safe little area and venturing into a big city. I am really a small town girl who doesn't like big cities much.

But life is all about change and growth. I started thinking about what would happen if a young man who's always only known his Amish community but struggled with a difficult father would do if he left that community . . . and then found he needed to return.

How would the woman he left behind feel about his return and his desire to rekindle their relationship?

I proposed the idea of an Amish series called Coming Home to my editor, Ramona Richards, and want to thank her for her enthusiasm for the project. Abingdon Press has been the home for my Amish books for a long time, and I appreciate everything Ramona and everyone at the company does to bring my work to readers.

I also want to thank my daughter, Stephany, and her son, Kasey, for finding me this home. They called me on her cell phone with the speaker on to tell me they had found this development which, I could hear him piping up, "has lots and lots of flowers . . . and bushes!" He sounded just like one of the hosts on the HGTV network shows he likes to watch with his mother.

Now I sit happily in a home office with a stencil on the wall behind me that says, "Home is where your story begins."

Of course, my biggest thanks goes to God for giving me life and helping me to tell stories of hope and faith and love.

1

"You're sighing again."

Lavina looked up from the baby quilt she was sewing and stared at Mary Elizabeth, her *schweschder*. "What?"

"You're sighing."

"I am not."

"You are," Rose Anna, her youngest *schweschder*, said quietly. "Ever since we sat down to sew." Her blue eyes were kind. "What are you thinking about?"

"Who," said Mary Elizabeth. "A better question is *who* is she thinking about?"

"I'm not thinking about anyone."

Both her *schweschders* frowned at her. Lavina was twenty-three, the oldest of the three, but the way they looked at her she felt as if she were a *kind*. The three of them were barely a year apart and looked so alike with their blonde hair, blue eyes, and petite figures they could have passed for triplets.

"Maybe I'm just tired." Lavina set the quilt aside, got up and walked over to look out the window. Leaves the color of gold, red, and orange danced in the wind, heralding autumn. It used to be her favorite season. The long, hot summer and all the work of harvest, canning, and preserving was over.

But weddings were taking place now. This time last year she'd thought she and David were getting married . . .

"She's doing it again," she heard Rose Anna whisper behind her.

"Tea," Lavina said, and she turned and gave them a bright smile. "Anyone want a cup of tea?"

"*Schur.*"

She walked into the kitchen, filled the teakettle, and put it on the stove. Her glance went to the calendar on the wall. She looked away at how many weddings were noted for the month.

This time last year she'd been planning on marrying David Stoltzfus and making a home for them.

Sinking into a chair at the table, she cupped her chin in her hands and waited for the water to come to a boil.

"Lavina?"

She looked up. "Hmm?"

"I've always found that if you want the water to boil you have to turn the gas on under the kettle." Mary Elizabeth demonstrated by turning the dial. Her mouth quirked in a smile.

"Oh, *ya*. Silly me."

Mary Elizabeth pulled out the chair next to Lavina and sat. "I'm worried about you."

"I'm fine. I was just thinking about something and forgot to turn it on."

"You're sad."

Lavina did her best not to sigh. "*Ya*. I'm sad. I'll get over it."

She racked her brain for something to talk about, a way to change the subject. Mary Elizabeth wasn't shy about pressing an issue when she wanted to.

"I think I'll have a cookie. Want one? *Mamm* made some chocolate chip."

"*Schur*. But— "

"Are you going into town with me to Leah's tomorrow?"

"Maybe next time. *Mamm* and I are going over to Waneta's house. Listen—"

"Leah's going to be happy I'm bringing her orders in a little early."

"I know."

"I think she's going to be really happy with that Sunshine and Shadow quilt you made."

Mary Elizabeth shrugged. "I like that pattern. And the tourists like the old traditional Amish patterns."

"Well, you did a great job on it."

"If I have time I want to do a Broken Star pattern before Christmas."

Lavina brought the cookie jar to the table and tried to hide her smile. Finally she'd distracted her *schweschder* from worrying about her.

They talked about quilt patterns for a few minutes and then the teakettle shrieked.

Mary Elizabeth got up to turn the gas off. She filled two cups and sat again.

"I should get tea for Rose Anna."

"She can come get it if she wants." Mary Elizabeth handed her a tea bag and then chose one for herself from the bowl on the table.

Lavina listlessly dunked the tea bag over and over in the cup until Mary Elizabeth took it from her and set it the saucer. "Go ahead," Lavina said. "Tell me I have to get over him."

"I'm not going to tell you that."

Lavina looked up. "You're not?"

"*Nee*. You love David and time apart isn't making you forget about him."

"He made his decision. And he didn't ask me to leave Paradise with him."

"Did you ask him?"

Shocked, Lavina stared at her *schwesder*. "You know I didn't! I couldn't!"

"You could have. You chose not to."

"I couldn't."

A windstorm of emotions swirled up inside her. Lavina rose, paced the kitchen. "I couldn't make that choice. You know I'd have been shunned. I joined the church. But David hadn't."

"I wonder—" Mary Elizabeth stopped, then took a deep breath. "Lavina, would you have been as miserable as you've been since David left? You'd have been with him."

"Well, that's blunt."

"*Ya,* you know I say what I think."

"There's just one thing you're forgetting. David didn't ask me to marry him. He didn't ask me to go with him."

"I know." Mary Elizabeth fell silent for a long moment. "I do understand what you're feeling. Only a few months after David left his *bruder* Samuel went with him and took part of my heart."

Lavina reached out her and touched Mary Elizabeth's. "I know."

Rose Anna wandered into the room. "I thought you were going to fix tea. You're having it without me." She put her hands on her hips and pouted.

Mary Elizabeth stood and poured another cup of hot water. "It's my fault. I was talking to her. We weren't trying to make you feel left out."

Rose Anna sniffed but took a seat to the right of Lavina. "What were you talking about?"

Lavina started to say it was nothing, but knowing how Rose Anna, the youngest, was acting, she figured it would just make her feel even more left out.

"Mary Elizabeth feels I should have gone with David when he left the community."

Rose Anna's face took on a dreamy expression. "That would have been so romantic."

"He didn't ask her to go with him," Mary Elizabeth said. "Remember?"

Lavina's heart sank. She felt sandwiched in by Blunt *Schweschder* on one side and Hopeless Romantic *Schweschder* on the other.

Could the three of them be any more different?

"It was bad enough he left," Rose Anna complained. "But he didn't have to take his *bruders* with him. I really cared about John . . ." Tears filled her eyes.

"We have to stop talking about this," Mary Elizabeth said. "We're just going to depress ourselves."

"I agree," Lavina said. And heard herself sigh. "I kept hoping he'd change his mind." She shook her head and stood. "I'm going for a walk."

"Take your jacket," Mary Elizabeth said. "It's getting a little chilly."

"Yes, *Mamm*," she said, making a face at her. But she took the jacket. And then, after only a moment's hesitation, she put some of the oatmeal raisin cookies they'd baked earlier into a plastic baggie and took them with her. Mary Elizabeth gave her a knowing look. She knew where Lavina was headed.

David's home—his former home—was just a half-mile from hers so it was no wonder they'd been close as *kinner*. They'd walked to *schul* together, played together, gone to youth activities at church together. As the years had passed they'd become such good friends. More than friends. She had thought they were going to get married and then, after repeated arguments with their bishop, he'd suddenly moved away.

She frowned as she neared the Stoltzfus home and saw Waneta, David's *mamm*, sitting on the front porch looking miserable.

"Waneta? Are you *allrecht*?"

"Lavina, *gut-n-owed*." She tried to smile. "I'm fine. Just getting some air."

"Chilly air." Lavina climbed the steps and took a seat in the rocking chair next to her. "I thought I'd take a walk and bring you some cookies we baked earlier."

"Such a sweet *maedel*. *Danki*."

Lavina took one of the woman's hands in hers and found it was cold. She chafed it. "Why don't we go inside and have some with a cup of tea?"

Suddenly there was the sound of breaking glass inside the house. Waneta jumped and glanced back fearfully.

"What is it? What's wrong?"

"Just my *mann* being careless," Waneta said. "You know men, so clumsy."

The front door opened, and he stuck his head out. "Where's my supper?" he demanded. Then he saw Lavina. "You come around to ask about David? Well don't! I don't have a *sohn*!" The door slammed.

Waneta jumped. "He doesn't mean it." But tears welled up in her eyes. "He's not well."

"Not well?" David had told her once that his *dat* sometimes drank . . .

Tears rolled down Waneta's cheeks. "The doctor told us today that he has the cancer." She pulled a tissue from her pocket and dabbed at her eyes. Then she looked at Lavina, seemed to struggle with herself. "Lavina, do you ever hear from David?"

She shook her head. "You know I would come tell you. We've talked about this. If either of us heard from him, we'd tell the other. It wouldn't matter if we're supposed to shun him. We'd tell each other."

"He needs to come home," Waneta said, sobbing now. "He and Samuel and John. They need to come home or they may never see their *dat* again."

David sat in his new-to-him pickup truck in the driveway of his *Englisch* friend Bill's house.

It had taken him a year to save up enough for the five-year-old pickup truck, but he'd firmly resisted the temptation to get a flashy new truck because it meant buying on credit. He wasn't dead set against credit. Sometimes a person had to use it. Land was expensive in Lancaster County. Unless you inherited it you often had to arrange for a bank loan.

The memory of the farm he'd grown up on flashed into his mind. He firmly pushed it away. He didn't miss all the arguments with his *dat* and with the bishop.

David missed Lavina, but there was no point in thinking about her. He couldn't have her so he had to keep pushing her out of his mind. After being away from her for a whole year now, he was down to only having to do that a couple of times a day.

He wondered what she would think of the truck. One of their favorite things had always been to go for a buggy ride.

"Ready for your first ride?" Bill asked as he got into passenger seat.

"Yeah."

"Where are we headed?"

David shrugged. "I don't know. Where shall we go?"

"Let's just do some country roads, get you used to the truck."

"And not scare you in Paradise traffic?"

"You didn't scare me when I was teaching you to drive."

"Right."

Bill chuckled. "Well, not much, anyway. Now, teaching my younger brother, that was scary. Kid has such a lead foot."

David went through the steps Bill had taught him to do prior to turning on the ignition. Fasten seat belt. Check. Position rear-view mirrors. Check. Check gas gauge. Check. Release parking brake. Check. Turn on ignition. Check. Put car in gear. Check. Look for traffic.

"You forgot a step."

David stopped the truck before he left the driveway and turned to his friend. "What?"

"You forgot to check out your appearance, dude." Bill pulled the visor down and checked his hair, smoothing it with one hand, then checked out his smile before he turned the visor back. "C'mon, don't be shy. You want to look good for the ladies when you cruise."

With a laugh, David pulled down his visor and checked out his appearance. After months, he was still not used to seeing himself with an *Englisch* haircut. He hadn't recognized himself in the glass store window he'd passed the day after the haircut. He'd had to take a second look, see that it was him, see the dark blue eyes and square jaw, the brown, almost black hair.

"And don't forget the shades," Bill said, passing him the pair he'd urged David to buy. "They're not just to look cool. You have to be careful about glare when you're driving."

"So much to remember. It was easier to just hitch up a horse."

"But wait 'til you get this baby out on the road and feel the horsepower under the hood," Bill said, stretching out his long legs. He tilted his own sunglasses down and looked at David over the top of them. "Not that I'm urging you to speed."

"Not going to do that," David said firmly. "Speeding tickets are a waste of good money."

"Wise man. Too bad I didn't think that way when I first started driving. 'Course, it's part of growing up, I guess. In my culture, I mean."

"Guys in their *rumschpringe* race their buggies," David said as he checked for traffic and eased out of the driveway. "You'd be surprised the speed some of them can get out of them. Sometimes the Amish buy horses that have been retired from racing."

They rode for a while in silence.

"How's the truck feel?"

"*Gut*—good," he corrected himself. "It will help me with work. Sometimes the boss needs something delivered and he doesn't have enough trucks."

"When you have a pickup people will be asking you to help them with all sorts of things," Bill told him. "I can't tell you how many people have asked me to help them move."

"I like to help people."

"I know. You're a good guy."

David didn't feel like a good guy. What would Bill think if he knew why he'd left his Amish community? If he knew he'd walked away from a woman he'd promised to marry? He wouldn't think he was so good then.

But Bill, thankfully, had offered friendship without prying. It was Bill who was good, helping him find a job, a place to rent and now a vehicle when he needed one. He'd invited David to his church but David wasn't ready for that yet. Maybe someday.

"You doin' okay?" Bill asked him.

David gave him a quick glance. "Yeah. Why?"

"You just seemed a little down when I got in the truck and you don't act like you're enjoying it. Are you sorry you didn't buy a new one?"

"No. I don't want something I can't afford. And this'll do fine for work."

"You're being smart. Let me tell you, I wish I hadn't gotten into so much debt buying my first truck." Bill tapped his fingers on his knee.

David found himself driving down roads he'd only driven in a buggy. Now he was in an *Englisch* vehicle and needed to slow down and be careful of the Amish buggies. He passed the buggies of two former friends, but they didn't recognize him in his truck and he didn't wave. No point in getting his feelings hurt if they didn't return his wave.

"Hey, you okay?"

He glanced at Bill. "Yeah, why?"

"How's it feel to be near the old neighborhood?"

"Fine."

But it wasn't. He hadn't been anywhere near his former Amish community since he'd left. Not having transportation had kept him in town and kept him from the temptation of trying to see Lavina . . .

"Hungry?" Bill broke into his thoughts. "There's a great place for burgers about a mile ahead."

It was a little early for lunch but that was fine. He nodded. "Sure."

Lunch might be a great way to thank Bill for helping him buy the truck. The restaurant was closer to where he used to live than he liked, but there probably wouldn't be anyone he knew having lunch in the middle of a workday. He parked and started to get out of the truck when a beep sounded. Startled, he looked back and found Bill grinning.

"Gotta take the keys if you want to find the truck here when you come back." Bill shoved his hands in the pockets of his jeans as he watched David retrieve the keys from the ignition and lock the truck. "What happens when someone tries to steal your horse and buggy?"

"No one does."

"Hmm."

They went inside and found a booth. David realized that Bill was watching him over the top of his menu. "What?"

"You sure you're okay here?"

What a friend. "I'm fine. You don't have to worry that someone's going to come yell at me for leaving the community."

"We haven't talked much about why you left," Bill said as he set his menu down. "Any time you want to I'm here for you."

"Thanks." He turned, ready to give his order to the server and saw a woman in Amish dress entering the restaurant.

For months after he'd left the Amish community he'd thought he'd seen her so many times. But it always turned out to be another woman.

Just like all those other times, the woman turned and he saw it wasn't Lavina but another Amish woman.

"David? You gonna order?"

He blinked. "Oh, sorry. I'll have the double cheeseburger and fries. Well done on the burger."

They ate their lunch, and David didn't look toward the door again.

"Beautiful work," Leah said as she stroked the quilt. "Just like always."

Lavina smiled. "*Danki*. I hope your customer who ordered it is happy with it."

"I'm sure she will be." Leah folded the quilt, put it in one of the Stitches in Time bags and set it under the counter. She went through the rest of the quilts Lavina and her sisters had sewn and approved all of them. "Let me write you a check."

The bell over the shop window rang. Several women walked in. Leah glanced around. All of her granddaughters were busy helping customers. "Excuse me for just a moment, Lavina."

"You don't have to worry about the check right now," Lavina said quickly.

"I'll be just a moment," Leah assured her. "Why don't you take a look at the new fabric we just got in?"

New fabric. Lavina couldn't resist. She had several bolts in her arms when Leah found her a few minutes later.

"I see you found the new fabric," Leah said with a smile. "Let me help you with those." She took several of the bolts and carried them to the cutting table. "How are you doing, Lavina?"

"*Gut. Danki.*" Lavina set her bolts down and stroked the material on one of them, avoiding Leah's gaze. When Leah didn't say anything, Lavina looked up.

Leah's faded blue eyes were kind. "Really, *kind*?"

"You know it's not easy to miss someone. Your first husband died."

"David isn't dead," she reminded Lavina.

"He has to be to me. He's gone, Leah. He's been gone a year. He's not coming back."

Leah sighed. "I don't know what to say. But I know this: God has a plan for each of us, timing that doesn't always please us, but he always knows what He's doing."

"I know."

"Do you, *kind*? Can you find the faith to believe it?"

"I've tried."

"Remember, 'we live by faith, not by sight.'"

"I know." Lavina sighed.

Leah unrolled a bolt of fabric. "So, how many yards?"

"Four of each."

Working competently, Leah cut the fabric, folded it and pinned a slip of paper with the amount to charge on each. She walked to the counter, and Lavina followed her. "Oh, I almost forgot your check." She pulled a checkbook from the drawer, made out the check, and handed it to Lavina.

"Waneta was in yesterday," she said as she tucked the fabric into a shopping bag. "She's worried about her *mann*. Maybe David will come back to help take care of him."

"I don't think he will. They didn't get along, remember?"

Leah handed her the shopping bag. "Maybe someone should let David know about his father."

"I don't know anyone who knows where he moved."

"There must be a way." Leah reached inside the cash register for a list. "Can you and your *schwesders* handle a few more orders before Christmas?"

"*Schur.* We appreciate the work, you know that."

Leah patted her hand. "I appreciate what you do for us. We can't possibly handle all the demand for quilts with just Naomi sewing them."

Lavina tucked the check in her purse and picked up her shopping bag. "Have a *gut* day!"

"You, too," Leah said. "And think about what I said."

She waved at Naomi as she left the shop. The temperature had gotten a little bit cooler, but the sun felt warm on her shoulders as she stepped outside. She stopped to look in the display window—she hadn't taken the time when she was carrying in the boxes of quilts to deliver—and smiled when she saw that one of her quilts was displayed next to Naomi's. Little leaves cut from fabric scattered on the floor of the window announced the season. Anna's hand-knit baby caps covered the heads of little dolls seated on one of Mary Katherine's beautiful woven throws. Leah's little cloth Amish dolls rode in a hand-carved buggy carved by Ben and Mark, twin cousins of the three Stoltzfus *bruders*.

The wind picked up, swirling her skirt. She hurried to her buggy parked behind the shop and began the ride home. She felt tired from the last-minute rush the past week, finishing the quilt order, but happy with the check tucked in her purse. And how nice to have new fabric to work with. A quilter always loved having a big stash of fabric waiting to be worked into a quilt. Her *dat* pretended to complain about how much fabric the women in his house accumulated but he'd converted the den in the house into their sewing room and lined the walls with shelves for fabric and supplies.

Her stomach growled. She'd left in a hurry that morning, taking time for only a cup of coffee. Up ahead was a restaurant/bakery that was a favorite of locals. She glanced at her purse and debated treating herself to a sandwich and taking home some baked goodies for her *schweschders*. The three of them deserved something special after their long hours.

She parked, entered the restaurant, and inhaled the delicious aromas. The door opened behind her as she stood waiting to be shown to a table.

"Lavina! I've been hoping to talk to you!"

She turned and found herself staring at Officer Kate Kraft. "Oh, did I do something wrong? Did I park in the handicapped spot or something?" The parking lot had been crowded and she'd been a little close to a pickup truck, but she thought she'd parked the buggy legally.

The other woman laughed. "Not at all. I'm looking for some fellow quilters to help me with a project. Are you having lunch? Maybe we could talk about it."

"Sure." Everyone liked Officer Kate. She had earned the respect of the Amish community by being deferential to their beliefs.

Here in Lancaster, the Amish and *Englisch* associated with each other more than they did in other areas. Lavina supposed that was because Lancaster Amish were involved in business and commerce more than farming because land had become so expensive.

Tourism had changed Lancaster County, but so far both groups had made it work.

They settled into a booth, and the server handed them menus then left to get their drinks.

"No need for me to look at the menu," Kate said without opening it. "I know it by heart. I try to pack a healthy lunch, but I don't always have time before I leave the house in the morning."

Lavina smiled. "It never changes. I want a cheeseburger and French fries. That's not something we cook often at home."

Her soft drink and Kate's coffee came. They gave their orders and then Kate leaned forward. "So, I wanted to ask you if you'd be interested in helping teach quilting in a program we've started at a domestic abuse shelter in town. It's based on a program a friend of mine started at a prison in Ohio."

"She teaches quilting in a prison?"

Kate nodded enthusiastically, barely noticing when their server put her lunch down in front of her. "Quilting changes lives, Lavina. We teach the women life skills while we're teaching how to put together a quilt. Some of the women have such low self-esteem. They've been involved in relationships with husbands, boyfriends, family that have made them feel like they can't do anything. They learn how to sew, learn how to feel pride in accomplishment, learn life skills that help them get jobs and help support themselves—and their children if they have them."

Kate paused to take a breath. "Sorry, I'm pretty passionate about what we're doing." She picked up her sandwich and began eating. "Leah has given us material and supplies. And I've gotten donations from the community. We teach the class from noon to 2 p.m. on Wednesdays. Do you think you'd be interested in stopping by this week to see if you'd like to volunteer?"

Lavina nodded. "I'll come and see if it's something I can help with." She sipped her drink. "I have a question for you."

"Sure." Kate smiled and watched the server refill her coffee cup. "What's your question?"

"If I wanted to find someone—someone who's moved away from here—how would I go about it?"

"There are a lot of things you can do," Kate said. "Do you know how to use a computer?"

"Not very well," Lavina admitted. "I've done some work on the ones in the library, but I'm not the best."

"Where do you think this person moved to?"

"He's still in the county."

"Hmm. It might not be that hard. Start with directory assistance first. You know, information on the phone. Here, let me give you some paper to write on." She pulled out a slim notepad and began ripping out a few sheets.

Lavina lifted her soft drink and glanced idly at a man passing their table on the way to the cashier at the front of the restaurant. Was she seeing a ghost? Her eyes widened, and her fingers went numb on the glass. It slipped from her grasp and shattered on the tile floor. "David!"

The man stopped and stared at her. "Lavina!"

2

David couldn't believe his eyes. He'd wondered if he'd ever run into her, and now here she was as he stood, tongue-tied, not knowing what to say.

"So, is this the man you were looking for?" asked the police officer Lavina was sitting with.

"Er, yes," Lavina stammered, blushing.

David tore his eyes from Lavina and noticed that the woman was a police officer. He frowned. "What, am I in trouble for something?"

"Nope," the officer said. "Well, that was fast work," she told Lavina with a smile. "I wish everything a citizen asked me about went as well."

She picked up her check. "Lavina, it's been fun. I have to be getting back to work. You give me a call if you're interested in volunteering, okay?"

"I will."

The server came over with a broom and dustpan. David watched Lavina apologize and try to take the broom to clean up the mess she insisted she'd made, but the server wouldn't let her. The job accomplished, the server left, leaving David and Lavina standing there staring at each other.

"You look well." He couldn't get enough of looking at her.

"You, too."

"You were asking that officer how to find me?"

"*Ya.*" She took a deep breath.

"Why?"

Bill walked up then. "David, I thought you were behind me and then I got up to the cashier and you weren't there. Hello," he said to Lavina. "I'm Bill, David's friend."

"Lavina Zook."

David dragged his gaze from Lavina. "Bill, could you give us a few minutes?"

"Sure. I'll wait for you up front."

"Thanks." David waved his hand at the booth, and Lavina slid back into her seat. He sat opposite her. "Tell me why you were looking for me."

Had she missed him as much as he'd missed her?

She bit her lip. "I talked to your *mamm* the other day. David, your *dat* is very sick. Your *mamm* said she was afraid that if you didn't come see him—" she broke off, obviously struggling for composure. She took a deep breath. "If you don't see him now, you might never get to."

"I'm sure she was exaggerating. He's never sick. He's too mean to get sick."

Lavina shook her head. "I don't think she's exaggerating." She took a deep breath. There was no easy way to say it. "She said he has cancer."

David felt the news hit him like a blow to the gut. He rubbed at his temple, feeling a headache coming on. "He won't want to see me. He's the reason I left."

"But if he doesn't have much time . . ." she trailed off. "David, if you can't do it for him, think about your *mamm*. She needs you right now."

"I'll think about it." He got to his feet.

"Should I tell her I saw you?"

"It's up to you." He stood there, staring at her. Who knew when he'd see her again. "Lavina, I'm sorry for the way I left."

"Are you?" she asked him. "Are you, David?"

She slipped from the booth and hurried away.

Torn, he started after her and then realized she'd gone into the ladies room. He glanced at the front of the restaurant and saw Bill standing there, looking out the window. Maybe it was best if he just left. He wasn't prepared for seeing Lavina, and the news about his father had unsettled him. He needed to think.

"Sorry I kept you waiting," he told Bill. He paid the bill, and they walked to the truck.

Lavina came out of the restaurant and walked to her buggy. They watched her, but she didn't see them—obviously not expecting David to be sitting in a truck outside.

"So is Lavina your girlfriend?"

David shook his head. "Was," he said. "Was."

He watched her drive the buggy away.

"Everything okay?" Bill asked him when David sat there without immediately turning on the ignition.

"She told me my dad's sick. Very sick."

"Man, that's rough. You gonna go see him?"

He'd told Bill a little about why he'd left the community, but he hadn't said anything about Lavina.

"I don't know," he said finally. "I just don't know."

He put the key in the ignition and started the truck. They drove back to Bill's apartment in silence, then sat there, the engine idling.

"You have my cell number if you want to talk."

David nodded. "Thanks."

"See you Monday on the job. Thanks for lunch."

"You're welcome. Thanks for help with the truck."

Bill grinned. "I'm sure the two of you will be very happy together." He got out of the truck and went into his apartment building.

David pulled out onto the road and drove back to his own apartment. The truck was just transportation to him. Expensive, challenging transportation. He hadn't left his community for things like trucks or drinking or . . . whatever. He'd left it because of arguments with his *dat* and the bishop.

Mattie, his landlady, was raking leaves in the front yard when he pulled into the drive. "Well, look at you now. Bought yourself a truck, huh?"

"Yes. Do you mind if I park it here?"

"Not at all."

"Let me do that." He reached for the rake and his eyes widened as the little elderly lady put up a determined struggle for it.

"I can do it."

"I know. But I'd like to. I miss doing things like this."

She gave him a long look and then handed him the rake.

He really did miss working on the yard, on the farm. When he left, he'd had to find a job in town. He was grateful for it, but as he raked up the leaves, he enjoyed the crisp fall air, the exertion. The chance to not think about what Lavina had said even if it only put off things for a little while.

"I'll go get some plastic bags," she said.

They worked together, Mattie holding bags so that he could scoop up the leaves into them. Then David hauled the bags to the curb.

"Yard looks really good now," she said when they were finished. "Thank you for the help."

"You're welcome."

"How about some supper? I've got a casserole about to come out of the oven. Ham and scalloped potatoes."

"Sounds wonderful," he told her and meant it. On a cool fall night like this it was the kind of supper his *mudder* or his *grossmudder* might have made.

Mattie's kitchen was small, but warm and smelled wonderful. He washed his hands at the sink and sat in one of the chairs, watching her pull the casserole from the oven. She served it with canned green beans and sliced bread. Simple, filling. David ate two servings of the casserole and hoped he wasn't taking food she couldn't spare. He figured she rented out the tiny apartment upstairs for extra money.

"That was good as my *mudder's*—my mother's," he told her.

"That's high praise," she said, beaming, and her face creased into many wrinkles. "The Amish are great cooks. And how are your brothers, David? I haven't seen them visiting you this past week."

"I'll be going by tomorrow to see them."

When it came time to leave she insisted on giving him a Tupperware container of casserole leftovers. As he climbed the stairs to his apartment, he thought about how he'd told her he'd be seeing his brothers the next day.

But he wasn't sure he was ready to do that yet. He wanted to give himself time to think about how he'd tell them, what he'd say. But he knew he had to do it soon so his *mudder* wouldn't worry and think they wouldn't come. But what if they didn't?

Lavina walked up to Waneta's house and frowned when she saw only one light showed in an upstairs window even though the day was growing dark.

She raised her hand to knock at the door then she bit her lip. What if David's *dat* came to the door? Remembering how he'd bellowed last time she visited made her hesitate and drop her hand.

Then she remembered how David's *mudder* had looked . . . how she had cried when she said that her *mann* was ill, and how she'd begged Lavina to find her *sohn* and ask him to come see his *dat*. She couldn't let the older woman down.

So she raised her hand and knocked, then knocked again, harder, when no one answered the door. Finally, when no one came after several minutes of knocking on the door, she gave up and turned to leave.

Then the door opened. "Lavina?"

She spun around and nearly slipped. "Waneta! I thought you might not be home when you didn't answer."

"I fell asleep," she said, straightening her *kapp* with an embarrassed smile. "Amos had a bad night and I was up with him."

"Oh, I can come back."

"*Nee, nee, kumm,*" she said, holding the door open. "We'll have some tea."

"I don't want to bother Amos."

"He's finally asleep. *Kumm.*"

Lavina walked inside and took a seat at the kitchen table. She watched Waneta bustle around making the tea. Her movements were quick, nervous. Lavina guessed that she was eager to learn if Lavina had found her *sohn,* but she wouldn't want to rush and ask her without offering some hospitality after Lavina's walk in the cold weather.

She waited until the cup of tea was set before her and Waneta had settled tiredly into her chair.

"I found David."

She shook her head as she remembered how they'd come upon each other that day. Was it coincidence—or God's plan?

Waneta's hand flew to her mouth and tears welled in her eyes. "You did? Already? *Mein Gott!*" Then her face fell. "But you didn't bring him." Her shoulders sagged. "He didn't want to come."

Lavina reached over and touched her hand. "He needs to think about it, Waneta." She fell silent for a long moment. "I'm afraid old hurts don't die quickly."

Waneta nodded and stared at her tea. "I know. They said many a harsh word to each other before David left. I know he and his *bruders* may never come home again."

"I'm sure he'll come," Lavina said reassuringly.

But she wasn't so sure. She and David had talked so often about their families. His *dat* was . . . difficult. David had worked so hard to help on the farm, getting up early without being asked, shivering in the winter, sweating in the summer, milking cows, and mucking out stalls. Planting crops and tirelessly nurturing them and then harvesting them.

But his *dat* had never been satisfied. Never. He'd criticized and yelled. She'd seen red marks on David's face that he wouldn't talk about.

David had taken it until his *mudder* had tried to step in and stop him, and the blow that Amos had intended for David had landed on her.

He'd gone to the bishop for help and been turned away. His *dat* was a *gut*, hardworking *mann*, he'd been told. David needed to do as he was told and not interfere between his parents.

How was that right? he'd asked Lavina. A man wasn't supposed to treat his *fraa*, his *kinner*, that way. She didn't know what to say. It hadn't been long after that conversation that she'd heard that David had left the community.

He hadn't come to say goodbye to her.

"I'm sorry, I don't have any cookies or anything to offer you with your tea. I haven't had time to bake this week with Amos being so sick from his chemotherapy."

"It's *allrecht*. I need to be getting home for supper."

She glanced around the kitchen. The room felt cold and only the overhead gas light lit it. Nothing was simmering on the stove or baking in the oven.

"Waneta, what are you doing for supper?"

She watched the older woman glance absently around the room. "Oh, I think I'll just warm up some soup I have in the freezer, make some sandwiches for Amos and me. I don't think either of us wants more than that tonight."

"You're sure I can't help you cook?"

Waneta patted her hand. "You've done more than enough contacting David. Now you need to get on home for your supper before your family worries."

Lavina hesitated. Her heart went out to the woman. She looked a little lost, a little lonely sitting here. In years past the table would have been filled with three big, strapping *sohns* and a *mann*, all acting starved after a long day working. There would be platters of food and elbow shoving if they weren't being passed fast enough.

Arguments over the last biscuit. Their *dat* had frowned a lot but ate his supper quickly and left the table.

Lavina didn't have to imagine it. She'd been David's guest for supper a couple of times and witnessed such. It had been quite an experience after the quiet meals she and her two *schweschders* enjoyed around their kitchen table. Her own *dat* was so warm, friendly, and different from David's. And her *dat*'s relationship with her *mudder* was so different from the one she saw Waneta had with Amos.

"I'll stop by tomorrow evening," she promised. "Is there anything you'd like me to bring? Anything you need?"

The minute the words slipped out she wanted to bite her tongue.

Waneta smiled sadly. "Just David and Samuel and John."

Lavina searched for a way to comfort. "It's just been a day," she said finally. "Give David some time."

"I don't know how much time . . ." Waneta trailed off.

"The doctors aren't saying he has that little time?"

"*Nee*," she said with a sigh. "It's just that a bad day can weigh so heavy on the heart. It hurts so much not to be able to help him feel better."

"I'm sure he's grateful for all you're doing."

"*Ach*, you're such a sweet *kind*. Amos has always been a very proud man. He doesn't like relying on me right now."

Her words reminded Lavina of David. He was much like his *dat*.

Sometimes she wondered if *proud* wasn't just another word for stubborn.

Lavina paused in stitching her quilt. She and her sisters and their *mudder* sat quietly, sewing and chatting before a crackling fire, their toes toasty and warm while rain pattered against the windows. The scent of a big pot of beef stew simmering on the stove in the kitchen filled the house.

She couldn't help remembering how Waneta's house had been dark when she'd visited the night before, how Waneta had been so tired from caring for her husband that she hadn't started supper and talked about warming up some soup and making sandwiches. She'd apologized for not having cookies to serve with the cup of tea she offered Lavina.

The community always rallied around one in need but Lavina suspected that the news hadn't gotten out yet that Waneta needed help. She and Amos hadn't attended church the past month . . .

"*Mamm?* Would you mind if I made some food to take to Waneta's?" She explained what she'd found when she visited and her mother frowned.

"Of course. I'll talk to some of my friends tomorrow, and we'll see what we can do to help."

Lavina set down the quilt and jumped to her feet. "*Danki, Mamm.*"

Mary Elizabeth set her work aside. "Can I help?"

"*Schur.*"

They walked into the kitchen and Lavina found a big bowl and the canister of flour. "I'm going to make some bread." She eyed the stew simmering for their supper. "I wonder if we have the makings for some more stew . . ."

She found a package of stew meat in the freezer and carrots, celery and onion in the refrigerator and pantry. "I'll start it and see if *Mamm* will let us take what she's made. The new pot should still be ready for our supper, but this way we can take the food over to Waneta before it gets dark."

"*Ya.* And maybe we can make up a basket of jars of canned vegetables and fruit. Amos needs to eat nutritious food while he's on chemotherapy, right? We don't know if Waneta was able to can before Amos got sick. Besides, even if she has plenty the canned goods will last on the shelf for some time."

"*Gut* idea. Ask *Mamm.*"

Lavina sifted flour and dry ingredients in the big bowl and soon the yeasty scent of bread rising filled the air. After she covered it with a towel, she turned to getting a big soup pot out. After flouring the meat she began browning it in the pot with some vegetable oil. She chopped onions and added them.

Mary Elizabeth glanced over. "You're crying!"

She grabbed a tissue from the box on the counter. "It's the onions."

"You're *schur*?"

Lavina nodded. It made her feel sad that David's parents were going through such a difficult time and the family wasn't together. Whether Amos healed from his cancer, she hoped the family would heal and be together.

For now, she and Mary Elizabeth could take some hot food and caring. And who knows, maybe at this very moment David was thinking of coming back.

Lavina shaped the loaves of bread into pans and set them aside to rise. She sighed. It was no good daydreaming about David coming back. She'd spent so much time doing that this past year . . .

She found an oven-safe dish and set it aside. As soon as the bread came out and cooled a little they could go. She raided the cookie jar and packed up the dozen or so peanut butter cookies. Later she'd bake some more and replace them.

"Rain's stopped," Mary Elizabeth said as she came into the kitchen.

"*Gut*. We can walk."

"Walk?"

"Don't whine. It's only a few blocks."

She rolled her eyes. "That's far enough. We'll be carrying stuff."

"I'll carry the stew. You can carry the bread and cookies."

A little while later they set out. The rain had cooled the air so it was a little nippy, but Lavina didn't mind. Mary Elizabeth chattered as she carried the warm loaves of bread in her arms.

A truck drove past them. Lavina frowned. A red truck that looked familiar somehow. It stopped then backed up. The passenger side window rolled down. "Need a ride?" the driver asked.

It was David.

3

David had been driving up and down the road of his old house for half an hour.

He just couldn't make himself stop, let alone get out of his truck and walk up and knock on the door. He was a coward. No question about it.

Then he saw two women in Amish clothing walking on the side of the road. As he passed them he saw that they carried something in their arms. One woman glanced over as he rode by. It was Lavina. He saw the flash of recognition in her eyes as their gazes met.

He stomped on the brakes, then put the truck in reverse and backed up. As he touched the button to roll down the passenger-side window, he realized that there could be no avoiding stopping at his parents' house tonight.

"Hi."

She nodded. "Hi, David."

His gaze went to her *schweschder.* "Mary Elizabeth."

"Hi, David. How are you?"

"*Allrecht.* Get in, I'll give you a ride."

"We're almost there," Lavina pointed out.

"And that casserole dish has to be getting heavy," Mary Elizabeth said. She opened the door and climbed in to sit on the bench in the back seat.

Lavina slid into the front seat and set the insulated carrier between her and David before she shut the door.

"So you decided to come back. I'm glad."

He put the truck in gear. "We'll see if I am." He knew he sounded grim, but that's the way he felt. Neither of them could ignore what had happened to make him leave just because his *dat* was sick.

Whatever Lavina had in the insulated carrier smelled like heaven. He realized he hadn't eaten for hours and was hungry.

The house came into view. David pulled into the drive, shut off the engine, and sat there for a long time staring straight ahead. Lavina and Mary Elizabeth got out.

"Are you coming?" Lavina asked him.

With a heavy sigh he pulled the keys from the ignition and left the vehicle. He followed them up the stairs and watched as the front door opened before Mary Elizabeth could knock. His mother smiled as she saw the two women and she invited them inside.

And then her gaze traveled past them and she saw David. The color fled from her face and she swayed for a moment. Mary Elizabeth reached out a hand to steady her and she shook her head. She stumbled forward, holding out her arms, clutching David and sobbing.

"You came! You came!"

She'd always been a robust woman, but she felt as if she'd lost weight. He finally set her from him. "We need to go inside, *Mamm*. It's too cold out here for you."

Nodding, she turned and stepped back into the house. Lavina and Mary Elizabeth had gone ahead into the kitchen and were setting the things they'd brought on the kitchen table.

"Stew and bread and some cookies," Lavina said, looking at Waneta. "Enjoy."

She and Mary Elizabeth started for the door.

"Wait!" Waneta cried. "Where are you going? You just got here."

Lavina glanced at David. "The two of you will have a lot to talk about."

"*Ya*, but no need to rush off," Waneta said quickly. "Please, sit, have some coffee. If it hadn't been for you, David wouldn't have known to come."

As if to add to his mother's invitation, David pulled out a chair for her and Mary Elizabeth.

She cast a helpless look at Mary Elizabeth, but her *schweschder* was no help—she shrugged and sat, so Lavina sank into the chair. She watched David's *mamm* bustling around the kitchen, and David sat silently looking ill at ease in the kitchen of the home he'd grown up in. Lavina wondered if Waneta wanted a sort of buffer since David had surprised her.

Only when everyone had shrugged off their jackets and had a mug of coffee in front of them did Waneta stop fluttering around the kitchen and sit at the table.

"Where's *Daed*?" David asked her.

"Upstairs resting. He should be up soon for supper." She traced a pattern on the top of the table. "He's been having chemotherapy for colon cancer."

"What does the doctor say?"

Waneta's lips trembled. "He says your *dat* has a very aggressive form of cancer so he started him on chemo right away. I—you need to ask your *bruders* to come see him, David."

He nodded. "I thought I would talk to you first before I went to them."

"I'm glad you came." She reached over and covered his hand with hers.

It was so quiet the clock ticking sounded like a loud heartbeat.

"I drove up and down the street and had trouble stopping," he blurted out. "I'm not sure he's going to want to see me."

"David gave us a ride," Mary Elizabeth spoke up.

"So you have a horse and buggy of your own now?"

"Not exactly. I have a truck."

Waneta stared at him. "A truck? Does that mean you've become *Englisch?*"

"*Nee, Mamm.* I needed a way to get to work."

Everyone glanced up as they heard feet land with a thump on the floor upstairs and then make their shuffling way toward the stair landing.

"We really need to go," Lavina said, looking uneasy. "*Mamm* is expecting us for supper."

"*Danki* for the food," Waneta said. "You're such kind, generous *maedels.*"

Lavina blushed at the praise and avoided David's gaze. He wanted to talk to her, but this wasn't the time or place.

"I'll stop by to see you tomorrow," David said quickly before his father could appear in the room.

She looked startled. "Um, *allrecht.*"

Amos Stoltzfus walked into the kitchen and stopped when he saw David.

"What are you doing here?" he bellowed, glaring at him.

David rose. "I came to see you," he said, lifting his chin. "*Mamm* said you were sick."

"So?"

He studied his *dat.* He'd lost weight since David had left, and his beard and hair were threaded with more gray. But his voice was as loud and abrasive as ever.

"We have nothing to say to each other," Amos said bluntly.

He walked to the sink, filled a glass with water and drank it down. Although he turned his back, David saw that his father's hand shook.

"Amos, *kumm*, sit," Waneta said, her tone placating. "Lavina and Mary Elizabeth brought us supper. Beef stew. And the bread's still warm from the oven."

He hesitated, turning to glare balefully at David. "Great timing, got here for supper. Always did show up at mealtime, didn't you? Well, if you're looking for a welcome like the prodigal son, you've come to the wrong place."

David felt the old anger rise to the surface. He eyed his jacket he'd hung on the peg by the kitchen door. Then he saw his mother follow the direction of his gaze, and she looked ready to cry.

So he took a deep breath and silently counted to ten. "Neither of us ever missed a meal, did we?" he told him easily and he smiled at his mother. "Do you need any help?"

"If you'll get some bowls, I'll slice the bread."

She lifted the casserole dish from the insulated carrier and set it on the table in front of David, then set the carrier aside on the counter. Getting a knife from a drawer, she placed the bread on a wooden carving board and sliced it.

Amos sat in a chair and watched her. It was as if David wasn't even in the room. When someone left the community the family often shunned them. He'd wondered if that was what his father would do if he came back . . . just sit at the table and ignore him.

He ladled a bowl of stew and handed it to his mother who turned and set it before her *mann*. Then he filled another bowl for her. Finally he served himself.

They bent their heads for prayer and then began eating.

It was a start, he thought as he dug his spoon into the bowl of stew. It could have been worse. His *dat* could have told him to leave and he hadn't. He said a silent prayer of thanks to his heavenly *Dat* and began eating.

David's head was pounding by the time he finished his bowl of stew.

He asked himself why he hadn't waited until after he'd eaten his supper to stop at his house and see his *mudder.*

Then he reminded himself that he hadn't intended to stop at all. He'd been driving up and down the road putting off stopping when he'd passed Lavina and Mary Elizabeth walking there and they'd seen him. Not wanting to appear the coward he really was, he'd felt he had to stop.

Now, here he was, trapped at the supper table between a disgruntled old man and his *mudder* trying desperately to act as if they were one happy family gathered again around her kitchen table.

David hadn't expected for his *dat to* kill a fatted calf for him. He knew not to expect to be treated like the prodigal son of the Bible but . . . he was going to have a whopper of a headache and maybe a really *gut* case of indigestion.

"Another bowl of stew?" his *mudder* asked him. "There's plenty for both of you to have seconds."

"Not for me," his *dat* said, pushing away his bowl half-eaten. "Don't feel much like eating. I'm going back to lie down."

Without saying another word he got up and shuffled back upstairs.

"Maybe I shouldn't have come," David said.

His mother got to her feet and poured them both a mug of coffee. She returned to the table and set them down, then opened a plastic container of cookies.

"Lavina and Mary Elizabeth brought these," she said, putting some of the cookies on a plate and setting it before David. "I haven't had time to bake. I went with your *dat* to his chemotherapy session today."

He picked up a cookie and bit into it. "It's *gut*." He figured Lavina had made them. She liked to bake. She hadn't known he'd be here. It was just a coincidence that she'd made peanut butter cookies, his favorite kind. *Ya*, and a coincidence that they had been walking to his house this evening when he was driving there.

Coincidence.

Suddenly something Lavina used to say came to him: "There's no such thing as coincidence." Everything was from God, she always maintained.

He wondered if he would have stopped at the house tonight if he hadn't seen Lavina and she'd seen him.

Oh, well, what did it matter? He was here now and what did it change.

Now he just had to decide what his next step was.

He felt his mother's hand on his. "*Danki* for coming."

"You thanked me already."

She sighed. "Your *dat* isn't an easy man but he's a *gut* one."

They heard a thump upstairs. Startled, she looked up and got to her feet. "I need to go check on him."

She started for the stairs, then turned and looked at him. "You're staying, right? I haven't changed it since you left."

"*Daed* hasn't moved his favorite horse in there?"

She chuckled. "*Nee*. I'll be right back."

David helped himself to another cup of coffee and a couple more cookies and sat down. He hadn't planned on staying the night. He hadn't planned on anything. They needed to talk some more, he and his *mudder*.

She came into the kitchen a few minutes later looking tired and worn. "He'll be down for the night now."

When had they gotten so old? he wondered. They'd been old—well, older than the parents of his friends. God hadn't sent them *kinner* until they were nearly forty and then, as if to make up for their faith in believing in Him, had sent David and his two *bruders* all within six years.

He got up to pour her a cup of coffee. "We didn't get to talk earlier with Lavina and her *schweschder* here. And *Daed* was in no mood to talk to me."

"I'm sorry, *sohn*. He'll come around."

David reached for her hand and studied how fragile it looked with blue veins showing beneath the thin white skin. "He's not going to change. I came to see if I can help you. I'll do my best to stay, but if he insists I get out, you know I'll have to leave."

She lifted her chin. "I have something to say about that. I won't let him order you from the house."

He lifted his eyebrows.

"But —"

"I mean it," she said firmly. "I should have said more to him. It wasn't right for him to treat his *sohns* the way he did."

"Or his *fraa*."

She shrugged. "I don't care about that. I care about losing my three *sohns*. I care about whether they'll walk away from their Amish faith, their community. I care about whether they have *kinner* of their own, whether I'll see them." She stopped, struggling for composure.

David didn't like to upset her more, but he needed to know more about his *dat*.

"Tell me about *Daed*. How bad is it?"

"It's bad. He has stage three colon cancer."

"How bad is that?"

"There's only one stage more. One worse, I mean. Then—" She couldn't go on.

"You said he's going for chemotherapy?"

She nodded. "He didn't want to at first. The doctor talked to him. I talked to him. He finally agreed. He's got a lot of treatments ahead of him."

"You're worn out."

"It hasn't been easy." She rubbed at her temple tiredly. "They're doing some tests next week to see how he's doing."

"Go on up to bed. I'll do the dishes." When she stared at him, he grinned. "I know how to do dishes, remember?"

"*Ya,* I remember you doing them two or three times."

"I did them more often than that."

She shook her head. "You broke too many."

"I think your memory's getting faulty."

She smacked his arm, but she was smiling. She hadn't smiled much that night.

"I'll be careful," he promised.

"*Allrecht*. I'm going to put the leftover stew in the refrigerator if you don't want any more. You didn't eat much at supper. That's not like you."

"Well, I might have a little more now that *Daed's* in bed."

She nodded. "*Gut nacht*. See you in the morning."

"*Gut nacht*." David helped himself to another bowl of stew and another slice of buttered bread. It felt better than he'd thought to be back in the kitchen of the home he'd grown up in. The room was a simple room, dominated by the big wooden table his father had carved after he'd built the house for himself and his new *fraa* when they were married. There was a *dawdi haus* on the back, like there was on so many Amish houses, for the two of them to retire to when a *sohn* took over the farm.

But Amos had argued that he wasn't ready to retire yet, even though his health had begun failing before the diagnosis of cancer had been made. Sometimes the oldest *sohn* didn't get the farm—sometimes a younger *sohn* did, and David honestly didn't mind if one of his *bruders* got it —but Amos had flatly refused to retire and simply drove his *sohns* harder and talked to them even harsher than before.

David finished the stew and bread, made quick work of the dishes and chose an apple from a bowl on the counter. He pulled on his jacket and walked out to the barn. When he slid the barn door open a chestnut mare stuck her head over her stall and neighed a welcome.

"Nellie," he crooned to her. "I've missed you, girl. Did you miss me?"

She nuzzled his neck and pushed her nose at his arm, pulling his hand out of his pocket. "Yeah, I think you miss me bringing you an apple more than you miss me."

He gave her the apple and then found himself wrapping his arms around her. "Oh, Nellie I missed you so. I'm back, Nellie. I don't know for how long, but I'm back."

She made a snuffling noise as if trying to comfort him. They stood like that for a long time until he finally went back into the house and climbed into the bed in his old room.

Sleep came hours later.

"Well, that was tense," Lavina said as they walked back home.

"David's *dat* sure hasn't changed. He's always been such a grump." She glanced over at Lavina. "I know, I shouldn't talk like that. But he is."

"He's not well."

"He's always been that way."

Mary Elizabeth was right, but still, they shouldn't talk about him like that. So she changed the subject as they walked and was grateful when they reached their house.

Everyone was gathered around the table. Lavina and Mary Elizabeth quickly shed their jackets and bonnets and joined their family for their own supper.

As she listened to Rose Anna chatter, glanced around the table and saw her parents and her siblings enjoying being with each other, Lavina couldn't help wondering what was happening at the Stoltzfus house. She didn't envy David sitting at their table with his *dat*. What if his *dat* had thrown him out of the house? What if David had left—after all, he'd done so voluntarily last time.

"*Gut* stew," her *dat* said. "Warms the belly on a cold day." He tore a piece of bread in half and used it to dip into the gravy.

"Lavina took a pot over to Waneta and Amos this afternoon," her *mamm* told him. "I'll take them my chicken and dumplings tomorrow."

"Take enough for three," Lavina said as she buttered a slice of bread. "David may be back."

"David?"

She nodded. "Waneta was hoping he'd come back since his *dat* is sick with the cancer. He was there for supper tonight."

"It would be so nice if that family could get together again. Especially now that Amos is sick. God wants us to care for each other."

She finished her stew and got up to get the apple crisp from the top of the stove where it had been cooling.

"He gave us a ride in his truck," Mary Elizabeth said as she got ice cream from the freezer.

"Truck?"

"He told his *mudder* he hasn't become *Englisch*. He bought it to get to work."

"Are his *bruders* coming back, too?" Rose Anna asked, sounding hopeful.

"I don't know. We didn't get to talk." Lavina hugged to herself the secret that David had said they'd talk tomorrow.

She accepted the bowl of apple crisp Mary Elizabeth passed her, breathing in the scent of the warm apples and cinnamon before she plunged her spoon into the dessert. Mary Elizabeth was telling them about how the two of them left when David's *dat* had come downstairs. Lavina tuned out what her *schweschder* was saying.

It was her turn to wash up, but Rose Anna helped while Mary Elizabeth took a cup of tea upstairs to drink while she read a book.

"How did David look?" she asked as she took a dish from Lavina and dried it. "Was it hard seeing him again?"

Trust Rose Anna to ask such a question. She had such a tender heart.

"He looked *gut*," she admitted. "Thinner," she remembered.

"Maybe he hasn't been eating as well as he did when his *mudder* cooked for him." She put a dish in the cabinet. "I'm glad he came back. It was the right thing to do. Now if John and Samuel will come back . . ."

Lavina handed her a dish, but when Rose Anna tried to take it she held on to it. She knew that Rose Anna loved John and hurt when he left just as Lavina had.

"Rose Anna, even if David and his *bruders* come back, it doesn't mean things will go back to the way they used to be."

The corners of Rose Anna's mouth turned down. "You don't know that."

"*Nee,* I don't," She sighed. "But I don't think we should get our hopes up. We don't know that David's come back for good."

She stared into the sudsy water as if she could see an answer there. "David's *dat* didn't seem all that happy to see him tonight. As a matter of fact, he was awful to David. I wouldn't have wanted to sit down at the table with him."

She handed her a dripping dish. "For all I know, he left shortly after we did."

Rose Anna dried the dish and fell silent. They worked together and finished the dishes, wiped down the table and counter tops. She didn't say another word.

They turned off the gas lamp and climbed the stairs to their room. There they changed into nightgowns, brushed their teeth, then climbed into their twin beds. Lavina pulled her quilt up to her chin and stared at the pattern the moonlight filtering through the bare branches of the tree outside made on the ceiling.

"Lavina?"

"*Ya*?"

"I hope things work out. With David, I mean. For you *and* for his family."

"*Danki,* Rose Anna. *Gut nacht*. Sweet dreams."

She was only twenty-three, but at that moment Lavina felt so old. Once she'd harbored simple dreams. A *maedel's* dreams. She and David loved each other, and they were going to get married. But life was more complicated than that. Things changed. People changed. She'd grown up this past year, accepted that David hadn't loved her or he'd have found a way to stay in the Amish community.

At the very least he'd have contacted her sometime this past year . . .

She'd thought David was the man God had set aside for her, but she'd been wrong. There must be someone else. He just hadn't shown up yet.

Sometimes God's timing wasn't what people wanted. She punched her pillow to make it more comfortable and closed her eyes, thinking how most of the time it wasn't. Look how one of her *mamm's* friends had prayed for a *boppli* for fifteen years and then had *zwillingbopplin* when others her age were becoming *gross-mudders*. A woman in her church had been widowed for twenty years and never thought she'd marry again. Then a man from Ohio moved here and they fell in love and married.

God hadn't sent her another man when David left, and now David was back. She didn't know what that meant for her . . . if anything.

She closed her eyes. She'd wished Rose Anna sweet dreams. Now she hoped for some of her own.

Snuggled deep in her quilt on a moon-washed, cold fall night, Lavina dreamed of the last day she had seen David. They'd taken a picnic lunch to eat in a nearby park.

"Have another piece of chicken?" she invited, holding out the plastic container.

David chose a leg. "Three's my limit."

Lavina set the container down on the quilt they'd spread on the grass and replaced the top. She knew he'd try to resist another piece and wouldn't be able to so she'd packed plenty. He loved her fried chicken. And like many hard-working Amish men, he could eat a lot and not gain weight.

The day was warm but pleasantly so. The delicate white seed tops of dandelions seemed to dance on the gentle breeze that blew over the nearby pond. Lavina poured cups of lemonade and wished the day wouldn't end.

They'd stolen a few hours for themselves after church. Summer was so busy with the harvest in and all the canning and preserving. But Sunday was a day of rest and there would be no work aside from the necessary daily chores of caring for and feeding the animals.

"More potato salad?"

*"*Nee,*" he said with a satisfied sigh. "I'm full." He leaned back on his elbows and stretched out his long legs. "We'll have to head back soon," he said. "It's going to rain."*

She frowned. "Not fair. Why does it have to rain on the only day we have off?"

"Sometimes things don't seem fair." Now it was his turn to frown.

"Did you speak to your dat*?"*

He shook his head. "He was in a bad mood yesterday and went to bed early. I'm hoping to talk to him after supper tonight."

His father was a difficult man, so demanding of David and his two bruders*. They worked so hard and yet it never seemed to be enough for him. But it seemed to Lavina he was hardest on David, his eldest* sohn*.*

She touched his arm. "I wish the two of you got along better."

"I don't think he gets along with anyone," David muttered. He reached for his lemonade, gulped it down, and crushed the paper cup in his hand. "I don't know how much more I can take." He stared down at the cup in his hand as if he had forgotten it. Sitting up, he tossed it into the picnic basket.

"Surely he'll retire soon and let you take over the farm. Your mamm *told me that the doctor told him he needs to slow down, that he's worried about his health."*

"He's too stubborn to retire. If he did that, he couldn't control my bruders *and me."*

"Be patient," she said softly. She hated seeing him unhappy.

They looked up as thunder rumbled. Reluctantly, she packed up the picnic things, and they gathered up the quilt and ran for the buggy as fat raindrops began pelting them.

"Guess it's time to head home," he said, sounding as if that was the last place he wanted to be.

She reached for his hand and held it as he took the long way home.

Lavina got into Officer Kate's car. It surprised her to see the woman dressed in a sweater and jeans and driving a vehicle other than her police car.

"I'm so glad you could come today," Kate told her.

"I'm looking forward to it."

A few minutes later she was surprised again when Kate pulled up in front of a simple three-story house on the outskirts of town. From the outside it didn't look occupied; the houses on each side of it didn't look like anyone lived there, either.

Once Kate used a code on the front door, though, it was an entirely different story. There were a half-dozen women sitting in the spacious living room and more *kinner* than Lavina could count. One woman sat in a rocking chair feeding a baby a bottle.

Kate had explained that the shelter wouldn't be marked with a sign because its location was kept secret for the safety of the women and children who stayed there.

A woman with a round face and a big smile hurried toward them wiping her hands on a dish towel. "Kate, good to see you! So who's this?"

Kate introduced Lavina, and the woman pumped her hand. "Glad to meet you. So happy you could come help the women with the quilting class."

"I'm happy to."

"I just put some coffee on up in the room, Kate. Let me know if you need anything. I'll be in the kitchen."

"Thanks, Pearl."

Lavina followed Kate up the stairs and down a hallway. She heard the whir of sewing machines and the chatter of women before they walked into a room that had been converted into a sewing room. It reminded Lavina of the room her *dat* had fixed up for her *mudder* and *schweschders* at home. There were several tables with sewing machines of various ages, another two tables with projects laid out on them and shelves and shelves of fabric and colorful yarns.

The women glanced up as they walked in. One of them looked startled, jumping up and dropping the fabric clutched in her hands.

"It's okay, Carrie," Kate said in a low-pitched, soothing voice. "It's just me."

The woman frowned. “I see that.” She sat and didn’t look at Kate again.

“Hello, good to see all of you again,” Kate greeted the women. “Lavina here accepted my invitation to join us this week. She’s a master quilter.”

“Well, I don’t know that I’d say that,” Lavina said, embarrassed, gazing around at the dozen or so women gathered in the room. She’d been taught to avoid *hochmut*—pride—practically since birth.

“If someone’s making her living from what she does, I’d say she’s a master at it,” Kate responded equably.

“Isn’t every Amish woman a quilter?” someone asked, sounding skeptical.

“It’s true most Amish women quilt, Carrie,” Kate said. “But not all of them have the skill Lavina has. She and her sisters supply two quilt shops in town with their work.”

Kate turned to a nearby shelf, plucked a box from it and set it on the table in front of her. “This is the week’s quilt block.”

She handed several to Lavina to pass out and began handing out others to women near her.

“Each woman makes a quilt to donate to the community,” she explained to Lavina. “Then she gets to make one for herself and her family.”

She liked that idea. Community—their own and the *Englisch* one outside it—was important to the Amish. Each year Lavina, her *schweschders,* and other Amish women made quilts to donate to the auction that raised money for Haiti. The Amish community had been doing it for more than twenty years, well before the last devastating earthquake that had caught the attention of the world.

Kate gave a brief lesson on how to construct the block, and then she and Lavina walked around the room offering help when it was requested.

Lavina paused beside the woman Kate had called Carrie. She was the one who’d been a little sarcastic about how she thought every Amish woman quilted. Carrie was struggling to thread the sewing machine. Looking disgusted, she slumped in her chair.

"Would you like some help?"

"You know how to thread an electric sewing machine? I thought you people didn't use electricity."

"We don't. But it looks like it threads in much the same way as my treadle machine at home."

"Whatever you say."

Lavina didn't take offense at the way she talked. Carrie seemed . . . unhappy to her. Sometimes unhappy people were unfriendly.

On the ride here today Kate had warned Lavina that the women at the shelter had been through rough times. They'd been forced to leave their homes because of violence—sometimes in the middle of the night with only the clothes on their back. Some of them had children, and all of them hid here at the shelter where their husbands and boyfriends couldn't find them. None of them had much money, and even worse, they had no self-esteem after months and even years of abusive behavior from those men.

Although Carrie looked about her age, she acted older, harder. She wore jeans that were worn and tight and a faded t-shirt. There was a colorful bruise under one eye.

Carrie stood and gestured at the chair she'd been sitting in. "Be my guest."

Lavina sat, studied the machine for a moment and then she guided the thread through the loops on the top and side of the machine and finally the needle. "There. See if it works now." She stood so Carrie could resume her seat.

Unsure whether she should stay and offer help or move on, Lavina studied the quilt block. "I don't know about you, but I don't mind working on something someone's ordered. But it's nice to work on one I want when I can."

She met Carrie's gaze. "Have you thought about what kind of quilt you'd like to make for yourself yet?"

Carrie jerked her shoulder. "Not really. I'm more concerned with what I'm going to wear for a job interview when I get one.

When I went back with Kate to get my clothes my boyfriend had torn up my clothes, the bas—" she stopped. "The jerk," she corrected with a sidelong glance at Lavina.

"I wonder—" Lavina paused and bit her lip. She had to ask Kate if she could offer to help her sew something to wear to an interview.

"What?"

"Maybe Kate knows where you can get something—"

"I'm tired of taking charity." Her lips pressed together, Carrie bent over the quilt block.

Lavina stared at her stiff posture, unsure what to do. She looked around and saw Kate on the other side of the room, bent over talking to a woman sewing on a machine. "Let me know if you want help on the block."

She moved on and found another woman her mother's age who glanced up and smiled at her. "Don't pay Carrie no mind. She's only been here two weeks. It's hard making the split, no matter how bad your man treated you, coming here with nothing and starting over." She held out her hand. "Hi, I'm Edna."

Lavina shook her hand. "Hi, Edna."

"Don't suppose you have this kind of problem in your community."

"I'm sorry to say we do."

"Really?"

"People are people no matter where they live or what religion they practice, don't you think?"

She thought of David's *mudder.* She hoped that all Amos did these days was yell . . . not that yelling wasn't bad enough.

"Women turn to the bishop for help in my community. He talks to the husband and tries to work things out."

"I kept trying to hold on," Edna said, pulling some straight pins from a pincushion shaped like a plump tomato. "Some people think holdin' on is a sign of strength, but there comes a point to where it takes more strength to just let go!"

She pinned a block and then started sewing it up. "My man wouldn't talk to our minister and said counseling was for dummies. It was bad enough that he hit me, but when he hit my little boy I knew we had to leave." She glanced around the room. "We came here."

She finished sewing a seam, lifted the foot on the sewing machine, and pulled out the quilt block. After she clipped the thread she held the block up and examined it critically. "What do you think?" She handed it to Lavina.

"Good job," she said. "Nice straight seams."

Edna took it back and pinned another piece. "This is fun. How long you been quilting?"

"My mother gave me a piece of fabric and a needle and thread when I was five," Lavina remembered. "I've been sewing ever since."

Lavina moved on when Edna went back to work. When she saw that Kate sat at a table doing some handwork on a quilt, she approached her and quietly told her about Carrie's dilemma.

"Pearl can help her with that," Kate said cheerfully. "She's started a clothes closet for the women for job interviews and such things. She put out a call to her female friends and there are some nice suits and dresses. I'll tell Carrie before we leave today."

The time flew by. It felt like they'd only been there a half hour, but before she knew it Kate began putting supplies back on the shelves. The women tucked their work in project boxes and stored them on shelves, saying goodbye as they left the room. Lavina checked the clock on the wall and saw that two hours had passed.

"I don't need you to fix my life!" she heard Carrie shout.

Lavina spun around and saw Kate frowning as Carrie stomped out of the room.

Kate sighed. "That went well." She carried the box of quilt blocks to the shelves and stored it, then turned to Lavina. "Ready to go?"

They walked outside and got into Kate's car. Lavina waited until they were out onto the road headed home.

"I'm sorry Carrie yelled at you," she said. "Should I have not told you what she said?"

Kate glanced at her briefly then focused on the road. "I get yelled at all the time. I'm a cop, remember? We're not real popular." She made a turn. "Don't worry about it. It's a difficult time for Carrie and the other women."

They chatted about the class and soon Kate pulled into the drive of Lavina's house.

"So," she said, turning and meeting Lavina's gaze. "Are you going to join us again next week?"

"I don't know how much help I was."

"You helped a lot. Don't let Carrie scare you off. We never know how much we can help just by showing up ready to try."

"Okay," Lavina said. "I'll be happy to."

"Great." Kate grinned. "See you next week."

4

Tell us all about the quilt class," Mary Elizabeth said the minute the three of them gathered in the sewing room the next day. "How was it? Did you enjoy it?"

Lavina thought about it as she threaded a needle. "I did. The shelter is a big old house just outside town. You can't tell it's a shelter from the outside because they have to keep it secret that it's where these women and children live to keep them safe."

"That's sad," Rose Anna said, her forehead puckering as she thought about it. "I can't imagine having to be afraid of my boyfriend or my husband when I have one."

"Or having to worry about having a place to live or clothes and food for myself and my *kinner*," Lavina said.

"Kate said sometimes the women have to leave their home with only the clothes on their back. Some of the women looked like they had so little."

She remembered the worn jeans and faded shirt Carrie had worn and how she'd wondered what she'd wear to a job interview.

"But when I walked in the door it looked like a home," she told them. "A group of women were sitting in the living room talking and a mother was feeding her *boppli* a bottle. Several *kinner* were watching television. A big yellow bird was talking about the alphabet and a blue puppet kept asking for cookies. It was called *Sesame Street* and the *kinner* were laughing and looking happy."

She knotted the thread. "It looked very much like a home, a regular *Englisch* home. And the sewing room where we taught the class—well, where Kate taught it and I tried to help—was very much like this one."

Picking up the quilt she'd been sewing, she smiled. "It made me feel good that the women and the *kinner* had a home after what Kate said they'd been through."

Rose Anna frowned. "Is there anything we can do?"

"You want to help with the quilting classes?"

"Well, that wasn't what I was thinking." She turned as their mother came into the room and took a seat. "*Mamm*, I was wondering if we had some things we could donate to the shelter Lavina visited yesterday. You know how places like that always need things."

"You mean some quilts?"

"I was thinking more like that fold-up trundle bed we haven't used in years."

"We could do that," Linda said, looking thoughtful. "There might be some other things we can donate. Ask the person who runs the shelter what they need, and then we can let people at church know."

"*Allrecht*."

There was a knock on the front door. Linda went to see who it was.

"I guess it makes you thankful for what we have, doesn't it?" Mary Elizabeth asked. "We have our parents, a warm home and good food, and our church."

Lavina nodded. She started to speak but stopped when her mother returned to the room.

"David's here to see you."

"*Danki*." She set the quilt she'd been sewing aside and hurried from the room.

She found David sitting on the sofa in the living room. He stood when she walked into the room.

"Could we go for a ride so we can talk?" He looked so serious.

"*Allrecht,*" she said. "I'll get my jacket." She grabbed up her jacket and bonnet and let her mother know she was leaving the house. When she walked outside with David she was surprised to see the Stoltzfus family buggy.

"Did you get rid of your truck?" she asked as she climbed into the buggy.

"*Nee*. Nellie needed exercising."

She studied him as he checked traffic and pulled out onto the road. She wondered if the horse really needed exercise or if he'd taken the buggy because he missed the old family horse.

They rode for a time without speaking, the only sound the clip-clop of Nellie's hooves on the road. The air was chilly, but she was warm enough in the buggy.

"I wanted to talk to you," he said finally, not looking at her.

Another long pause followed. He found a place to pull over and turned to look at her. "I wanted to ask your forgiveness. I shouldn't have left without seeing you first."

"*Nee*, you shouldn't have," she said, trying to stay calm. "How could you?"

Before he could speak, the words poured out of her. "Do you know how I felt? I thought we meant something to each other."

"We did." He stared down at his hands, then looked up and stared at her. "Can you forgive me?"

"I've tried," she admitted, tearing her gaze from his to stare out the window. "You don't know how hard I've tried. A year, David. You were gone a year, and you couldn't even write to me. I didn't know where you were, if you were *allrecht*, anything."

She heard the pain and accusation in her voice and bit her lip. What good did it do to say these things now? But emotions—pain and anger and feelings of rejection—were welling up, boiling over. She didn't know she felt so strongly. She'd been taught to believe in extending forgiveness to those who wronged her all her life, and the one time she'd been given the opportunity to practice what she believed she failed miserably.

"I hurt you. I'm sorry."

She didn't need to look at him to know he meant it. She heard the regret in his voice.

"Why didn't you ask me to go with you?" she asked quietly.

When he didn't respond she summoned the courage to look at him. She'd never spoken to him like this. But she wanted answers.

"What could I offer you?" he said finally. "I had practically no money. No property. No job." He sighed. "No future."

She stared at him. "You had yourself. You had your two hands and a strong back to make your future with me by your side." She paused. "You had your heart that I thought held love for me. What more could I want?"

Turning, she stared out the window, not seeing the landscape outside. "I would have gone with you."

"Like Ruth in the Bible?"

"*Ya*."

"I didn't want you to give up your family."

Confused, she turned back to him. "What?"

"They would have shunned you if you'd left the community."

"You said you hadn't decided to become *Englisch*."

"I haven't."

"So you haven't decided to leave the church?"

"I hadn't joined the church so there was nothing to leave. You know that."

"What I don't know is why you asked to talk to me today."

She watched him sit there staring ahead. Then he took a deep breath and turned to her. "I'm coming back to do what I can to help *Mamm* since *Daed's* sick. But I'm coming back for more than that, Lavina. I came back for you. Will you give me another chance?"

Lavina wasn't the most talkative person, but he could tell he'd shocked her speechless.

When silence stretched between them he felt a sickening lurch in his stomach. What had he been thinking? He should have waited, let her get used to seeing him for a while before he asked her to give him another chance.

Then an awful thought struck him: what if she was seeing someone? For all he knew she was engaged to be married. It was that time of year when Amish couples were getting married. Sometimes there were several weddings each week during the fall months . . .

Maybe he'd returned too late. Maybe too much time had passed, and she was too angry with him for abandoning him. Maybe—

"You want another chance," she said slowly. "After all this time, you came back and you want another chance."

"*Ya*," he said, carefully watching her expression. He couldn't read it.

"You want me to trust you after you betrayed my trust."

"*Ya*," he said.

"After what I just said to you?"

"Lavina—"

She held up her hand. "*Nee*, I can't think of such a thing. Not so suddenly. You've been out of my life for a year and suddenly you're not only back, but you're wanting us to go back to what we used to be."

A tear trickled down her cheek, and she angrily swiped at it with her hand. "I don't know if I can go back to that, David. I don't know if I should—if we should."

"We were *gut* together," he told her, reaching for her hand. "You know that."

She sighed and nodded. "*Ya*, we were. But that was then. This is now. We're different people now."

"I haven't changed," he said earnestly. "I haven't."

"But I have." She lifted her chin. "I learned to live without you. I learned I had to think about life without you. I had to learn to survive without you in my future."

David felt a wave of panic wash over him. He'd told himself that she could turn him down, but he'd forced that thought from his mind. He hadn't been able to think it could happen. She'd been part of his life for so many years. The Amish usually lived in the same community all their lives—generation after generation. They went to *schul* together, attended church together. Participated in work frolics and community activities. Their lives were so entwined. They became friends and married the boy or girl they'd known all their lives.

But she was saying he'd ruined things by abruptly leaving and not contacting her for a year. He'd been the biggest fool ever thinking it would be easy to just come back, apologize, and everything would be *allrecht*.

And he still didn't have anything to offer her. Despite what she said, he felt any woman would want to know he could provide for her.

He pulled the hand he'd offered back, picked up the reins and jerked them. Nellie stepped back onto the road and began pulling the buggy down the road.

"David—"

He held up his hand. "*Nee*, I understand."

"Do you? If I let you that close again and you left, I don't think I could survive. *Nee*, David, you ask too much."

She'd just broken his heart again so he knew what she meant. She probably didn't know how he'd felt when he walked away from her—when he'd felt forced to leave his home, his community, everything he knew and cared about a year ago. He'd been so angry with his *dat* he hadn't even been aware of how he'd felt when he woke up the day after and it really hit him what he'd walked away from. He'd lost the church and community he'd grown up in, but most importantly, it had hit him that he might never see Lavina again.

But he hadn't gone back. He'd told himself he had nothing for her. He still didn't, but he'd taken one look at her and knew he had to find some way to make things work. Maybe his father would realize that he was just so sick he had to retire and take it easy. Maybe . . .

Maybe he just needed to accept that he'd come back for two reasons—for his *dat* and for Lavina—and it appeared now that it wouldn't be for Lavina. If he was honest, neither of them wanted him. He'd known his *dat* didn't before he stepped back into his old home. He'd feared Lavina wouldn't, either. But he'd had to take a chance on it.

How he wished she'd give him a chance.

He pulled up in front of Lavina's house, and before he could get out she'd slipped from the buggy and was running toward the front door.

"Lavina!"

But she kept going. She raced up the steps to the porch and threw open the front door.

David stood there, debating going after her. Then he shook his head. She probably wouldn't even answer the door if he knocked.

His shoulders slumped, he walked back to the buggy and got into his seat. "Take us home, Nellie," he said. "Take us home."

She began plodding toward the house down the road.

Usually he liked the relaxed travel a buggy provided. His mother had always said the *Englisch* rushed about so in their automobiles, and that they should slow down and learn to "smell the roses."

Tonight he found himself wanting to hurry Nellie and get home quickly so he could lose himself in the oblivion of sleep. He'd had two bad days in a row—the first returning home to hear how sick his *dat* was and to have the man show him just how little he cared about his returning home.

And then today, hearing Lavina tell him how much he'd hurt her, how she couldn't trust him not to do it again. Talk about rejection.

He drove down the long, dark road, feeling depressed and more than a little lonely. It wasn't a new feeling . . . it had been the story of his life for the past year. Sometimes he didn't think he'd have made it through without the friendship of Bill, his *Englisch* friend, and his *bruders* when they had left the Amish community and moved near him.

With Nellie in charge of getting them home and no need to concentrate on the road with no other vehicles on it, David's thoughts wandered back through the years, back to memories of rosy-cheeked Lavina, her braids flying as she played tag on the school playground during recess. How he'd felt to know she'd sit with him for hours and listen as he poured out his pain at trying to get along with his father, and how her blue eyes would fill with warmth and compassion and she'd hold his hand. The happiness in those eyes when he asked her to accompany him to their first singing when she was a young *maedel*. Then utter joy years later when he asked her to marry him and the sweet taste of their kiss sealed the engagement.

Tonight he'd looked into the face of a young woman, not a *maedel* from his childhood, and seen how she'd turned away from him for the pain he'd caused, and he felt a soul-deep bleakness and despair.

An owl hooted in the woods lining the road, its call echoing in the silence. The wind grew colder and found crevices to creep into around the windshield and the doors of the buggy, seeping into his bones and making him feel old. It made him long for the comfort of his truck; watching the back of old Nellie, knowing she'd guide him home as she'd done for years and years, was a comfort he'd missed. She, the buggy, the family farm, the Amish way of life were such a part of him, just as much as his blood and bone and sinew.

He'd missed so much. He had to find a way back, not just to help his *mudder* with his *dat* and the farm, but to find himself again.

He told himself he couldn't let himself get depressed over two bad days, rejection from two people who meant something to him. *Gut* things didn't always come easy even when all came from God, from His plan for your life and according to His will.

There was something to be learned from every road He took you down, every hardship you faced, as well as every joy.

Maybe Lavina wasn't the woman God had set aside for him. Maybe there was another he'd find joy in loving, find happiness in marrying, and having the *kinner* he hoped God would send. Who knew? He sighed. It was evident he wasn't supposed to find out tonight. Maybe not for many nights.

He pulled into the drive of his home and got out of the buggy to unhitch Nellie. As he stood there giving her an affectionate hug, he told himself to be grateful for the moment, for the peace of the still night, for the safety and security of a home and a warm bed for the night. He said a prayer of thanks and asked for guidance, and then he led Nellie into her stall for the night before heading to his own solitary bed.

5

They say you can't go home again."

"Who's 'they'?" David picked up a box he'd collected from the grocery store and began to fill it with items from one of his kitchen cupboards.

"It's an expression." Bill opened the refrigerator and looked inside. "There's no beer in here. You have to have beer if you want someone to help you move."

"That's a rule?"

"Yeah. And pizza. Gotta have pizza, bro." He sat down at the tiny kitchen table. "Anyway, Thomas Wolfe said you can't go home again. We had to read him in high school. You didn't?"

"No."

David leaned into the open cupboard to make sure he'd gotten everything out. *Allrecht,* so it wasn't really that he was trying to make sure he got it emptied and cleaned out. He was really trying to avoid talking about *schul.* He'd always felt he'd gotten enough education, but once he lived and worked in the *Englisch* world, it was a real negative that he hadn't graduated from a high school.

Back home, it was considered more than enough *schul* to attend for eight years and then apprentice for your life's work. He'd learned to farm alongside the most demanding teacher in the world—his *dat*—and that was more than enough training for what he'd do for a living.

Not that learning stopped when *schul* did. He, like many Amish, loved reading. He knew the *Englisch* enjoyed their television, but most nights he didn't turn on the small set that was part of the small furnished apartment; instead, he indulged in his love of reading. He was sure Bill would be complaining when he had to haul the boxes of books already packed to go in the truck.

David used the cleaning cloth to do a last swipe of the shelf in the cupboard and shut the door. That was it for the kitchen. He'd cleaned the refrigerator the day before, and it was as spotless and empty as the day he'd moved in.

He hefted a box and turned to Bill. "Ready to start loading?"

Bill rolled his eyes and sighed. "Sure."

"I'll buy us a pizza when we have everything loaded."

"It better be loaded."

"The truck?"

"The pizza."

"Okay."

They were sitting in a favorite restaurant eating a slice of Bill's favorite meat lover's pizza when David remembered what his friend had said.

"So why does this Wolfe guy say you can't go home again?"

"Hmm? Oh, Wolfe. Well, you know, nothing's the same. You can't recapture the memories, your dreams of glory, that sort of thing." He shrugged and grinned. "I don't remember much of the book. I did the Cliff's version."

"What's that?"

Now Bill looked embarrassed. "It's a booklet students buy to read a summary of the book, so they don't have to read the full book."

"Why wouldn't someone want to read the book?"

He shrugged again. "Not enough time. Not what you want to read. Rebellion against your teacher who assigns it or your parents. All sorts of reasons."

David loved to read, so what Bill was saying didn't make a lot of sense. "The night I went home my father told me I better not expect to be welcomed back like the prodigal son. You know, like in the Bible."

"Now I do know that story. We learned about it in Sunday school when I was a kid."

"I liked that story." Better not think about it, he told himself. His *dat* wasn't going to change.

Bill wiped his hands on a napkin, took a sip of beer, and eyed the last piece of pizza. "You want?"

David shook his head. "No, take it."

"I've already had three more than you."

But Bill reached for the slice. He chewed for a long moment, his gaze steady on David. He finished the pizza, took a long swig of beer, then balled up his napkin and tossed it on his plate.

"I know you're moving back home. But do you want to?"

He shrugged. "I don't have a choice." He looked up with a smile when their server brought him another soft drink.

"Sure you do. We always have a choice."

They both looked up as the door opened and a pack of teenagers streamed in, filling the near-empty restaurant with noise. They settled at a table close to the video games. David couldn't help feeling old as he watched them horsing around, flirting with the waitress who looked about their age and trying to wheedle her into bringing them a pitcher of beer. She took their order and brought them a pitcher of soft drink.

He knew they should get going so Bill could get home to his ESPN. It was his favored evening activity. And delaying moving into his old room wasn't going to make it any easier.

"Didn't mean to make you feel bad," Bill said as they walked out to David's truck. "I know you feel you have to help your mother. But no one would blame you if you didn't go back. Not the people who know how your father was, how he threw you out."

"I left."

Bill settled in the passenger seat and reached for his seat belt. "What?"

"I said I left. He didn't throw me out."

"From what you said he made your life a living he—" he stopped. "He made your life miserable." Leaning forward, he fiddled with the radio. "Was he the same way with your brothers?"

"Yes."

"What did they say when you called them? Are they going back, too?"

David winced. The phone calls with Samuel and John had been short and curt.

"He's not going to die," Samuel had told him. "He's too mean to die."

"Mean people die every day," David said. "*Mamm* said he's really sick. I saw how he looked after his chemo treatment." He searched for the right words to get Samuel to do the right thing. "*Mamm* needs us. Don't do it for him. Do it for her."

"Is that what you're doing?"

David had rubbed at the ache building behind his eyes. "Look, don't say no. Think about it. Just don't think about it for too long." He sighed. "I have to talk to John. Is he there?"

The response he got from John, the youngest, wasn't any better. David could hear hard rock blaring in the background. Of the three of them, John had been the one who most enjoyed the *Englisch* world.

"I'm sorry, I'm not going back," John said bluntly. "Don't try to guilt me into it, either."

The ache built to a vicious headache. "Like I told Samuel, just think about it. I'll need the help with planting come spring."

John muttered a curse. "If you're still there then, we'll talk. I gotta go. I have company."

With that, he hung up. David shoved the memory of the calls aside as he pulled into the drive of his home.

Nee. It wasn't his. If his *dat* had his way it never would be. What Samuel had said hadn't been kind but he couldn't blame him for saying it. Their *dat* had been equally rough on all of them, but it had seemed to affect John most of all, perhaps because he was the youngest.

"We can turn around," Bill said. "Just make a U-turn. I'm sure your landlady would let you have your old place back in a heartbeat."

David put the truck in park and turned off the ignition.

The front door opened and Waneta stepped out, wearing a big smile. She looked at Bill. "Hello, I'm Waneta, David's mother."

"This is Bill, *Mamm*."

"*Wilkumm*. I just made a fresh pot of coffee. Do you like snickerdoodles?"

"I sure do, ma'am."

"Wish my mom baked cookies," Bill told David as he lowered the tailgate on the truck and pulled a box toward him.

"Everybody's mom bakes cookies."

"Okay, she occasionally baked cookies." Bill hoisted a box and started for the house. "The dog refused to eat them."

Leave it to Bill to lighten things up, David thought. Too bad he couldn't live here with him and make things bearable.

"You know, there's a way to get fresh-baked cookies every day," he said as he followed Bill up the front steps.

Lavina loved sewing. She really did. But sometimes it gave her too much time to think. And too often those thoughts circled back to David.

How was he doing with his *dat*? Were they getting along or arguing as they always had? What was his day like? David had always loved working on the farm. It was the slow time of year for farming now, when the land lay resting, becoming colder and harder as the temperatures grew colder. This was a time when farmers turned to repairing equipment, to planning and browsing through seed catalogs. Some made furniture in their barns or basements or worked part-time, seasonal jobs.

She knew Amos had to go for chemotherapy treatments and wondered if he let David drive him. She didn't think she'd ever known a more difficult man than Amos.

"Lavina? Where did you just go?"

She lifted her eyes from the quilt she was hand-finishing. "Hmm?"

"You've been sitting there not listening to us for the past ten minutes."

"Oh? Sorry."

"I think you've already left the house."

"What? I'm sitting right here."

"She's right," Linda said as she used her scissors to snip a thread. "It's like when *Daed* is getting ready to go off to an auction. His body's still here but you can tell his mind's already racing ahead to the auction."

"I'm only going to the quilting class," Lavina said.

Better to let them think she'd been thinking about that rather than David. Then they'd start questioning her and worrying over her.

She glanced at the clock. "Guess I should be getting ready to leave. Kate will be here soon to pick me up."

"Busy young woman," Linda said as she sewed. "Adding a volunteer class on to her job as a police officer and raising a family."

"Her husband volunteers, too," Lavina said as she folded her quilt and stored it on a shelf. "Oh, not with the quilting. He volunteers at the veteran's center since he was in the military."

She started for the kitchen and then turned back. "*Mamm*, have you heard from *Grossmudder* and *Grossdaadi* this week?"

Linda shook her head. "I haven't checked the mailbox today." She sighed. "I know they're having a *gut* time in Pinecraft but I miss them so."

Lavina walked over to hug her. "We all do. Every time I walk past the door to their *dawdi haus* I think they'll be there."

"I do, too."

"Well, maybe there'll be a postcard today. Or they'll call. Listen, do you mind if I take some cookies for the ladies in the class?"

"Take as many as you want. There's a loaf of pumpkin bread in the freezer, too. It'll thaw in no time and you can slice it when you get there."

Kate pulled into the driveway a short time later.

Lavina buttoned her jacket, picked up her purse and the tote with the baked goodies, and hurried out to the car.

"I'm so glad you could join us again." Kate glanced over at Lavina. "I wasn't sure if Carrie might have chased you away."

"I enjoyed myself last week," Lavina told Kate. "And I wonder if I could be pleasant to other people if I was going through what she is. I've never been without a home. Without my family."

She turned to Kate. "We both know what she's going through isn't just an *Englisch* problem. It happens in my community, too, but the bishop often can work things out with the couple." She paused. "Well, sometimes. We don't believe in divorce."

"And many women—Amish or *Englisch*—don't think they can break out of the cycle of abuse."

Kate turned into the driveway of the shelter, put the car in park, and turned off the ignition. "Well, let's hope we have a quiet morning." She shot Lavina a grin. "I pray for quiet everywhere. At work. At home. "

Chuckling, she punched in the code on the front door. "I get less of it at home than anywhere. I have two kids," she explained as she opened the door and waited for Lavina to precede her.

A little girl jumped up from in front of the television and ran to hide behind her mother on the sofa.

Kate stopped. "Sweetie, it's okay."

"Ellie, don't be scared," her mother soothed her. "We're safe here. This is Kate. She came to help us the night Daddy was hurting me." She looked up at Kate. "She's still a little skittish."

"I'm going upstairs to teach the ladies to sew," Kate told Ellie. "You're about five, right? I was around that age when I learned how to sew a dress for my doll. Do you want to come up and watch?"

Ellie stayed behind her mother.

"Maybe next time," her mother said.

"You're welcome to join us whenever you like. I think you'd both have fun. I started sewing with my mom when I wasn't much older than Ellie."

Kate and Lavina passed out the week's block and walked round helping the women with it. When there was a lull in questions, Lavina sat down with a quilt block, threaded a needle and began sewing. She glanced over when Kate paused at the window and appeared to be looking at something downstairs in the front yard. Then Kate walked over to her and bent down.

"I have to go downstairs for a minute," Kate said quietly in her ear.

Lavina looked up, saw the frown on Kate's face. "Is everything okay?"

Kate nodded. "I'll be right back." She strode quickly from the room.

Women chatted, sewing machines whirred, and the sounds of children playing downstairs drifted up. It was a happy place, thought Lavina. Not just a safe one. She'd never really thought about it, but she supposed you had to feel safe to feel happy. She knew she was lucky that she'd never had to think about being safe . . . she'd always felt safe, cared for. Looked over by her parents but most of all by God.

She hoped these women would feel that way soon. Assured that no one needed her, Lavina excused herself and went in search of a restroom. As she came out she saw Kate and Carrie talking in the hallway. Carrie stood with her arms crossed over her chest and a mutinous expression on her face.

"I was just having a smoke," she muttered.

Lavina, walking past her, could smell the acrid scent of cigarette smoke.

"You know the rules," Kate said quietly.

"I was smoking outside. Not in the house."

"You were smoking in front of the house. That's not allowed."

"So what's the big deal?"

"Someone who knows you could drive past. We have to keep the location secret to keep everyone safe."

Lavina hurried back to the sewing room so they wouldn't think she was eavesdropping.

A few minutes later Kate returned to the room followed by a glowering Carrie, who slumped into an empty chair in front of a sewing machine.

"What's the point of sewing a quilt?" she asked the room. "It's not like I'm going to get a job sewing a quilt." She gave Lavina a baleful look. "Maybe you can get a job doing that if you're Amish but not if you're American like me."

Lavina wanted to say she was American, too, but she didn't want to engage in an argument with the woman.

"You don't have to stay if you don't want to," Kate said calmly. "This is an entirely voluntary activity."

Carrie expelled a gusty sigh as she picked up the fabric pieces for her block and pushed them around on the table the sewing machine rested on. "Got nothing better to do in this dump."

Kate sat down at a nearby table and pulled a quilt from a tote. Lavina saw that it was composed of fabric in many patterns, all red, white, and blue. Kate glanced up and saw Lavina's interest.

"I'm making a quilt for a friend of my husband who's recovering in an Army hospital," she said, spreading it out on the table before her. "Each month one of the quilting magazines features a special patriotic quilt to sew for men and women who serve in the military. Malcolm still has a lot of friends in the service, so I make one for them once in a while."

Kate sighed. "I'm nearly finished with this one. It feels like it's taken forever. I've only been able to work on it for short periods of time what with work and kids."

She glanced over Lavina's shoulder and tensed, then stood and slowly moved toward the doorway. Was there trouble again? Lavina wondered.

"Ellie? Ellie, where are you?" they heard a woman call up the stairs.

Kate appeared to relax immediately. She crouched down. "Ellie? Come on in, let's have some fun sewing."

The little girl walked into the room, wide-eyed, sucking her thumb. Kate held out her hand and after a moment Ellie took it.

Her mother appeared a few seconds later and stood in the doorway watching as Kate settled her daughter in a chair and gave her a colorful square of material.

"Hi, Mom, come join us," Kate said easily. "We're going to sew."

David stood in the driveway and watched the van leave with his parents.

He'd offered to drive them to his *dat's* chemotherapy appointment but he'd been brusquely turned down. Oh, his *mamm* had looked pleased at the suggestion when he made it at the breakfast table. She'd looked expectantly at Amos, but her smile had quickly faded when he shook his head vehemently and left the table.

David walked out onto the fields and felt at home for the first time since he'd moved back. He'd been barely able to walk when his *dat* first took him out into them one day. He'd watched his *dat* scoop up a handful of rich earth and let it drift through his fingers. David had dug his own pudgy hand into the earth and laughed at the feeling of it and wanted to stay there all day. His *dat* had showed him how to put seeds in the earth, and as the crops grew David had grown and never thought a day in the fields was anything but play.

He didn't remember exactly when the two of them had begun disagreeing, when his father had turned sour and angry. His bad moods and dictatorial behavior wasn't just directed at David, as much as he'd have taken on the full brunt of it to save his *bruders*. It wasn't just his *sohns* who endured such. As he grew older he saw how his *mudder* flinched at the harshness in her *mann's* voice, how her shoulders slumped.

David knew a man was supposed to be the head of his home, but he didn't believe God ever meant for a *mann* to treat his *fraa* and family with anything but love and guidance.

Walking the fields, David wondered what would be planted this spring. He seriously doubted his *dat* would be able to do the work, but going by past behavior he would undoubtedly insist on dictating what would be planted in what field and exactly how and when to do it.

David had some ideas about what he'd like to see planted. But he doubted his *dat* would be interested in hearing them. Whenever he'd tried in the past they'd been dismissed as "new-fangled" and "not the way we've always done things."

With a sigh he turned to walk back to the house. He had to head into work soon. His boss had agreed to a part-time schedule until David figured out what to do. He'd started to resign, but his boss had told him he was one of his hardest-working employees and pressed him about why he wanted to leave. So he'd explained and David had had to agree that until planting season came he might have time on his hands. If he needed time off to drive his father to chemotherapy and so on, all he had to do was ask for the time off and he'd get it.

Not that he'd needed it today after all. Stubborn old man. He'd rather pay an *Englisch* driver to take him to the hospital than let his son drive him.

A horn honked. David looked out the road in front of the house and saw a familiar beat up white car pull into the drive. The car stopped, but the engine didn't. It coughed and wheezed and finally rattled to a stop.

David grinned at his *bruder* Sam. "Surprised this thing is still running."

"Hey, don't knock it. Sally here's paid off." He looked at the house. "Thought you said you'd be taking *Daed* to chemo today."

"He didn't want me to."

"Why do you bother?"

David shrugged. "I told *Mamm* I'd come back to help, and that's what I'm trying to do."

"And what if he doesn't let you?"

David kicked at the gravel beneath his feet. "I guess I'll deal with that when I have to."

He looked out at the fields, remembering how he'd wondered what he'd be planting in the spring, wondering if his *dat* would allow him to make some changes . . . he swung his gaze back to his *bruder.* The three *bruders* looked much alike, born just a little over a year apart.

"So what are you doing here?" he asked Sam.

"Just happened to be in the neighborhood," he said casually, resting his arm on the car window.

"Oh yeah?"

"I drive through the old neighborhood occasionally," Sam finally admitted. "Don't try to tell me you didn't do it sometimes, too."

He had. "Well, I have to get to work. My boss gave me the day off to drive *Daed* to the hospital, but since I don't have to I may as well go on in. Speaking of work, what are you doing away from it in the middle of the morning?"

"Running a couple of errands for the boss." He turned on the ignition.

David put his hand on his *bruder's* arm. "Sam? What about coming by later for supper?"

Sam scowled at him. "No. And don't try to give me a guilt trip. I'm out of here." He threw the car in reverse and backed out so quickly gravel spurted up from his tires.

Sighing, David watched Sam drive away. Apparently guilt worked only on him. Or perhaps it was that he wasn't as *gut* at it as their *mamm*. So what he needed to do was get the two of them together and she could work on him.

He frowned as he remembered the way Sam talked. He sounded more *Englisch* than the last time they'd talked. He wondered if his *bruders* would stay in the *Englisch* world or return to their Amish roots . . .

What a chain of events he'd set off when he'd left here. First one *bruder* had left home, then another. Within a year there were no *sohns* in the Zook house, only Amos and Waneta. No arguments. No help with the chores.

How David wished things had been different.

Now his *dat* was fighting the battle of his life. Who knew if he'd survive? It was like people said. You never knew how long you might have someone in your life so it was best to try to get along.

But he'd tried so hard. Honestly, he didn't know what else he could have done. If only he could have stayed silent, bent to his *dat's* will.

Guilt weighed heavy on his shoulders as he walked back into the house.

6

Lavina was driving home in the family buggy when she spotted a man dressed in Amish clothing trudging down the road ahead of her. His shoulders were slumped and his steps were slow, as if he was old and tired.

But when she pulled even with him she saw that it was David. He glanced up as she called his name.

"Can I give you a ride?"

He stared at her for a long moment, then glanced back, checking for traffic. "*Danki*."

They rode in silence for a few minutes. "Where's the pickup?"

"Back at the house. I needed to walk for a while."

He'd said house not home. "How is your *dat*?"

"He's at the hospital right now having chemo." He stared out the window. "He wouldn't let me drive him. I asked."

"I'm sorry, I really am."

He glanced at her, then away. "I know. *Danki*."

This time she didn't jump in and fill the silence. She waited. Sometimes people needed a listening ear. A listening heart.

They passed his house and if he noticed he didn't say anything. Whatever was troubling him ran deep. He'd hurt her deeply, but she didn't like to see anyone in pain. He obviously needed a friend.

A few minutes later he roused himself. "I'm sorry. We went past my place. Why didn't you stop?"

She bit her lip. "You seemed distracted. Like you didn't want to go in."

He sighed. "I don't, but that's not your problem. You must need to get home."

"In a bit. Do you want me to turn around and take you home? Or is there someplace else I can take you?"

"I don't have any friends here."

"You have friends."

"Not any more. I didn't keep in touch with anyone here in the community."

"No one?" She'd thought he'd just avoided her and his parents.

He shook his head, his expression bleak. "My *bruders* and I didn't live together, but without the tension from our *dat* and being strangers in the *Englisch* community we got closer. But they won't come back. Neither of them. Nothing I've said to them will change their minds." He glanced at her. "Maybe I should get you to talk to them."

She tried to smile. "Maybe it wasn't a good thing that I talked to you about it. I've never seen you so unhappy."

"It's *allrecht,*" he said with a big sigh. "You didn't twist my arm."

"*Nee?*"

"*Nee.*"

She pulled into his driveway, but he didn't get out immediately. A brisk wind swirled down the road, sending a rainfall of golden leaves showering down. The trees were nearly bare now. Fall was turning into winter.

"I don't blame you, Lavina. Honestly. It's my fault. I knew it wouldn't be easy." He grimaced. "An *Englisch* friend of mine said you can't go home again."

"What?"

"It had to do with some book he read." He told her what Bill had said about the book. "He's a *gut* guy, but I don't always understand what he's talking about."

He took a deep breath. "Anyway, *danki.* I appreciated the ride and you listening. I didn't deserve it after the way I treated you."

Lavina studied him. She remembered how she'd flung angry words at him, telling him that he'd broken her heart when he'd left and remembered how he'd said he'd broken his own heart. She'd hurt for more than a year and no matter how sorry she might know he felt now, she didn't know if she was ready to forgive him.

If she could ever forgive him.

He stepped out of the buggy, then turned back to look at her. "Be careful driving home. It's getting dark and you know how drivers can be."

"I'll be careful. It's not far. David?"

"*Ya*?"

"Don't get discouraged." She remembered what Leah had said to her that day in the shop. "Remember, 'we live by faith, not by sight.' Things will get better."

"I hope you're right." He looked toward the road. "I think that's *Mamm* and *Daed* coming home now."

"Then I'd better go so they can pull in. Be well, David."

"You, too, Lavina."

Their eyes met and she felt the warmth and regret in them as he stepped back so she could drive away.

As she headed for home Lavina glanced back and saw that it was indeed Amos and Waneta getting out of the van. David held out his hand to help his *dat,* and the older man ignored him.

Feeling sad, she turned her attention to the road. When she got to her own driveway, she saw her father closing the door to the barn. He smiled when he saw her and walked over to help unhitch the buggy. Before he could do so she wrapped her arms around him and hugged him.

He hugged her in return, but when she continued to hold on to him, he pulled back a little and studied her face. "*Kind*, what is it? Are you *allrecht*?"

"*Ya,*" she said, dropping her arms. "I was just thinking that I don't let you know often enough how much I love and appreciate you."

"*Schur* you do. What brought this on?"

"I just came from David's house. *Daed,* his *dat* is so unpleasant to him. Always has been."

"I know. You've told me through the years."

Together they unhitched the horse from the buggy. Lavina led Daisy into her stall while her *dat* stored the buggy.

"You go on in the house and I'll finish," he told her, measuring out Daisy's feed.

"You're just in time," her *mudder* said as she walked into the kitchen.

Lavina walked over and kissed her *mudder* on the cheek before she shed her jacket and bonnet and hung them on pegs near the door.

"I would have been home earlier, but I saw David walking on the road, and I gave him a ride home."

"Did his truck break down?"

She washed her hands, dried them, and then reached into a cupboard for dishes. "He was just taking a walk. It doesn't sound like things are going so well with him and his *dat*."

"It's early days yet." Linda opened the oven, pulled out a roasting pan and set it on top of the stove.

"Mmm, pot roast. My favorite."

Her father walked in just then. "She made it because it's my favorite," he corrected with a grin.

Linda laughed. "I made it because it's everyone's favorite in this family."

A few minutes later, her family gathered around the table, her *daed* asked for the meal to be blessed, and the platter of pot roast was passed around.

And not for the first time Lavina sent up a silent prayer that peace would descend on David's home.

David should have been prepared for his *dat* to shove his offer of help inside the house aside.

But was anyone ever really prepared for rejection?

"Here, David, pay the driver for me," his *mudder* said, pushing the bills into his hands. "Thank you," she said to the driver and then she hurried after her *mann*.

David passed the money to the driver and thanked him. As he turned the driver said his name.

"I hope your father feels better. Chemo is rough. My dad had to do it, too."

"I see. I hope he's well now?"

"Sure is. Took two rounds but he made it. Your father will, too. Take care. Tell your mother to let me know when she needs me next. 'Night."

"Good night."

He followed his parents into the house. His *mudder* helped his *dat* off with his jacket, smiling patiently as he grumbled that he wasn't a *kind* and could do it himself. He settled himself in a chair at the kitchen table, looking pointedly at the stove.

"I'll have fresh coffee made in just a minute," she said, pulling off her jacket and hanging it up quickly. "David? Coffee?"

"*Schur*, sounds *gut*."

He took a chair opposite his *dat*. Amos looked at him. "So you got time for riding around with Lavina instead of work, eh?"

"I went into work today," he said, refusing to let him rile him. If he'd known his *dat* wouldn't let him drive him to the hospital for his treatment, he could have put in a full day not just an afternoon . . .

He bit back a sigh. Water under the bridge, he told himself. He shouldn't have assumed his *dat* would want him to drive him.

His *mudder* set mugs of coffee in front of them then hurried to get milk from the refrigerator. She stood beside Amos. "What do you feel like for supper?"

He shrugged. "Not hungry."

"If you eat some supper you'll feel better," she said. "Then a nice rest." She sent David a desperate look.

"You look tired, *Mamm*. Why don't you sit down and have your coffee?"

"But—"

He rose, poured the coffee himself, and set it down on the table in front of the chair where his *mamm* usually sat, then waited until she sat before he resumed his seat. "Do you want me to go get something?"

"What? Like pizza?" his father asked sharply.

"*Schur*, if that's what you'd like. My treat."

"Waste of money. Cooking's her job," he said with a jerk of his head toward his *fraa*.

And she looked exhausted to the bone. She caught his eye and shook her head, sending him a silent message not to say anything. So he stayed silent.

"How about something warm and comforting like a grilled cheese sandwich and tomato soup?" she asked Amos. "And we have some apple cobbler left over from last night I could warm up."

That sounded pretty *gut* to David, but he was afraid to say anything. If he knew his *dat*, he'd want the opposite of whatever David said. So he stirred sugar into his coffee and drank it and stayed silent.

Amos shrugged. "Got any ice cream for the cobbler?"

"*Schur* do. And you can eat dessert first if you want."

"*Allrecht*, since it'll take you a while to get supper on the table."

David bit his tongue. The man had just a few minutes before claimed he wasn't hungry. Grumpy old goat. He rose and pulled on his jacket. "I'll go check on Nellie."

Amos harrumphed and held out his mug for a refill on his coffee. Waneta set the pan of cobbler and carton of ice cream on the table and hurried to get the coffee pot. The minute her back was turned, Amos dug a spoon into the cobbler and shoved it into his mouth.

Waneta turned and caught him in the act. She winked at David over his *dat's* head as he started out of the room.

Nellie put her head over the stall and neighed as David entered the barn. "Is it me you're happy to see or this?" he asked as he always did when he offered her the apple he brought.

But he didn't really care if it was the apple. At least she acted happier to see him than his *dat* had.

Supper was a silent affair but David didn't mind. His father ate half of his grilled cheese sandwich and slurped his bowl of soup and then trudged upstairs to rest. His *mudder* didn't eat quite as much. Too tired, he suspected. She sat nursing her cup of coffee and talked quietly about the chemo treatment that day and said his *dat* had a round of tests coming up soon to see if the chemo was working.

That's when he saw her mouth tremble, saw tears rush into her eyes. He reached across the table and took her hand. "It's going to be *allrecht*, *Mamm*. You have to believe that."

She nodded and used her napkin to wipe away the tears. "I know."

"Why don't you go put your feet up while I do the dishes?"

"I won't argue with you," she said with a tired sigh.

"That's *gut* because I get enough of that with *Daed*."

"I know."

"I'm sorry."

"For what?"

"I'm sure it wasn't pleasant having to be in the middle of our disagreements all these years."

"Sometimes *dats* and *sohns* rub each other the wrong way. At least you did the right thing and came home when you were needed."

"Not that he's letting me do anything for him."

"You've taken on his chores. They were too much on me on top of taking care of him and the house. We still need to talk about what we'll do when spring planting time comes around. But not tonight."

"*Nee*, not tonight. Now go on, relax."

Taking her coffee, she went into the living room.

David filled the sink with warm water and dish soap and found himself staring out the kitchen window and remembering how he and Lavina had talked that afternoon. His *mudder* wasn't the only one he'd put in the middle of things. How often had he complained to Lavina about a fight he'd had with his *dat*? She'd listened and kept him from blowing up more times than he could remember. So what had he done? Left her, hurt her terribly, more than he'd even dreamed, and yet she still talked to him as if she cared for him.

In the end, was he any better than his *dat*? He stopped, struck by the thought. He'd never considered that he could be like him but was there much difference? While he'd never been verbally abusive to Lavina, wasn't the emotional pain he'd caused her just as bad?

He stood there staring unseeing out the window. Was it women's lot in life to put up with men such as his *dat* and him?

Lavina walked into Stitches in Time, a big box of quilts in his arms. Her eyes widened. "Jenny! I haven't seen you in weeks!"

"I know. I've been finishing up a book deadline."

There were no celebrities in the Amish community, but Jenny was well-known for her books that touched many in and out of it. She'd come here as an *Englisch* television reporter injured in a bomb blast overseas, and while staying with her Amish *grossmudder,* fell in love with the boy next door and joined the Amish church.

Jenny held a cute little boy in her arms. She looked too young to be a *grossmudder.*

Lavina set the box down on the counter. "Is Leah here today?" she asked, glancing around.

"Yes. She just went into the back to get a special order for me. Looks like you've been busy."

"It's a busy time of year. My *schweschders* and I are grateful for the work—work we love."

Jenny smiled. "There's nothing better, is there? Doing work we love. I hear you're finding time to help Kate with her special project."

"I'm enjoying it. I don't know how much help I'm actually being."

"I'm sure you're a lot of help. The women are learning new skills that may help them get jobs, and everyone needs to do something they enjoy—just for themselves." She looked at the box. "Can I peek at what you've brought in today?"

"*Schur.* I have another box I need to bring in."

Jenny lifted the lid. "Need some help?"

"*Nee*, I can manage."

"I love this one," Jenny said, running a hand reverently over the quilt on top. "Oh, I think I'm going to have to ask Leah if I can buy it if she hasn't got a commission for it."

"*Danki*, but maybe you want to wait until you see all of them," Lavina said. "I'll be right back."

When Lavina returned, Leah was standing at the front counter watching Jenny admiring the quilts in the first box. She set the second on the counter and Jenny gleefully opened the second box.

"Beautiful work, just beautiful."

"No one sews finer quilts than Lavina and her *schweschders.* Lavina, I told Jenny no one had commissioned the quilt she likes so she may buy it." She watched Jenny lift another from the second box, and her faded blue eyes gleamed. "If you buy two you can have a discount."

Jenny glanced up. "Oh, you are such a crafty shopkeeper, Leah. How much of a discount?"

"Fifteen percent."

"Make it twenty and you have a deal."

"You are such a crafty customer, Jenny." But Leah wore a satisfied smile as she rang up the order.

"I have two very special people these are going to for Christmas," Jenny said as she handed over her credit card.

She gazed around the shop, looked out the windows at the people passing by carrying shopping bags.

"I wouldn't be here, in this community, married to the man I love, with the children and grandchildren I have, if my grandmother hadn't sent me a quilt when I was lying injured in a hospital. She sent a note with it telling me to come home and heal."

She shook her head and smiled mistily as she took back the card and tucked it into her purse. "What a plan God had for me, and it started with a quilt from my grandmother."

She gathered up her bags. "See you both at church on Sunday."

Lavina walked around the shop, a wicker basket on her arm, choosing a few items as Leah insisted on writing her a check before she left.

"Christmas gifts?" Leah asked when she rang up the contents of Lavina's basket.

She nodded. Some of them were going to be early presents, she'd decided. She couldn't wait to give them out.

Kate apologized when she arrived late to the class. "Sorry. I had a court date this morning and then I had to change." She glanced at the shopping bags in Lavina's hands. "What's all that?"

Lavina shrugged. "I just got a few things."

"Now don't you go feeling like you have to spend money bringing things to the class."

"One bag is some fabric we had lying around. You know how it is. Everybody who quilts or sews ends up with too much fabric. *Daed* said he's going to have to add on another room if we keep buying fabric."

"Malcolm built some shelves in the closet of his man cave for my fabric."

"Man cave?"

Kate laughed. "He likes to call our den his man cave. He sits in there watching football games with his friends on the weekends. I swear, the TV in there is almost as big as a movie screen. Fortunately he isn't as rabid about the games as some men."

She parked in the driveway of the shelter and helped Lavina carry one of the shopping bags. "Some of the women in here have been abused by their husbands and boyfriends after the big bowl games. The men drink too much and get too upset about their teams losing." She shook her head. "For some it doesn't take much for them to think they can use a woman for a punching bag."

Lavina made a practice of being grateful for her life, for the people in it. She felt especially grateful after hearing things like that. She was beginning to think what had started out as a way to volunteer was turning out to be an opportunity for her to think about being grateful for the people and things she had in her life . . .

A few more women had joined the group. Kate introduced herself and Lavina and then welcomed them. The next few minutes were busy as the aims of the class were explained and the new quilt blocks were handed out.

Ellie sat in a chair near the back, swinging her legs as she watched her mother sew.

When the class settled down Kate and Lavina took seats at a front table. Kate pulled out the quilt she was making for a wounded soldier. Lavina reached into one of her shopping bags.

"I bought something for you," she whispered. "Well, it's for you to give to a certain someone."

Kate set the quilt aside and studied the package Lavina handed her. "Oh, a kid's beginner quilt kit! How clever! For Ellie, right?"

Lavina nodded.

"That's sweet, Lavina. Let me pay you back."

She shook her head. "It's my gift to you to give to her. I see how much you enjoy getting someone excited about sewing and quilting."

"Someone did that for me when I was a little girl," Kate said. "There was this dime store in the small town where I grew up. It had a fabric and craft section, and I became fascinated with all the fabric and patterns. I would use my allowance to buy an eighth or a quarter of a yard of material and make dresses for my Barbie doll. I thought I might be a designer when I grew up. The clerk there was always encouraging me and having me bring in the doll to show her what I'd made."

She glanced up and scanned the room to see if anyone needed help. Everywhere they looked heads were bent and sewing machines whirred.

"Anyway, one day my mother went with me, and when I went to the fabric counter and asked the clerk to cut an eighth of a yard, she got embarrassed and began apologizing to her. But the woman said she was so happy to see someone young interested in sewing. She was the first to encourage me to try quilting. And the rest, as they say, is history. I started taking classes with Naomi at Stitches in Time when I moved here, and it's my place to get away for some quiet time with friends each week." She grinned. "Kind of like Malcolm's man cave and football games but quieter. And no beer."

She got up. "I think I'll go see if Ellie's interested in learning to quilt."

And if Lavina knew Kate as she was coming to, she'd interest Ellie in quilting and she'd make a friend as well.

7

David woke suddenly in the middle of the night. He lay there, staring into the dark, wondering what had woken him.

There was a rap on his bedroom door "David?"

"*Kumm.*" He sat up in bed, reaching for the battery-operated lamp on his bedside table.

His mother opened the door and stuck her head into the room. "David, I need help. Your *dat's* sick."

"I'll be right there." He threw back the covers and reached for the flannel robe he kept at the end of the bed.

He heard retching noises as he approached the bathroom. His mother hovered over his father who was kneeling on the floor in front of the toilet.

"Sometimes chemo affects him like this," she told David as he stepped into the small room. She turned and ran cold water over a washcloth and pressed it to Amos's neck.

"Leave me alone!" he snapped. "I'll be fine. Give me that and get out of here."

Waneta did as he asked, moving out into the hallway.

He wiped his face then tossed the cloth into the bathtub. "It's stopped."

As he struggled to his feet he turned and saw David. "What are you doing in here? I don't need you."

Then he swayed and would have fallen if David hadn't reached out and grasped his arms. "Let me help you back to bed."

"I said I don't need your help." He shoved at David's hands but there was little strength in him.

"You might not want my help, but you need it," David said, not taking offense. "Let me help you. *Mamm* looks exhausted."

Amos grunted. "She didn't need to get up with me."

Obviously she had, David thought. The man was so weak he could have fallen right into the toilet.

As they moved into the hallway Waneta hurried ahead to smooth the sheets on her *mann's* side of the bed. Then, once he lay down on the bed, she covered him with the quilt. "Can I get you anything?"

"Water," he said gruffly. She handed him the glass on the bedside table and he drank, then sank back against the pillows. He glared at David. "You can go now."

His mother started to say something to him, but David shook his head at her. He didn't need his *dat's* thanks. Didn't want them.

"Hope you feel better," he said simply. He glanced at his mother. "Let me know if you need me."

She nodded, sending him a grateful smile.

David walked out of the room and as he neared the bathroom his steps slowed. It wasn't a pleasant job cleaning it up, but it only took a few minutes and he figured it saved his mother from having to do it. And he reasoned she'd probably had to do it a number of times for him when he'd been sick as a *kind*.

She appeared in the doorway just as he finished. "Oh. *Danki*."

"Go on to bed," he told her. "I might not be as good at cleaning as you, but this is *gut* enough for tonight. Get some sleep."

"You too."

He watched her as she turned and trudged back to the master bedroom. She smiled before she went inside and shut the door.

Caring for his *dat* was taking such a toll on her. Here he'd been depressed and feeling sorry for himself. . . . His *dat* had rejected his help earlier; he wasn't any more pleasant than he'd been before he left home. Nothing had changed.

Now he was ashamed after seeing what his *mamm* obviously had to contend with sometimes after the chemo treatments. He'd come here to help her, and while he'd hoped he and his *dat* could resolve their differences, he'd warned himself not to expect too much—certainly, not to expect any improvement too quickly.

He had to keep the main goal in mind: he'd promised his *mudder* that he'd return and help her. He needed to focus on that and stop being selfish and thinking about himself.

His ears perked when he heard the squeak on the stairs a little while later. Who was up? It must be his *mudder*—his *dat* had been too unsteady on his feet to venture downstairs.

David got up and pulled on his robe and a pair of socks. He went downstairs, his steps silent on the stairs.

"Can't sleep?"

His mother spun around, one hand pressed to her heart. "Oh, my, you scared me!"

"I heard that top stair squeak. Guess you didn't because of that." He gestured at the teakettle that was just beginning to hiss.

She nodded and turned off the flame.

"I remember that stair got me into trouble a few times," he told her.

"The stair did, eh?"

He chuckled. "You always knew when one of us sneaked in late. I'd have thought you'd have had *Daed* fix it after all this time."

"No need to after all of you left."

He touched her shoulder. "I'm sorry."

She shrugged. "What's done is done." She poured boiling water in a mug. "Want some tea?"

He made a face. "I don't suppose we have some hot chocolate mix?"

"*Schur.*" She started to walk toward the cupboard, but he shook his head and went looking for himself.

"Get me a chamomile tea bag, would you?"

They fixed their hot drinks and sat at the table. The scent of flowers and chocolate filled the room.

"There are some cookies if you want them."

The memory of cleaning the bathroom just minutes before was still too vivid. He shook his head. "Is he asleep?"

"The minute his head hit the pillow."

"Does this happen after every treatment?"

She shook her head and took a sip of her tea. "The doctor gave him something for the nausea, but he won't take it." She rubbed her forehead and sighed.

"You need to get some rest."

"I think I'm too tired to sleep."

"I hope his tests are *gut* next week, and he won't have to go through any more chemo."

"Some of the women from church stopped by yesterday to tell me everyone's praying."

David felt a stab of guilt. He hadn't prayed for his *dat*. He hadn't talked to God for a long time. While he'd lived at home he'd asked God for help and he hadn't gotten it. Finally, in desperation, he'd had to leave home.

So he hadn't thought to pray to God when he heard his *dat* was ill. Now, after he hadn't so much as thanked God for a meal, would God listen to him?

"*Allrecht*, ready? We lift on the count of three. "One, two, three!"

Lavina and Mary Elizabeth lifted the rollaway bed up onto the spring wagon. Lavina sagged against the back of the wagon. "That was heavier than I thought it was."

Mary Elizabeth curled her fingers into a fist and they fist-bumped. "But we did it." She looked over past Lavina. "Leave it to a man to come along after we've gotten the job done."

Lavina turned and saw David pull into the drive. She sighed. "Tell me my face doesn't look sweaty," she muttered.

"You look fine."

David climbed out of his truck and walked up to them. "*Guder mariye*. Do you need some help?"

"Lots more in the house," Mary Elizabeth told him.

"She's joking," Lavina said quickly. "Unless she's willing to give up her bed."

"Can I take this somewhere for you?"

She shook her head. "*Danki*, but we can handle it."

Kate had warned her that the address of the shelter had to remain secret.

"You *schur*? Looked like it was a bit much for the two of you."

"Guess you never heard that *Englisch* song? 'We are women, hear us roar.'"

"Uh, *nee*, can't say I have."

"She has an *Englisch* friend who calls herself a feminist. Very into women's rights," Mary Elizabeth explained. "Not at all like most of the women here."

"I see."

Lavina thought David looked a little confused.

"Well, we have to get going," Lavina told him, feeling awkward. She sent Mary Elizabeth a look, and her *schweschder* climbed into the passenger seat of the wagon.

"If you're *schur* I can't follow you and help you."

"*Nee*, don't follow me!"

He frowned. "I won't. I'm not in the habit of going where I'm not wanted. Well, not usually."

He turned to walk to his truck.

Now she felt terrible. "I appreciate your offer," she said quickly. "But Mary Elizabeth and I want to do this."

"*Allrecht*."

"David?"

"*Ya*?"

"How is your *dat*?"

"Not feeling so *gut* after his last treatment. *Mamm* says this happens sometimes."

"I'm sorry. Maybe we can stop by with some food later. I'm *schur* she's tired from taking care of him."

"She'd like a visit, I'm *schur.* See you later."

Lavina climbed into the wagon, ignored the curious look Mary Elizabeth was giving her and called to Daisy.

"I appreciate your helping me with this."

"You've been telling me how much fun you're having. I can't wait to see the quilting class."

Pearl was delighted with the bed, and Lavina was delighted to find that the woman's husband and her teenage son were on hand to help unload it.

"What a wonderful idea," Pearl said as Lavina and Mary Elizabeth followed the men into a bedroom to show them how to set up the bed and pull out the trundle. "Some of the children—especially the youngest—are so scared when they come here they want to sleep with their mothers. This way they can be close but she'll still get her rest."

"I was thinking this might be good for Ellie. Kate called her a Velcro kid. She said the kids get so scared they stick to their mothers like Velcro. "

Pearl nodded. "I think we'll move her and her mother into this room this afternoon if they like it. Thank you so much, Lavina, Mary Elizabeth."

"You're very welcome." It felt *gut* to Lavina to see something that hadn't been used in some time be put to use. God wanted people to circulate things they no longer needed. One of the lay ministers had read the Bible verse about it from the Book of John last Sunday, and it had really touched her.

Kate had already arrived and many of the women taking the class were at their machines. Mary Elizabeth wasn't shy, but after Kate introduced her to the class she kept in the background and observed.

Halfway through the class Carrie came in, got her project box from a shelf, and took a seat in the back near Mary Elizabeth.

"Another Amish chick, huh?"

Mary Elizabeth grinned at her, ignoring her sarcastic tone. "*Ya*, nice to meet you. I'm Mary Elizabeth, Lavina's sister. Are you enjoying the class?"

Carrie shrugged. "It's something to do. It's pretty boring around here."

"Really? What do you like to do?"

Lavina bit back a smile as she watched the two. Mary Elizabeth loved to talk but even more she loved meeting new people, especially *Englisch* people since she didn't venture out much.

Another shrug of the shoulders. "I like to cook. Not that the jerk I was married to was ever happy with anything I cooked."

"I love to cook, too," Mary Elizabeth said. "What's your favorite, cooking or baking?"

"Baking."

"Me, too. I like making bread. It's simple, but I like the smell and kneading it."

A few minutes later when Lavina looked over the two were deep in discussion, the sewing in front of Carrie was forgotten and the sullen look she usually wore was gone.

Lavina glanced around the room. Women were chattering as they sewed, comparing their quilt blocks and projects.

"What is it?" Kate asked quietly.

"The class used to be quiet. Now look at it."

"I know." She smiled as she looked out at the class. "They're learning to connect with other women. Making friends again. One of the first things an abusive husband or boyfriend does is separate his wife or girlfriend from her friends and family. That way they don't know what he's doing and she has no support system she can depend on when she realizes she's trapped in a web of abuse."

She turned to Lavina. "Some of the women will be here for a short time before they find jobs and apartments they can rent.

Others will stay longer." She sighed. "And others will return to their husbands and boyfriends as they find they can't break the cycle."

Lavina didn't like thinking about that.

The women began putting their projects in their storage boxes and placing them on the shelves. They said goodbye and filtered out of the room

Ellie and her mother were the last to leave. Ellie put her project box on the lowest shelf.

"Mommy, can we go home now?" she heard Ellie ask her mother.

"No, sweetheart. I'm sorry."

Ellie puckered up. "When, Mommy?"

Her mother looked ready to cry herself.

Lavina turned to Kate and saw her blinking hard.

"It's all so rough on the kids," she said in a low voice. "She left her home that night with the pajamas on her back and her teddy bear in her arms. And that was it."

"Pearl said she's going to put the bed Mary Elizabeth and I brought today in their room. Maybe you can tell her that."

"Good idea, thanks." She got up from her chair, walked over to Ellie and her mother and crouched down. "Sweetheart, this is home," she said, gesturing at the child's mother.

Ellie shook her head. "That's Mommy."

"Home is wherever you and Mommy are."

Lavina watched the little girl tilt her head to one side and consider that.

Kate stood and said something Lavina couldn't hear to Ellie's mother. Whatever it was made the woman smile. The three of them left the room together.

Lavina tucked her quilt into her tote and stood. Mary Elizabeth was still chatting with Carrie. She didn't remember ever seeing Carrie talk so much with anyone. She couldn't wait to find out what the two of them had been talking about.

"That was fun!" Mary Elizabeth said the minute they were in the wagon heading home. "Are we going to go to David's house later this afternoon?"

It took her a moment to answer. She'd been so sure Mary Elizabeth was going to say something about the class or Carrie. "*Ya*, why?"

Mary Elizabeth turned to her, her expression serious. "I'm going to ask David to take me to talk to Samuel."

David pulled into his driveway and found himself smiling when he saw Lavina and Mary Elizabeth getting out of the family buggy.

He turned off the ignition and hopped out of his truck. "*Gut-n-owed*. Can I offer to carry anything inside?"

"Of course," Mary Elizabeth said. "We brought food."

He looked in the back of the buggy, choosing the smallest, lightest dish. "Got this one. You getting the rest?" he asked Lavina with a grin. He handed it to her and took the two heavy casserole dishes from the buggy.

"Smells *gut*," he said, taking a big sniff. "*Mamm* would have been happy with a visit. You didn't have to bring food, too."

"We'll take it back then," Mary Elizabeth said.

"Always joking." He held the dishes out of her reach. "It's really helping *Mamm to* have the meals. And earlier today two of her friends helped by doing some housework." He paused. "She had more friends before *Daed's* grouchiness drove them away." Then he shook his head. "Sorry, I shouldn't talk about him that way."

"Well, he did drive a lot of people away, including his own *sohns*."

"Mary Elizabeth!"

She lifted her chin and met her *schweschder's* shocked gaze. "Well, it's true and we all know it."

"It's not our place to judge."

Mary Elizabeth sniffed but she stayed silent as they climbed the porch steps and went into the house.

David was glad he'd asked Lavina and Mary Elizabeth to visit. His *mudder* greeted them warmly and thanked them for the food. She pulled the foil from both casseroles and told him to choose which one he wanted for supper.

"Maybe we should let *Daed* decide."

"He's taking a nap and since he wasn't feeling so *gut* this afternoon I'm not going to wake him."

"Then chicken and dumplings."

"What, you don't like my baked pork chops?" Mary Elizabeth asked, sulking.

"The baked pork chops, then," he said quickly.

She laughed. "I made the chicken and dumplings."

He looked at Lavina. Did you make the pork chops?"

She shook her head. "Our *mudder* did. I baked the cookies."

Her cookies—whatever the variety—were the best. But he wasn't going to say so in front of Mary Elizabeth and have her sulking again—joking or otherwise.

So he did what any man would do. He made his escape.

"Chores," he said, starting for the back door. "Back soon as I finish."

Nellie was happy to see him even though he'd left the kitchen without remembering her apple. "I'll make it up to you,'" he promised. "I'll bring it out after supper."

He lingered over the chores. After all, he'd asked Lavina and Mary Elizabeth to stop by and visit his *mudder*. From what he could tell, she hadn't been out of the house except for going with his *dat* to chemotherapy and doctor appointments for months.

So he fed Nellie and talked to her and puttered around giving the three women time to talk about whatever it was women talked about.

It came to him suddenly that he missed talking to Bill and to his *bruders* Sam and John. He took a moment to go to the phone shanty and call Bill, and make plans to have lunch on Saturday.

Then he started to call his *bruders,* but decided he'd drive by their place after work tomorrow instead.

He sniffed the air when he walked out of the phone shanty. He smelled snow in the air. An early winter had been predicted. Winters in this part of the country could be long and bitter. He supposed he should be making sure the windows and doors on the farmhouse were sealed tight. That there was enough firewood for heat. He knew the routine from living at the house where he'd been born, but it occurred to him that he could ask his *dat* what needed to be done and they might have an actual conversation.

And then again they might not, considering the way they got along. But better to find out now what he needed to do to keep them warm and safe this winter. His *dat* was in no shape to be working on the home in his condition, getting overtired, cold, or wet.

When he returned to the house he was surprised to see Mary Elizabeth sitting at the kitchen table drinking tea by herself.

"Your *mudder's* upstairs checking on your *dat,*" she said when she saw him look around. "Lavina went home because there's something I wanted to talk to you about."

He washed his hands at the sink and sat down. "What's that?"

"I want you to take me to see Sam."

If she'd set out to stun him she couldn't have done a better job. "Why do you want to do that? If you're hoping he'll come back like I did, I have to disappoint you. The last time I spoke to him he refused."

"I want to ask him."

Feeling frustrated, David ran a hand through his hair. "Like it worked so well that I came home," he muttered.

"But you don't know it'll be the same for Sam."

"*Daed* treated all of us the same," he told her bluntly. "Equally badly."

"But maybe since he's been so sick he'll be different." She looked at him earnestly. The three sisters looked so much alike it was hard to stare into her blue eyes.

"He wasn't as of last night." He stood so suddenly the chair he'd been sitting on scraped the floor like a fingernail against a chalkboard. "He was retching in the bathroom and I was trying to help him and he ordered me out. He doesn't want me here, Mary Elizabeth! Is that what you want for Sam?"

Tears welled up in her eyes. "*Nee!* I just want Sam to come home! I want to see him again. Don't you realize I love him?"

With a sigh he sat again. "I love Lavina, but it didn't change anything when I came back."

"We're all different. You don't know it won't be different for Sam and me."

"He still won't have anything to offer you any more than I have anything to offer Lavina."

"*Ya*, their *daed* has to die for them to have the farm, and so far I haven't cooperated, have I?" his father rasped as he walked slowly into the kitchen.

"Amos! Don't talk like that!" Waneta cried as she followed him into the room.

Aghast, Mary Elizabeth stared at him. Her mouth worked as if she struggled for words. "What a horrible thing to say!" she cried and then she raced from the room.

"It's the truth," Amos pulled out a chair, sat, and glared around him. "What does a man have to do to get supper around here?"

"Be nice for once!" Waneta burst out. "David, go after her!"

He grabbed his jacket. "My pleasure. I won't be back for supper."

"Now look what you've done," he heard his mother saying as he left the room.

It was the first time he could remember her ever speaking up to him.

"Mary Elizabeth! Wait up!"

She stopped and turned. "I'm sorry."

"For what?"

"I had no idea your *dat* could be so horrible. I mean, Lavina's told me some things over the years but never anything like what he just said."

David shrugged. "Well, I think he might have set a new record." He saw her shiver. "Get in the truck. I'll give you a ride home."

"*Danki.*"

He started the truck and turned the heat on high. "It'll take a minute."

"I'm *allrecht.*" She sat, staring at his house as he let the vehicle warm up. "What did you mean about you and Lavina?"

David searched his memory. Now, with the bitter words from his *dat* hanging like a cloud over his head, he just couldn't remember exactly what he'd said.

"You said, 'I love Lavina, but it didn't change anything when I came back.'"

"We haven't gotten back together. Didn't she tell you?"

"*Nee.* She won't talk much about you."

"I hurt her too badly. I didn't realize how much. I was too wrapped up in how miserable I was when I left . . . I didn't think of anyone but myself. I'm not sure she'll ever get over it."

He pulled into her driveway. "Sorry the heater's just now getting it warm in here."

"Don't worry about it." She unfastened her seat belt but made no move to get out of the truck. "I can help you." She turned to him. "I can help you get back together with Lavina. You take me to see Sam, and I'll help you get back together with my *schweschder.*"

8

So when is David going to take you to see Sam?" Lavina asked Mary Elizabeth as they sat quilting the next day in their home. It was just the two of them working today since Rose Anna had gone into town with their *mudder.*

"What makes you think I talked him into it?" Mary Elizabeth asked coyly.

"You usually get your way." Lavina said it without malice.

She grinned. "*Ya.*"

Mary Elizabeth had such a charming way about her, you just couldn't hold it against her that she knew how to get what she wanted. She supposed as Mary Elizabeth was the middle child in the family—in between her and Rosa Anna as the youngest—Mary Elizabeth had had to find a way of getting attention, of getting what she what she wanted.

"I'm not going to ask how you persuaded him. I know David misses his *bruders* and he knows his *mudder* wants them to see their *dat* since he's so ill."

Lavina laid her quilt down. "I don't know. It's been so hard on David being back." She watched Mary Elizabeth sober. "What's wrong?"

"I guess I always thought that you were exaggerating how badly David's *dat* treated him. But I saw last night."

"What happened?"

Mary Elizabeth set down her own quilt. She repeated what Amos had said.

Lavina closed her eyes and shook her head. "David's never told me something like that. It really shows how sick his *dat* is to say something so cruel."

"You can't blame the cancer. It takes a really awful man to say such a thing."

Lavina rubbed her temple. "I feel so guilty. I talked David into coming back home."

"He didn't have to. He could have refused you. After all, you haven't got my persuasive skills." She batted her eyelashes.

"Oh, Mary Elizabeth," Lavina said, unable to hold back a chuckle. She stood. "*Kumm*, let's have some lunch."

Her *schweschder* stood and slipped her arm into Lavina's. "Where do you suppose they're having lunch? We should have gone. We could have talked *Mamm* into taking us to that new restaurant."

"We have too much work to do."

Mary Elizabeth wrinkled her nose. "Work, work, work." Then she laughed. "I'm just joking. I love what we do."

Lavina sliced bread. "Tell you what. Next time we take quilts into Leah's shop the two of us will go and we'll have lunch at that restaurant."

"Your treat?"

She laughed. How like Mary Elizabeth to ask such. "*Schur.* Get what you want for your sandwich from the refrigerator. I'll have the egg salad left over from yesterday."

Mary Elizabeth brought the container to the counter. "Me, too." They made their sandwiches, and Mary Elizabeth looked in a cupboard and found a bag of potato chips.

They took their plates to the table and said their blessing over the meal. Mary Elizabeth began eating, but Lavina sat staring at her plate.

"Aren't you hungry?" Mary Elizabeth popped a chip in her mouth.

"I was just thinking about what Kate said to Ellie the other day at the quilt class. Ellie asked when she and her mother were going to go home and Kate said home is where your mom is."

She set her sandwich down uneaten and looked at Mary Elizabeth. "It hasn't been a home, a happy one, for David and his *bruders* for a long time. Maybe it isn't fair to ask Sam to come back."

"Then he can find a different place to live. I want him to come back for me."

"I see."

"I know you probably think that's selfish of me, but you can't say that wasn't part of the reason you wanted David to come home."

"You're wrong. I asked him to come back because his mother asked me to find him and tell him his *dat* was sick."

"But you have feelings for David."

"Did."

"Did?" Shocked, Mary Elizabeth stared at her. "But you were ready to marry him before he left." She put her sandwich down. "Aren't you glad he came home?"

Lavina sighed. "I'm glad he came home for his family. But it doesn't mean we're going to get back together." She rose and went to the refrigerator for a pitcher of iced tea.

"David still loves you," Mary Elizabeth said quietly.

She set the pitcher down and sank into her chair. "He told you that?" Her eyes narrowed as Mary Elizabeth avoided her gaze. "Mary Elizabeth, were you talking about me?"

Her sister shrugged. "Well, your name came up just because he said I shouldn't expect that if Sam came back, the two of us would get together. He said the two of you hadn't."

The statement took Lavina's breath away. She clasped her cold hands under the table.

"Are you *allrecht*?"

"*Schur*, why wouldn't I be? Why don't you get some glasses for our tea?"

When Mary Elizabeth got up to get the glasses Lavina took a deep breath to steady herself. Why was she getting so upset? she asked herself. Hadn't she been the one who'd told David they couldn't get back together?

But hearing her *schweschder* telling her David had said that . . . it made it feel so real. So permanent.

Mary Elizabeth filled the glasses with tea and sat to resume eating. "Anyway, David's taking me to see Sam this Saturday."

"*Gut*," She took a sip of tea to soothe a suddenly dry throat and listened to her *schweschder* chatter about how she was looking forward to seeing Sam again, how she wondered how he'd feel about seeing her . . . the words just washed over Lavina.

"Hurry and eat your lunch. We need to get back to work. The sooner we finish our quilts the sooner we can go to that new restaurant."

Lavina tried to smile as she picked up her sandwich. She loved egg salad, but right now it just looked too yellow, too oozy. She forced herself to take a bite, then another. When Mary Elizabeth finished her lunch, got up to put her plate in the sink and left the room, she quickly tossed her lunch into the trash and put her plate in the sink. She hated wasting food but she just didn't feel like eating.

She sighed. Back to work. It was what had kept her from wallowing in depression for the past year. At least she had her work.

David debated calling his *bruder* Sam and decided it wasn't a good idea. Sam would undoubtedly not want to meet with them, seeing it as an attempt to persuade him to return home.

At this point David just didn't care if Sam returned. It was bad enough the way his *dat* had talked to him last night. He loved his *bruders* and just didn't think he could subject him to that kind of abuse. The three of them had loved their *dat* like *gut sohns* were supposed to do and all three had finally given up and moved away.

David had blamed himself for influencing Sam and John, but he'd come to realize that if they had been happy they never would have left.

Saturday couldn't come soon enough—for a purely personal reason: Mary Elizabeth had promised she was going to find a way to get Lavina to see him. He knew Mary Elizabeth was persuasive, but he wondered if she really could pull this off.

A horn honked behind him. He waved a hand in apology and stepped on the gas. That was what thinking about Lavina had gotten him.

Bill was waiting for him in his favorite pizza place. He rose and gave David the kind of pounding slap on the back that was his sign of affection. David returned the gesture.

"So how are things going?" Bill asked as soon as they ordered.

"Not so good," he admitted, leaning back in the booth. "He's just as hard to get along with as he's always been. Maybe worse. I guess you're going to say I told you so."

Bill frowned. "I wouldn't do that. I had a feeling your father might still be difficult. People don't usually change, especially when they get older. Or sick."

He looked up and smiled at the server when she brought their soft drinks. His smile faded when she left and he turned his attention to David.

"How is he doing?"

"He's been very sick from the chemotherapy. My mother says he's supposed to get tests to see how it's working soon."

"Well, it hasn't been good. Then again you didn't expect it to be. But I think you felt like you had to go at least for your mother's sake. I don't think you'd have forgiven yourself if you hadn't gone."

"Maybe. Mary Elizabeth, Lavina's sister, wants me to take her to see Sam, see if he'll come home."

"Yeah? You think he will?"

"She's very persuasive."

Bill moved the salt and pepper shakers out of the way so their server could set the pizza in the center of the table.

"Sounds like there's more to this story."

David served them both their first piece of pizza, but Bill just sat there with his slice on his plate.

He shrugged. "She thinks she can get Lavina and me back together."

"Are you saying she's going to play matchmaker?"

"I guess you'd call it that."

"Well, she's sure got her work cut out for her. The last time we talked you said Lavina didn't want anything to do with you."

David winced. "Well, she didn't say it that way."

"Same difference."

"What?"

"Different words, same message." Bill picked up another piece of pizza. "Hey, I'm on my second piece and you haven't touched your first one."

He started eating but he wasn't feeling very hungry

"I think you're depressed."

"I don't think I'm depressed. I wouldn't say I'm wildly happy right now, but I don't think I'm depressed."

"Yeah, well if you're not, I'd wonder why not. I mean, with the situation with your old man, your girl, not doing the work you like . . ." Bill trailed off when he saw David set his slice down half-eaten. "Sorry."

David sighed. "No, you're right. Things aren't going great right now. But they'll get better."

"You want to catch a movie? Or go for a drive?"

"Maybe a short drive. I can't stay out late. Work tomorrow." He checked the bill and pulled out money to pay his share while Bill asked their server for a box to take home the uneaten pizza.

"So are you keeping the truck?" Bill asked as they drove along a country road.

David nodded. "Who knows if I'll end up staying in the community at this point. *Daed* could always end up getting into a mood and asking me to leave and *Mamm* wouldn't stand up to him. Besides, I use the truck for deliveries sometimes. You know that."

If he stayed and took over the work of the farm for his *dat* until he recovered he wouldn't need the truck. And there was the decision of getting baptized. He'd put it off for a long time but it wasn't something he could delay forever. If he did join the church he'd have to give up the truck. He'd miss it but he didn't think he'd become obsessed with it the way some men he knew had. The fact was he'd missed working on the farm so much. He'd missed Lavina so much.

He saw a man dressed in Amish clothing striding along the side of the road. There was something vaguely familiar about him.

"Someone you know?" Bill asked as David looked over. "You want to stop and give him a ride?"

The man turned his head to look at them, and David shuddered. He nodded in acknowledgement but drove on.

"Who was that?"

"The bishop."

"Oh. I don't guess you want to give him a ride."

"Well, I would even though we've . . . disagreed, but he lives in the next house."

"Reminds me of Ichabod Crane."

"Who?"

"You never read *The Legend of Sleepy Hollow*?"

"Not that I remember."

"Crane was this tall, thin guy in a story written by Washington Irving. It was cool. I actually liked reading it."

David shrugged. "I've read more this past year when I lived alone and had time on my hands in the evening than I did in several years, I think." He paused. "Well, I did watch a lot of television. Since there was one in the apartment and I wanted to see why the *Englisch* liked it so much."

"And?"

"It's addictive," he said, grinning.

"My sociology professor in college said its invention caused the downfall of the American family. People sit around and watch it and don't talk to each other even when they're in the same room."

"Kind of the way they were doing back in the restaurant with their cell phones?"

"Yeah."

David thought about it. They didn't talk much at his house and they didn't have a television. Actually, it might give his *dat* something to do rather than sit or lie around and focus on how unhappy he was. Or did he even know he was unhappy? David tried to remember a time when his *dat* had looked happy.

They rode around for an hour before David took Bill back to the restaurant so he could get his pickup.

"It was great seeing you again," Bill said as he unbuckled his seat belt.

"It was fun. Thanks for listening."

"No problem. Call me or drop by if you want to talk."

"I will. Don't forget the pizza." He grinned since Bill was already reaching for the box.

"Sure you don't want it?"

"No. If my father sees it I'll just get a lecture about wasting money."

"My father had some great advice about life."

"Yeah?"

"He always said let problems roll off your back, like water rolls off a duck's back. Simple, but it works for me. See you. And thanks for the pizza."

"You're welcome." Chuckling at the homespun advice, David backed out of the lot and drove home.

"I don't want to go. I don't need to go."

"Come on, Lavina. I need your support."

Lavina snorted. "You're up to something. You have never needed anyone's support. You're one of the strongest people I know."

"Strong people need support, too. I want to see Sam, but it's been a year. What if he won't have anything to do with me?"

"David shouldn't be taking you without asking his *bruder* if he wants to see you first."

"He doesn't think he should call first."

Something smelled fishy, and Lavina didn't think it was the tuna salad sandwich she was eating. "Why don't you ask Rose Anna to go with you?"

"You must remember what it felt like when you went to see David after you hadn't seen him for a year." Mary Elizabeth looked at her earnestly.

"She's right," Rose Anna said as she poured glasses of water. "You'd be much better going with her than me."

Lavina narrowed her eyes as she looked from one to the other. Mary Elizabeth was *gut* at talking their younger sister into things. Rose Anna stared back at her with innocent blue eyes.

She sighed. "I'll think about it."

Mary Elizabeth threw her arms around her. "*Danki!*"

"I said I'd think about it."

"I know."

Lavina opened the refrigerator to put the plastic container of tuna fish away, and when she turned suddenly to ask if anyone wanted lettuce she saw her two *schweschders* exchanging a look.

Fishier and fishier she thought. She returned to the table and sat to eat her lunch. Mary Elizabeth chattered away about the upcoming trip to see Sam, and Rose Anna listened avidly. The two of them didn't say anything when Lavina finished her lunch and left the kitchen.

Two days later she found herself following Mary Elizabeth out to David's truck parked in their driveway. She held open the door so her *schweschder* could climb inside and sit in the middle of the front seat.

"Oh, I forgot something!" Mary Elizabeth exclaimed. "I'll be right back."

Lavina sighed. "I'm sorry, David."

"It's not a problem. Get in, it's cold."

She hesitated and then climbed inside the truck. There was no point in standing there getting chilled.

Silence stretched between them. She felt awkward remembering the harsh words she'd thrown at him the last time she'd seen him.

"Mary Elizabeth said your *dat* is supposed to have some tests?"

"Soon."

Lavina shifted in her seat and looked out the window. What was taking Mary Elizabeth so long?

Finally she rushed up, opened the door and before Lavina could get out, climbed inside and scooted over, pushing Lavina closer to David. "*Allrecht*, let's go."

"So what did you forget?" Lavina asked Mary Elizabeth as David pulled out onto the road.

"Hmm?"

"What did you forget?"

"Oh, I had to tell *Mamm* we were leaving."

"We did that on the way out of the house," Lavina reminded her.

"*Ya*? Guess I forgot," she said airily. "Isn't it just beautiful today? I love this time of year."

Lavina wished there was a way she could move further away from David. Sitting this close, she could feel the warmth of his body, smell the clean male scent of him. It was torture.

If he had any reaction to her he didn't show it. Instead, he kept his eyes on the road as he drove toward town.

Mary Elizabeth chattered away about the weather, about the displays of fall pumpkins at roadside stands, about anything and everything.

She's nervous, Lavina realized, surprised. Mary Elizabeth was never nervous. Maybe she really had wanted someone to support her as she'd said. Feeling a little guilty at how she'd been suspicious, Lavina reached over and squeezed her *schweschder's* hand.

"Nervous?"

"A little." She took a deep breath. "Tell me where Sam's been living. You two didn't share a place?"

He shook his head. "I moved out first and found a little attic apartment. When Sam needed a place there wasn't room for him there. He found a small apartment, and when John decided to leave home he moved in with Sam."

"What if he's not home?"

"He'll be home. There are football games on today." He glanced at them. "On television. He and John never leave the apartment when they're on."

"What about you?" Lavina asked him.

The corner of his mouth quirked in a grin. "I was glued to the television when they were on, too," he admitted.

"Does Sam have a truck, too?"

"*Nee*. He hasn't saved up enough yet. A friend gives him a ride to work."

"How much longer?"

"Not long."

A few minutes later, David pulled into the parking lot of a modern looking apartment complex. He shut off the engine and turned to look at Mary Elizabeth. "This is it. Apartment 3C, right over there."

Mary Elizabeth grabbed the door handle and opened it. She was halfway out of the truck before Lavina could grab her arm.

"You want me to go with you?"

"*Nee*, I'll be fine."

"Mary Elizabeth?"

She stopped and looked at David.

"If he says he'll talk to you we'll go get some coffee and come back for you in half an hour, *allrecht*?"

"*Ya*, David." She hurried toward the apartment.

"And here I thought she was nervous." Lavina realized she was still sitting close to David. She moved to her right, over to where Mary Elizabeth had sat.

They watched as she knocked on the door. Sam opened it and stared at her in shock. Then Mary Elizabeth went inside and the door closed.

"She shouldn't be in there by herself with him," Lavina fretted. She reached for the door handle.

Then she felt his hand on her arm. "She'll be fine."

"If the bishop—"

"He's not around. Let's give them a chance to talk."

Lavina looked down. He hadn't removed his hand. She looked up, and their gazes locked. His eyes were warm, serious. She shivered and rubbed her arms. The truck had grown cool inside with the heater off.

David started the truck and warm air rushed out the vents again.

"Let's go get that coffee."

"We shouldn't leave her—"

"I brought my cell. Sam can call me."

"*Allrecht,*" she said finally. If they went for coffee they wouldn't be sitting so close together in his truck. It would be easier to guide the conversation to impersonal topics.

He drove them to a coffee shop, and she saw that maybe being in a different location wasn't going to make things so impersonal after all. Her heart sank. Why had he chosen this place? Didn't he remember it had been their favorite place to get together when they dated? It wasn't fancy but the coffee and pastries were *gut* and more important, less expensive than the places that attracted tourists. David didn't have much money back then, and he wouldn't hear of her paying sometimes.

As she got out of the truck she wondered if he remembered that this was "their" place and that was why he'd chosen it. If it was why he'd chosen it to appeal to her memories of it, she wasn't about to let him know that she remembered.

But when they went inside, the memories came rushing back. There, in the corner, she saw the table they'd sat at so often. She could see them as they'd sat there talking endlessly, laughing together, him distracting her and sneaking bites of her favorite dessert, the pear tarts. They'd talked of getting married when they visited that last time.

She blinked furiously so he wouldn't see the tears that rushed into her eyes. No way could she let him slip into her cracked and broken heart.

They got into the line of several people.

"Do you want your usual?" he asked.

Did he remember what it was? He hadn't called her in a year but he remembered what she liked here?

"*Nee*, I'll have the pumpkin coffee and a piece of spice cake, please. And I can pay for my own." She dug into her purse for some bills and when the person in front of her moved aside to the pick-up counter, she gave her order.

"Nice to see you," the clerk said. "Haven't seen either of you in a while. How have you both been?"

"Good," they said at the same time.

Lavina didn't know if David meant it, but she knew she'd just lied.

9

David took his coffee and slice of pumpkin pie and followed Lavina to a table. She chose one near the front window of the shop, not the table that had become their own most of the time when they used to come here.

When she stirred a packet of sugar into her coffee, then took a sip he noticed she avoided looking at him.

Maybe this idea of Mary Elizabeth's wasn't so good after all . . .

He dumped two packets of sugar into his own coffee and started eating his pie while he figured out what to say. Conversation had always been so easy for them. He'd felt so close to her all his life, sharing his thoughts and dreams and despair with his relationship with his *dat*.

Was that going to be a thing of the past? What if he couldn't build a bridge over the angry words and bitterness she'd thrown at him the first time he'd tried to talk to her after returning?

She sipped her coffee but didn't immediately start eating her dessert.

"You're not eating your spice cake," he said. "Do you want to get something else?"

"This is fine." She picked up her fork and took a bite.

"The pie is great." Wow. Sparkling conversation. "I love this time of year when there's a lot of pumpkin pie."

"You never met a pie you didn't like."

He grinned. "True."

"You'll even eat rhubarb." She shook her head. "I always felt it tasted like a mixture of strawberry and . . ." She appeared to search for the proper word.

"Battery acid. That's what you used to say."

"Right."

She smiled slightly. It was the first time he'd seen her smile since he'd left.

"If you tried a piece of my *Aenti* Ruth's rhubarb pie you might change your mind."

"You're wrong. I've had it. She brought one to church this summer." She took another bite of cake.

He looked over her shoulder. "John just walked in."

Lavina turned to see, but as she did she put her hands protectively over her cake. "What's he doing here?"

"Maybe he didn't want to play chaperone." He waved to his *bruder*, then looked at her and grinned. "I wasn't going to sneak a bite you know."

"That used to be your favorite way of getting some of my dessert. I'm on to your tricks."

Not all of them. It wasn't looking easy, but he was determined to win her back.

"Hi, Lavina." John pulled out a chair at their table and sat down.

"Thought I'd come grab some coffee and let Sam and Mary Elizabeth talk."

"Don't let us keep you from it," David said with a meaningful look.

"David! Don't be rude!" Lavina chided him. She turned her attention to his *bruder*. "Hi, John. How are you doing?"

"*Gut*. You?"

"Very well, *danki*."

He turned to David. "Hey, how about getting me a cup of coffee?"

"How about you get it yourself?"

"C'mon, I want to talk to Lavina for a minute."

Sighing, David got up and went to get him his coffee. When he returned John and Lavina were deep in conversation. For a moment, he felt jealous of his own *bruder*. Lavina looked animated, engaged in talking with John. Then he realized John was asking about Rose Anna, and he saw John hanging on to Lavina's every word.

He missed Rose Anna the way David had missed Lavina.

David set the coffee down in front of his *bruder* and then went back to the counter and bought him a piece of pumpkin pie. John blinked in surprise when he returned to place it before him. He thanked him and then immediately turned back to talk to Lavina. David sat down and finished his coffee and waited him out.

Lavina was the one who glanced at the nearby clock a little later and said apologetically that they had to leave and get Mary Elizabeth.

David looked at John. "Do you want a ride back?"

John nodded, bolted down the rest of the pie, and carried his coffee out to David's truck. John caught his look and waved Lavina inside saying he'd be getting out first. Once again David enjoyed Lavina sitting next to him.

When they arrived at Sam and John's apartment John hopped out. "*Danki* for the coffee and pie, David. Lavina, tell Rose Anna I asked about her?"

"I will."

"I'll send Mary Elizabeth out."

He hurried into the apartment and several minutes later Mary Elizabeth and Sam emerged arguing with each other. David couldn't hear what the argument was about without opening a window, and he didn't think Lavina would approve.

Mary Elizabeth held up her hands and shook her head, and then she stomped away from Sam. Lavina opened the door and she fairly jumped into the truck, slamming the door behind her. She turned her back on Sam, who was saying something they couldn't hear.

"Let's go."

"You sure?" David asked.

"Please, let's go." She fastened her seat belt and wrapped her arms around herself as if she hurt.

"Oh, honey, it didn't go the way you hoped?" Lavina asked her.

"*Nee*," Mary Elizabeth said, and David could hear the tears in her voice. "Men are such jerks!"

David winced. "Not all men."

She sniffed. "Sam sure is."

David and Lavina exchanged glances. Lavina shook her head slightly. He nodded and started the truck.

When he pulled into their driveway Mary Elizabeth thanked him quickly and bolted from the truck. Lavina started to move away, and David touched her hand.

"I'm sorry she was upset by the visit."

Lavina sighed. "She was determined to go. I couldn't talk her out of it."

"Did you tell her it hadn't been a *gut* idea to contact me?"

She turned horrified eyes on him. "She told you that?"

He nodded.

She looked away. "I'm feeling very . . . mixed up. I was angry at you while you were gone. Now you're back, but things are a mess between us." She stared at her hands folded in her lap. "But I'm not sorry that I talked to you as I promised your *mudder*. She needs you. Your *dat* does, too. He's just not willing to admit it yet."

"He probably won't ever do that."

"I'm sorry about that."

"*Danki*."

"Anyway, I do appreciate your driving Mary Elizabeth to see Sam."

"You're *wilkumm*. I hope I didn't make you unhappy taking you to that coffee shop today. I always had such a good time with you there."

She looked uncertain and didn't speak at once. And then she shrugged. "It's *allrecht.* I know you didn't take me there to make me unhappy."

"Could we at least be friends, Lavina?"

She met his gaze directly. "Maybe not today, David. But maybe one day."

He squeezed her hand. "I hope so."

She slipped from the truck and hurried into her house. David sighed and headed home.

"Go ahead. I know you want to say it."

"Say what?"

"You know you want to say I told you so."

Lavina stared at Mary Elizabeth. "I would never say that to you."

"But you're thinking it." Mary Elizabeth crossed her arms over her chest and stared at the wall in the sewing room.

"I am not thinking it." Lavina set down the quilt she was working on. "I only wish you hadn't gone because you got hurt."

Mary Elizabeth shrugged and then her face contorted. "He doesn't want me," she cried as she dug in her pocket and pulled out a tissue. "He said he's not coming back. Ever." She blew her nose and then looked miserably at her. "I wish I'd listened to you."

Lavina patted her hand. "I wish you had. But you always have to find things out for yourself."

"Are you calling me hard-headed?"

She bit her lip. "Well, you like to learn from your own experience."

Mary Elizabeth laughed and shook her head. She stuck the tissue in her pocket. "I guess that's better than calling me hard-headed."

"Remember we're going to the quilting class today. That'll be fun."

Of course, Mary Elizabeth figured out how to turn a trip into town into something fun. Some would have said she used Lavina's sympathy and "milked" things . . .

"You remember what you promised," she told Lavina later that morning as they carefully packed the quilt orders for Stitches in Time.

"I know what I promised. We're going to have the fancy lunch out like you want."

"Your treat."

"My treat."

The man who married her *schweschder* was certainly going to be led down a merry path. Mary Elizabeth knew what she wanted, and she went after it. Her quilt had been completed in record time because she wanted to go for her fancy lunch.

Lavina had watched her in the days after Mary Elizabeth had insisted on visiting Sam. She'd moped and been a little tearful for two days, and then she seemed to brighten up a bit. Lavina had seen her writing furiously in her journal. Somehow it must have helped because Mary Elizabeth had returned to being her usual cheerful self.

Until her crying spell today, that is.

"Wish we could go to lunch first," Mary Elizabeth said, almost bouncing with excitement as they rode to the quilting class.

"We ate breakfast two hours ago. You can't possibly be hungry already."

"I'm not. I just can't wait to go to the restaurant."

Lavina was glad to see she was enthusiastic about something again. "You had fun at the class last time."

"I know. I'm sure it'll be fun again." She smoothed the skirt of her best dress. "Think we're dressy enough for the restaurant?"

"You look very pretty."

"You, too," Mary Elizabeth said generously. "That shade of dark green is good on you. I haven't seen you wear it in a long time."

It had been David's favorite color on her. So the dress had been shoved into the back of her closet for quite a while. She didn't know why she'd chosen to pull it out and wear it today.

They stopped at Stitches in Time first to drop off the quilt orders, then proceeded on to the class.

All the regulars were there, including Ellie and her mother. And a sullen Carrie who barely returned Mary Elizabeth's greeting. She accepted the new quilt block, setting it aside without looking at it, then, looking bored, sewed on last week's block for a few minutes before getting up and leaving the room.

Lavina glanced at Kate who shrugged. After a few minutes, Kate slipped out. When she returned a few minutes later, she placed the blocks in Carrie's project box and set it on a shelf.

Ellie walked up to Kate and shyly showed her the small quilt she was making with her mother's help. "It's almost big enough for my doll baby."

"It sure is. And you're doing such good work. Maybe when you get done with this one you and your mom can make one for your bed."

Ellie grinned, revealing two missing teeth. She ran back to her mother and clung to her side as they worked on their quilts.

"I'm so glad you got the quilt kit," Kate said quietly. "She seems happier today, don't you think?"

Lavina nodded. It was a world she'd never known about, this place full of women who were very different but who shared a time when they were forced by circumstances to be together for shelter, for food, for friendship and emotional support.

After the class was over, she and Mary Elizabeth drove to the restaurant.

"You're quiet," Mary Elizabeth said.

"Just thinking about something Kate said today."

"I tried to talk to Carrie, but she wouldn't have anything to do with me. Something must be bothering her."

"It's not hard to figure out. Imagine having to stay in a shelter with strangers, because you have no place else to go because your husband beats you."

Mary Elizabeth nodded. "Remember when John Troyer hit Mary and the bishop talked to him? That stopped that."

"We have to hope so."

"What do you mean?"

"Sometimes the bruises don't show. And sometimes, they hurt you with the words they say."

"Lavina, you're not saying David—"

"He never hit me. But his leaving without telling me was like a slap . . . " she trailed off and squinted. A familiar figure was walking on the right side of the road ahead of them. "Is that Carrie?"

As they came abreast of the woman she turned and they recognized each other.

Lavina pulled over. "Can we give you a ride?"

Carrie eyed the horse dubiously. "I've never been in a buggy before."

"Hop in. You'll like it," Mary Elizabeth said. She climbed into the back so Carrie could take her place in the front seat.

"So where are you going?" Lavina asked as she checked for traffic and they got back on the road.

"I'm allowed to leave the shelter for a walk," Carrie responded belligerently.

"I just wanted to know where we could drop you." Lavina made her tone mild.

"Oh." She named a restaurant about a mile ahead. "Is that on your way?"

"It's on our way," Mary Elizabeth leaned forward to say from the back seat. "Lavina is treating me to lunch."

"So she had to pick the most expensive one in town," Lavina pretended to complain. "It's a reward for her getting her quilt done early."

Carrie's eyebrows went up. "So quilts do that well for you, huh?"

"We do okay," Mary Elizabeth said. "We're so grateful we can do what we love and bring money into the family."

"I don't like to sew," Carrie said. "I don't know why I went to the class."

"I think the class is something Kate thought would be fun and maybe help the ladies learn a skill so they can find a job." Lavina stopped and bit her lip. She didn't need to defend Kate or the class. "Quilting isn't for everyone though as a hobby or a job. What kind of job are you looking for?"

"I liked my job bartending, but my old man got jealous of the other men."

It took Lavina a moment to remember that some women called their husbands "old man."

"So you should get to do the job you like, and he needs to trust you," Mary Elizabeth said.

"Mary Elizabeth, it's not our business to tell other people what to do!" Lavina chided her.

"Well, it's not right."

"You're not like any Amish woman I know," Carrie told Mary Elizabeth. "You're not like your sister at all."

"We're not all alike anymore than the *Englisch* are all alike," Mary Elizabeth said tartly.

"I just mean you're more outspoken."

"She is that," Lavina agreed. She pulled into the parking lot of the restaurant. "How are you going to get back?"

Carrie shrugged. "I'll walk if I can't get a ride. It's not far."

She got out and walked away without saying thanks. Mary Elizabeth returned to her seat in the front.

As Lavina turned her attention to leaving the parking lot Mary Elizabeth touched her hand. "Look!"

Lavina looked in the direction her sister pointed. A man got out of a pickup truck and kissed Carrie.

"Do you think that's her boyfriend?"

She felt a chill race over her skin. "I hope not. You should have seen how bruised her face was the first week I went to the class."

They watched the two walk into the restaurant. Lavina sighed as she guided the buggy onto the road. "Kate said some of the women go back to their husbands and boyfriends, sometimes several times."

"Even when they beat them? Why would they do that?"

"There's a lot of reasons, I guess. Kate said it's a hard cycle to break."

"If I had a *mann* and he hit me . . . well, he just better never," Mary Elizabeth said, frowning fiercely.

They rode in silence to the restaurant. Lavina wondered if she should tell Kate about Carrie meeting the man. Would that be the right thing to do? Or was it being what they used to call a tattletale in *schul?*

David came out of work to find his *bruder* Sam leaning against his truck, his arms folded across his chest.

"Sam." He came to a halt. "What brings you here? Is something wrong?"

"I'm not happy with you."

"What'd I do?"

Sam glared at him. "You know very well. You drove Mary Elizabeth to see me. Without any warning."

"It's cold out here. Let's go get some coffee."

"Fine. Then you can give me a ride home."

"*Schur.*" He unlocked the truck, and they climbed inside. David started the engine and turned the heater on.

Sam fastened his seat belt and looked around. "You still happy with the truck?"

"Runs great. It'll take a minute to warm up." He drove them to the same coffee shop he'd visited with Lavina and tried not to think about how that had gone. "You want your usual?" When Sam nodded he went to place their order.

"Look, I'm sorry I sprang Mary Elizabeth on you," he began as he sat down at the table. "But she wanted to see you."

"She wants me to come back." Frowning, Sam dumped sugar and creamer in his coffee. "I can't do that. Not even for her."

"Not even for *Mamm*?"

"Low blow. You talk like that, and I'm leaving."

"Stay put. I'm sorry. I got you a piece of pie. Your favorite."

Sam smiled at the young *Englisch* woman who brought it to the table, but his smile faded when he looked at David. "If *Daed* hasn't changed—and you said he hadn't the last time we talked—why should I put myself through it all again?"

When David opened his mouth to speak Sam raised his hand. "Let's not talk about it. I just wanted to tell you not to do that again."

Ignoring the pie, he bent his head and stared into his coffee cup. "All I did was hurt her," he said in a low voice David could barely hear.

He raised his head. "Is she *allrecht* now? She was crying when she left."

"I don't know. I haven't talked to Lavina since that day."

"So you two haven't patched things up yet?"

David shook his head. "I'm not sure I'm going to be able to."

Sam leaned back in his chair. "Women."

"Yeah." But David knew he was to blame, not Lavina. Sam did, too.

A cell phone rang. Several people around him—*Englisch* and Amish—checked to see if it was theirs. Lancaster county bishops were more lenient about their flocks owning a cell phone for their work. David pulled his out and saw the number of his *mamm's* phone in the outdoor shanty.

"It's *Mamm*," he told Sam as he took the call.

"David! You have to come now! Your *dat's* fallen, and I can't lift him."

"Be right there." He stood. "Come on, we have to go. *Mamm* said *Daed* fell."

"You go. I'll get a ride home."

"Sam, come on! Do you want her to strain herself helping me?"

Groaning, Sam stood and followed him out to the truck. "This better not be a trick," he said as he stood waiting for David to unlock the truck.

"Oh, *schur*, I sit around and think up tricks to get you home." Disgusted, David started the truck and backed out of the parking lot.

"Hey, slow down! You don't want to get us killed."

David looked at the speedometer and lifted his foot from the accelerator. Sam was right. He didn't want to get into an accident or get his first speeding ticket. If his *mamm* had thought his *dat* was in an emergency situation she'd have said so or called 911.

They found their mother upstairs kneeling by their father, her face pale and pinched with worry. Her eyes lit up when she saw Sam, but she rose and stood back to let them help her *mann* back to bed.

Amos stared at Sam. "What are you doing here?"

"Helping you."

"Don't need your help!" he snapped.

"Well, you're getting it," Sam said without rancor as he and David eased him into bed.

"You *schur* you shouldn't go to the hospital to get checked out?" David asked him as his mother covered Amos with a quilt.

"Just got up too quick, had a weak spell, and my knees wouldn't let me get up," he muttered, looking embarrassed.

"Get some rest and I'll bring your supper up here," Waneta said.

The fact that he didn't argue with her, that he'd actually agree to eat in bed, which he'd always seen as a sign of weakness, told David he was hurting more than he'd admit. His eyes met his *mudder's*, and she nodded. They'd talk downstairs.

He turned his back on them. They left the room, and the minute they got downstairs to the kitchen Waneta threw her arms around Sam. "Oh, thank God, you came back!" she cried.

Sam looked at David over her head, seeking help. But he didn't push her away; he simply stood and held her and let her cry.

"*Mamm*, Sam's not coming back," David said after a long moment. "We were having coffee when you called, and I asked him to come help me with *Daed*."

Looking stricken, Waneta backed away and stared up at Sam. "You're not?"

He shook his head.

She burst into tears and fled the room.

Sam closed his eyes and shook his head. "I shouldn't have let you talk me into coming here."

David sank into one of the kitchen chairs. "Does she look strong enough to have helped me? He was dead weight lying there on the floor."

Sam pulled out a chair and sat. "She looks almost as bad as he does."

"Cancer has more than one victim." David felt a hundred years old sitting there. "Let me make sure she's *allrecht* and then I'll drive you home."

Sam nodded.

When Waneta walked in a few minutes later her eyes were red from crying, but she was composed. "I'm sorry, Sam. I shouldn't have said that to you. I don't have the right to put pressure on you."

He reached out and squeezed her hand. "It's *allrecht, Mamm*."

"Can you stay for supper?"

Sam looked at David. "*Schur*."

David smiled at him.

10

Rose Anna set aside her quilt and stood and stretched. "Time for a break."

"I'll be there in a minute."

When Rose Anna didn't move Lavina looked up from her quilt. "What?"

"You need to come now. It's your turn to make supper for David's family."

"It's Mary Elizabeth's."

"She's lying down. I told you she thinks she's coming down with a cold. Weren't you listening?"

Lavina knew she was a little distracted, but didn't realize she hadn't paid attention to Rose Anna. But her youngest sister loved to chatter as she sewed, and it was easy sometimes to let it wash over you, she thought.

"Sorry." She set aside her quilt and stood. "I'll go check on her."

"*Nee*, you don't want to wake her if she's sleeping. Come on, I'll help you."

"*Danki.*" She smiled and slipped her arm around her *schweschde*r as they walked downstairs.

"It'll be nice having tea just the two of us today." Rose Anna said as she put on the teakettle.

"*Ya*, we don't get enough time to talk," Lavina said dryly.

Rose Anna elbowed her.

Lavina gathered together the vegetables she needed and sat down with a paring knife at the table.

Rose Anna stared at the small mountains of potatoes, carrots, and onions. "That's an awful lot."

"We might as well make two batches and have one for our supper."

"That's a lot of peeling," Rose Anna set two steaming mugs of tea on the table. "You know, Mary Elizabeth's been quiet since she went to see Sam. I guess it didn't go well? She won't talk to me about it."

Lavina shook her head. "Sam doesn't want to come home like David did. That's all I know."

"What did you and David do while Mary Elizabeth and Sam were talking?" Rose Anna asked casually as she picked up a carrot.

Lavina's head came up. She'd had a suspicion that Mary Elizabeth had recruited Rose Anna in her matchmaking scheme.

"We just went for coffee and talked."

"At that place you used to love? That must have been nice."

"Not exactly." Lavina dumped a peeled potato in the pottery bowl in front of her. "It just brought back old memories that made me sad." She focused her attention on a carrot and then put it down without peeling it. "David wants me to forget about this past year, and I'm not ready to do that yet."

She looked at Rose Anna. "You know, I have my suspicions that Mary Elizabeth asked me to go along with her as a way to throw me together with David."

"Really?" Rose Anna peeled a carrot quickly and efficiently.

"*Ya*. I think she was playing matchmaker."

Rose Anna finished the carrot, tossed it into the bowl, and started on another. "Would that be a bad thing?"

Lavina narrowed her eyes. She couldn't tell if her *schweschder* was being careful of her fingers or avoiding her eyes.

The back door opened, letting in a gust of cool air. Their *mudder* walked in, her cheeks pink from the cold.

"You're home early," Rose Anna said, rising to help her mother take off her jacket. "Tea?"

Linda untied her bonnet and hung it on a nearby peg. She rubbed her hands to warm them. "*Ya*, that would be nice. Hannah Miller wasn't feeling well so I gave her a ride home."

"We're cooking supper for David's family and thought we'd make a double batch so it would be our supper as well."

"Make the oven work twice. I have two smart *dochders*. Where is Mary Elizabeth?"

"Said she wasn't feeling well, so she's lying down."

"I'll go check on her." Linda started to get up, but Rose Anna jumped up, telling Linda to drink her tea and warm up.

"Something going on?"

Lavina looked at her. "I don't know. They've both been acting odd lately."

"How?"

"I think Mary Elizabeth's been playing matchmaker, and Rose Anna knows about it but won't tell me." She told her about the visit into town so Mary Elizabeth could see Sam, and how she and David had ended up having coffee together.

"Sounds harmless enough."

"It should be up to me if I see David."

"True. Do you want me to speak to them?"

"*Nee*. I'll take care of it." She finished the vegetables and rinsed them at the sink. "I thought I'd make some rice pudding. It might be a good bland dessert for David's *dat*. David told me Amos has had some trouble with the chemo treatments."

"*Gut* idea. Maybe a double batch so your *dat* has some, too? He has a fondness for it especially if you put raisins in it."

Mary Elizabeth was still in bed when it came time to deliver supper to David's *haus*, and Rose Anna had decided to make a pan of cornbread. So Lavina slipped on her jacket and bonnet and took the two hot carriers and set out on her own.

David opened the door himself when she knocked. He took the carriers and invited her in.

"I shouldn't," she said. "We're about to eat supper."

"*Mamm* will be upset if she doesn't get to thank you. She's upstairs with *Daed* and will be right down."

"*Allrecht*." She followed him into the kitchen and watched him put the carriers on the counter.

"Have a seat," he invited. "I'll let her know you're here."

But before he could move to the stairs that led to the bedrooms, there was a knock on the door.

The bishop stood on the porch, dressed in a severe black coat that flapped in the wind like the wings of a great black bird.

"Bishop," David said as he swung the door open. "What can I do for you?"

"The first thing is to invite me out of the cold," the man said tartly. "I want to talk to you."

"It's not a *gut* time."

The bishop stepped in, ignoring his words. "Is that because you're entertaining a *maedel* without a chaperone?" he asked, fixing Lavina with a cold stare.

David had been trained since he was a small *kind* to respect his elders—particularly the bishop.

But rude was rude, and the man had no business entering someone's home without being invited. He and the bishop had clashed before, and he had no patience with him invading the house.

"You'll have to come back another time," he told him. "Call first."

"*Mein Gott*! David! What are you saying?" His mother rushed up and stared at him, aghast.

"If someone wants to talk to me, he shouldn't just show up without warning," David told her. "We've had enough of his talks in the past that I know how this one would go. I thought you were upstairs tending to *Daed*."

"I was. He wants to come down to supper. Can you help him so I don't worry about him falling on the stairs?"

"*Schur.*" It was looking to be one of those nights.

He walked into the kitchen and Lavina stood. "I should go."

"We both will," he muttered. "Just let me help my *dat* down the stairs and I'll drive you home."

"You don't need to drive me—"

"I do," he interrupted her. "I need to get out of here for a while if the bishop is going to stay and talk to my parents. Please?"

She looked at him for a long moment then she nodded. "*Allrecht.*"

He started for the stairs and found his *dat* halfway down them. "Let me help you."

"Don't need any help," his *dat* said brusquely.

"*Allrecht,* then I'll stay a step down from you, and if you fall it'll be a soft landing. *Mamm* asked me to help you and that's what I'm going to do."

He heard a snort behind him as he turned and did what he'd said he would, moving down a stair below his *dat*. Once he'd been assured his *dat* made it down the stairs and was safely ensconced in his chair at the head of the kitchen table, he grabbed his jacket.

The bishop was standing near the table taking off his coat. Waneta stood at the stove pouring coffee.

David looked at Lavina. "Ready?"

She nodded and stood.

"You're not staying for supper?"

"*Nee, danki*, I have to get home. *Gut-n-Owed*, Amos, Bishop."

David handed Lavina her jacket and bonnet and wasn't surprised when she put them on as she hurried to the front door. He could be wrong, but it seemed to him that she wanted out of there as badly as he did.

"*Danki*," he said as soon as they were safely inside his truck.

"For what?"

"You know very well. For getting me out of there before I had words with the bishop or my *dat* or both of them."

"Probably both of them," she said seriously.

He thought he saw the corners of her mouth lift in a faint smile.

"Probably both," he agreed as he started the truck. "Do you really have to get home?"

"Why?"

"I thought I'd thank you by taking you out to supper."

"You don't need to do that."

He glanced at her, then back at the road. "Maybe don't need to. But want to. Would you go out to supper with me, Lavina?"

"I'm not so sure that's a *gut* idea."

The car in front of him stopped and waited to make a left turn. David took his eyes off the road and looked at her. "*Schur* it is."

She hesitated and a car honked behind them. The driver up ahead had made his turn and David was slowing things down. He accelerated.

"Well?"

"Maybe just this once," she said finally. "If we don't talk about the past."

"What past?" he asked lightly, although he felt a little pang as he said it.

"I have to stop by the house and let *Mamm* know."

"No problem."

He drove her to her house and waited while she ran inside. She returned and a rush of cool air invaded the cabin. He turned the heater on high.

They discussed where to go. David tried to think of someplace they hadn't been. There was a new one he'd heard of—a bit pricey but he figured he could do it once.

When he named it, she laughed.

"Mary Elizabeth and I just went there the other day for lunch." She narrowed her eyes at him. "She didn't tell you to take me there, did she?"

"*Nee*, why would she do that?"

"Because I think she's been matchmaking. She'd like to see us back together."

"Back together? But that would imply we had a past and we agreed not to talk about it, right?" As if that would erase it, he gave her a smile as he drove.

She gave him a measuring look.

"So do we go there or are you tired of it?"

"No one could be tired of going there again even on the same day. But it's a little expensive, David. We don't have to go someplace that nice."

"I never got to take you anywhere nice," he said flatly.

The words hung in the silence. Both of them knew he'd never had money because he and his *bruders* worked on the farm without pay. He'd earned a small amount of spending money by finding occasional part-time work for other farmers. A coffee date had been a big event for them. David had too much *hochmut*—too much pride to let her help pay for anything.

"We went here the other day as a treat," she said as he pulled into the parking lot a few minutes later. "I'd promised Mary Elizabeth we'd go if she finished a quilt order early. Of course she got me to pay."

"She's *gut* at getting her way," he said with a smile so she knew he didn't mean it critically. He turned off the ignition.

"She's always been a charmer. We're not at all alike."

"I think you're charming," he told her quietly.

She glanced at him then away. "I wasn't fishing for a compliment."

"I know. And I meant it. But you're charming in a different way than Mary Elizabeth. She uses charm to get her way. You don't use it at all . . . you're a pleasure to be around because you're interested in others, not getting something for yourself."

He stopped, afraid he'd say too much, make her uncomfortable and not want to be with him. Pulling the keys from the ignition, he got out and hurried to open her door before she could.

"Wait and take a look at the menu before we go in," she said, pointing to a framed menu near the door. "You might not like what they serve."

"I'm *schur* it'll be fine. It wouldn't be this busy if it didn't serve *gut* food."

He gestured at the nearly full parking lot with one hand while he held the door open for her and she was forced to step inside. He loved her for being sensitive of his wallet, but he had the money to pay. They deserved a nice night out.

"Dinner prices are higher than they were for lunch," she murmured. "Why don't we just get dessert and coffee and go?"

"Why don't you stop worrying?"

"I made beef stew. Your favorite. You could go home and have that. We could ride around for a little while to make sure the bishop is gone."

"But then I wouldn't get to have supper with you."

He smiled at her and watched the way color rose in her cheeks at the compliment. Had he paid her so few compliments in the past that giving her one now made her blush?

He started to reach for her hand but a woman appeared at the table.

"Good evening, folks. I'm Shirley and I'll be taking care of you this evening," their server said as she lit the candle in the center of the table. "Let me tell you what the specials are."

David pretended to listen but he couldn't have cared less what they had to eat. He'd never heard of beef bourguignon or coq au vin, but he'd have cheerfully eaten dirt over noodles if it meant he got an hour with Lavina looking so lovely in candlelight.

The server took their drink orders and left them with menus. David was grateful that there were explanations under each entrée that was unfamiliar to him. The beef bourguignon actually sounded a lot like beef stew. He knew he could have Lavina's beef stew later if he wanted. Coq au vin sounded like drunken chicken. Steak. Hmm. He didn't have that often at home. Meals were simple and filling, but steak was expensive so it didn't often appear on the family supper table.

"I'm having the steak. Don't go ordering a salad to save me money."

She smiled. "*Allrecht*. I think I'll have the pork roast with apple stuffing. Sounds like something I might want to try making at home if I like it. *Daed* loves pork."

As he sat there enjoying the meal and the time with Lavina, David realized that the evening that had started out with an unpleasant visit from the bishop had turned into a very pleasant evening indeed for him. He silently thanked God for the unexpected blessing and promised he'd be more polite to the bishop next time he saw him.

Well, he'd do his best anyway . . . when it came to him and the bishop, he couldn't promise anything.

Lavina lay awake for a long time that night after she came home from supper out with David.

Although they hadn't talked about anything serious—and certainly not about the past—it still was more than just two friends having supper together.

He hadn't looked at her like she was a friend, but like a woman he wanted to be more than a friend with. She was a practical woman, one who now knew to guard her heart. Candlelight might make the atmosphere romantic but there had been more . . . there was no disguising the way he'd looked at her all evening, even if he was careful to keep things light and friendly.

And he'd taken her hand as they walked to the truck.

The ride home seemed too short. If he'd taken the family buggy there would have been more time to talk, to enjoy the moonlit night.

The truck itself posed a problem. The fact that he had it meant he could so easily ride it back to the life he'd lived in the *Englisch* world. Sometimes after the tension with his *dat* he wanted to do that . . .

Mary Elizabeth had looked up from her seat on the sofa with avid curiosity when she'd walked in the door, so Lavina said she was tired and going to bed early. She'd changed quickly into a nightgown, brushed her teeth, and slipped into bed before Mary Elizabeth could ask any questions. In minutes she was tucked under her quilt, the battery-operated lamp on her bedside table turned off.

Footsteps paused at her door and then moved on. Lavina smiled in the dark. Knowing Mary Elizabeth, she was probably dying of curiosity.

Moonlight filtered into the room, sending shifting patterns of light and shadow through the bare tree branches a few feet from her window, as she thought about her evening out.

She felt herself softening toward David and told herself that could be dangerous for her. Kate's words came back to her—the conversation they'd had about how sometimes the women in the shelter returned to their abusive husbands or boyfriends. How they couldn't break the cycle.

If she let David back into her life, into her heart, she could be hurt again if he left the community. She had no guarantee that he wouldn't return to the *Englisch* world if the relationship between him and his *dat* didn't change. David was in such a terrible position: if his *dat* survived he might tell David he didn't need him anymore. If he died, David and his *bruders* would inherit the farm and he'd stay.

She prayed his *dat* would recover and live for many more years, all the while she knew what consequences that might have for David, the man she knew she still cared for so much. God had a plan for everyone and lying here tossing and turning, worrying about David was wrong. God knew best. Phoebe King, Jenny Bontrager's *grossmudder*, always liked to say that worry was arrogant because God knew what he was doing.

So she told herself to think of something pleasant. Supper at such a fancy place had been so wonderful. She wanted to try duplicating the pork roast with apple stuffing one night. It looked simple enough on the plate—the roast had a hole cut in the center and it was packed with stuffing made with bread cubes and onion and chopped apples, and some spices like cinnamon and maybe nutmeg. Maybe she could even look for a recipe on the computer at the library one day or just try improvising with a recipe for roast pork.

She sighed when she remembered the dessert she'd shared with David. She could almost taste the ladyfingers soaked in coffee and the luscious filling. The server had written down the name of the exotic sounding dessert. Tiramisu. Paradise on a plate, she remembered with a smile. She'd look that up on the computer, too. It was unlike the simple Amish desserts she was used to but everyone should try an adventure with food now and then. Maybe David's mother would enjoy getting a piece of it when she made it. Linda seldom got out of the house except to go with her *mann* to medical appointments.

Lavina snuggled deeper under her quilt and thanked God for the unexpected pleasure of an evening out. Whether she and David ever became more than friends again, it would be a lovely memory. There had been menus the restaurant patrons could take home, and she'd slipped one into her purse. Tomorrow she'd tuck it into her journal.

A couple at a nearby table appeared to be celebrating a special time—perhaps an anniversary. The man had surprised the woman with a vase of red roses brought to the table, and they shared a bottle of wine. The maitre d' had poured the wine into fluted glasses, and it had looked bubbly and golden in the candlelight on their table. It made the woman giggle after she drank a glass. Remembering how happy the couple had looked, Lavina smiled and found herself fantasizing how it would be to be married and celebrating being happy together.

She fell asleep and dreamed.

She wore a dress the color of a robin's egg on her wedding day and felt she must be glowing like a candle as David joined her and they walked to meet the minister. So many of their family members and friends gathered in her home. Mary Elizabeth and Rose Anna and Sam and John were among the newhockers, *the attendants.*

She'd never felt so loved, so surrounded by wishes for joy and happiness that could be felt radiating from all whom they loved and who loved them.

But just as the minister was about to pronounce them mann *and* fraa, *she saw David begin to fade, to become transparent and then he was gone. She stared wildly around her, crying out his name, wondering where he'd gone.*

"David! David! Where are you?"

She woke, sitting up and reaching out for him. But she was alone in her room in her narrow bed. She wiped the tears from her cheeks and lay back against her pillow again.

It had only been a dream, a bad one.

She hadn't been married after all. But David was still alive, probably sleeping in his bed in his home not far from hers. He'd slipped away from her in the dream, and he'd slipped away from her life for a year.

But he was still here, still wanted her. And the future was unknown, but she'd do her best to just take things one day at a time and trust this path God had laid out for her before she was born. She knew he'd set aside a *mann* for her. She didn't know if it was David, but she had to trust His plan and His timing.

Lavina pulled the quilt up around her shoulders and closed her eyes. A Bible verse drifted into her thoughts. *I will both lie down in peace, and sleep; For You alone, O Lord, make me dwell in safety (Psalm 4:8).*

Comforted, she slept dreamlessly.

11

I've been thinking about what you said."

Lavina blinked in surprise. She hadn't seen Carrie slip into a seat at the back in the quilting class. "You know, about how you said sewing skills might help me get a job."

She smiled. "Well, that's actually what Kate said."

"I like bartending, but it'd be nice not to have to be on my feet, you know? I've been looking for something different. I mean, you sew sitting down, right?"

This was the most that Carrie had ever said to her. And she wasn't wearing the sullen expression that she usually wore.

Lavina nodded. "You put in pretty long hours sometimes, whether you're sewing on a machine or by hand."

"Amish quilts cost a lot, don't they? The tourists don't seem to mind what they pay for them."

"They're not cheap," she agreed. "That's because they take a lot of time to make. Some of the patterns are complicated."

"You think someone would buy one from a person who isn't Amish?"

"I don't know. I guess you could ask Leah. She owns a shop called Stitches in Time."

"I know that one." Carrie glanced toward the front of the room where Kate stood helping one of the class members, then back at Lavina. "Thanks for the ride the other day."

"You're welcome."

"It was good to get away from here for a while, you know?"

Lavina didn't really know what to say so she nodded. Carrie bent her head to her block and began sewing again.

"Nice to see you again," Fran, a woman Lavina guessed to be her mother's age said as Lavina stopped to admire her progress. "Carrie was quite talkative just now. Maybe she's feeling a little happier these days."

She paused and looked thoughtful. "I don't know if I could have made the break with my boyfriend at that age. I didn't think I could live without my husband when I was thirty-five and he was hurting me. And I had two little ones. I thought they needed their father." She shook her head. "Then one day I realized I couldn't let them see him hitting me. It was better for us to come here. Thank God for a place like this."

Kate announced it was time for the class to end, and Fran began putting her block into her project box. "The time just flies by when I'm sewing."

"I know. I'm glad you enjoy it. See you next week."

Pearl, the woman who ran the shelter, met Lavina and Kate when they descended the stairs. "We're having a little surprise party for Iris, one of the women in the quilting class. Hope you can join us."

"I'm sorry, but I have to be in court," Kate said. "Lavina?"

She liked Iris. The woman was quiet, a little shy, but she always smiled when Lavina stopped by her seat and asked if she needed any help. She nodded. "I'd like to stay. Can I help with anything?"

Pearl put her to work setting up in the dining room, and while someone kept Iris busy elsewhere, other women began filtering into the room to help, bringing little gifts they placed on a table, chattering and looking excited.

A short time later Pearl gave the signal for someone to get Iris and the women cried, "Surprise!" when Iris stepped into the room. She promptly burst into tears.

Pearl, a robust woman with graying hair and kind blue eyes, hugged her.

"Make a wish!" someone called as Pearl led her over to a birthday cake with candles on it. Iris closed her eyes and blew them out. Everyone applauded and took their seats as Pearl cut the cake, put slices on plates, and handed them to Lavina to pass out.

"Sit down, have yourself some," Pearl invited when everyone had a piece of cake before them.

"I never expected this," Iris told Pearl.

"We're family here," Pearl said. "You just remember that. We're all here for each other at Sarah's Place."

"He said no one else loved me," Iris said quietly. "He said no one would want me after he put his hands on my face."

"Well, he was wrong. Dr. Elton fixed your face, and that soon to be ex-husband of yours can't keep that sweet heart of yours from shining unless you let him."

Iris opened her presents and thanked everyone profusely. So profusely Lavina wondered if she'd received many presents in her life.

"Thank you for staying," Pearl told her as Lavina carried plates into the kitchen.

"I enjoyed it. And the cake was good."

"My mother's recipe. Sarah's Place is named after her. My father beat her for years and then one night he killed her in front of us kids. I was eleven." Her tone was matter-of-fact as she started another pot of coffee.

"That must have been awful for you."

Pearl nodded. "I like to think she'd be happy that women like her have a place to be safe." She looked at Lavina. "I'm so glad you've come to help Kate with the quilting class. I noticed more women are joining you each week."

"I don't know how much I've helped, but it's been fun," Lavina told her. "Some of the women are doing some very creative work. I think we all need something like that."

"I agree. I like to knit when I watch television in the evenings. Maybe one day we could offer a knitting class."

"And you could teach it."

"If I could find the time." She sighed. "I stay so busy running the place."

"I'm going to go see if there're are more dirty dishes."

Lavina went into the dining room and found that the party was still going on. The women were enjoying the last of the cake and coffee while Iris exclaimed over each present she opened.

These women behaved like long-time friends—family, even—Lavina thought. And yet she knew they hadn't been at the shelter long. The shelter was a temporary home but they'd formed a bond, reaching out to each other from a place of personal pain and were helping each other in the way that women everywhere did. It felt much like her own community, her own church, here today, she realized.

She'd come here to give of her time, but it seemed to her that she was seeing how other people gave of themselves to each other. She might never have known if she hadn't left her home, her community, her own idea of safety and security, and ventured here.

This day, the class, was an unexpected gift. It seemed to her that she should find a way to thank Kate for inviting her to help with the class.

On his way home from work David passed the restaurant where he and Lavina had eaten supper last night. He found himself smiling as he remembered what a wonderful evening he'd had. He hoped Lavina had enjoyed it, too. She'd seemed to.

The meal and tip had taken quite a bite out of his wallet, but they'd both deserved it after miserly dates at coffee shops and that sort of thing for years.

A couple near their table had obviously been celebrating a special occasion. David remembered how the man had red roses delivered to the table, and the waiter had served champagne that had made the woman giggle.

He'd persuaded Lavina to go to supper with him on the spur of the moment so there had been no chance of getting her flowers. There was a small florist shop a mile or so ahead. He could stop for some now. Supper had cost a lot but he'd seen signs outside the florist advertising something called a "fun bunch" for $5.95. He could afford that.

The shop was bright and cheerful and there, just inside the door, were the bunches of flowers that were "fun"—he wasn't sure what kind they were but he'd never seen flowers of fluorescent pinks and lime green and purple.

Then he spotted a bunch of dried pussy willows sticking out of an earthenware jar. They reminded him of a time when he and Lavina had been taking a leisurely buggy ride one day, and she spotted a stand of them growing in a pool of water beside the road. Lavina had always had a fondness for them. He'd climbed down an embankment and landed in muddy water and scared her, and then delighted her with an armful of the branches with the gray catkins that she said looked so much like kittens climbing a tree.

He checked the price and found he could afford them so he carried them to the counter to pay. As he carried the jar out to his truck and carefully set it on the floorboard of the passenger side, he wondered if she'd remember how he'd landed in the muddy water when he went to cut some for her.

Last night they hadn't talked about the past. But they had one and he hoped this would remind her of it.

He stopped by her house and Linda, Lavina's mother, opened the door. "Why, David, what a nice surprise. *Kumm*, I'll tell Lavina you're here."

David stood, shifting from one foot to the other. He hadn't really known what to expect from her. The Amish were forgiving, but he'd hurt her daughter, and this was the first time he'd seen Linda since he came back.

Lavina appeared and she looked as surprised as her *mudder* had been minutes before. "David? Is everything *allrecht*? Your *dat*?"

"He's still with us," he said quickly. "I wanted to bring you these." He held out the jar.

"Pussy willows!" She smiled. "I love these."

"They're dried. I got them from the florist."

"So they'll last a long time."

He nodded. "They're not roses but—"

"I like them better. Always have."

"Lavina, ask David if he'd like to stay for supper," Linda called out from the kitchen.

"I shouldn't," he said. "Today *Daed* had chemo, and I should be home in case *Mamm* needs help with him."

He'd rather stay. He was sure he'd get a lecture from his *mudder* about his being rude to the bishop.

"At least take home one of the pies we baked today."

He brightened. "I can do that."

She smiled. "You didn't ask what kind it is."

"It's pie. That's all I need to know."

"Men," she said, shaking her head. But he heard the smile in her voice as she turned and headed for the kitchen.

He headed home in a better mood, the pumpkin pie sitting on the passenger seat filling the truck cabin with its spicy scent.

When he walked into the house, it felt strangely quiet. That shouldn't have surprised him. It had been since he and his big, noisy *bruders* had left. But usually at this time of day he heard the sounds of his mother preparing supper. Delicious aromas met him at the door.

He started for the kitchen and as he neared it he heard the sound of quiet weeping. His *mudder* sat at the table, her face buried in her hands, her shoulders bent.

"*Mamm*?"

He set the pie on a counter and rushed to her, kneeling beside her chair. "What's wrong?" When she didn't respond fear swept over him. "*Daed*. Is *Daed* gone?"

She lifted her face. "Gone? Where would he go?" Then a look of understanding came over her face. "*Nee*, he's resting."

"Then what's wrong?" He rose and pulled out a chair to sit.

She wiped her eyes with a paper napkin. "He didn't have a good doctor's visit today. He's losing weight and his counts are still down. He's been so tired and sick. I think he just wants to give up."

"He's too stubborn to give up."

Her breath hitched. "I used to think so. But this is a battle sheer will won't win."

David could see it was taking a huge toll on her as well. He remembered how Saul Miller's parents had traveled the terrible road of cancer years ago. First his mother had fought breast cancer and then a year later, his father had gotten colon cancer. Both had survived, but it had been such an ordeal for both of them. It wasn't that cancer was contagious, Saul had told him one day when David visited Saul's store. It was that the spouse of the person with cancer became so burdened physically and emotionally that their own immune systems ran down and became susceptible to the terrible disease.

He started to tell his mother she needed to take better care of herself or she'd get sick, too, and remind her of what had happened to Saul's *dat*.

But she looked worn out. The last thing she needed was a lecture, however well-phrased or well-intended it might be.

"What can I do?" he asked her.

She shook her head. "It's enough that you took over your *dat's* chores." She glanced around the kitchen. "I need to start supper. See if I can get him to eat something. He didn't eat much lunch."

"Is there any of that stew left that Lavina brought over yesterday?"

"That's right, there's plenty since you didn't eat with us last night and your *dat* wasn't very *hungerich*," she said, getting up to pull it out of the refrigerator. "It won't take long for it to warm."

"Lavina sent a pie," he told her, gesturing at it sitting on the counter. "*Daed* loves pumpkin pie. Bet he'll eat some of that."

"So did you eat at Lavina's last night?" she asked as she put the stew in the oven.

"I took her out to eat."

When she continued to stand there, looking at him, he told her where they'd gone. Her brows went up at the name of the restaurant.

"Heard that's pricey."

"It was. But I've never had the money to take her anywhere special."

"Was it a special occasion?"

David shook his head. "Just a spur of the moment thing." He frowned. "I don't know if we'll ever be close again," he said slowly. "I hurt her a lot when I left. I'm trying to make it up to her. Not with fancy dinners but just trying to be friends with her again."

"She's a nice young *maedel*. I always liked her."

"I know." He grabbed an apple from a bowl on the counter and reached for his hat on the peg on the wall. "I'll go take care of Nellie and be back as quick as I can."

"*Gut*. Oh, and David?"

"*Ya*?"

"Don't think I've forgotten how you talked to the bishop last night."

He crammed his hat on his head and started for the back door.

"And don't think I didn't see you roll your eyes at me, young man!"

He grinned as he went out the door. She might have said stern words, but he'd heard the humor under them. She was already sounding better than she had when he'd come home.

Lavina spread the orders out on the table in the sewing room. Mary Elizabeth and Rose Anna and their mother gathered around.

"Which ones do you want?" she asked them. "There are enough orders for each of us to choose two. Rose Anna, you really like doing the Around the World quilt."

"*Ya*, and I'll take the Sunshine and Shadow unless you want it."

"That's fine. *Mamm?* Want the wedding ring quilt?"

She nodded and picked up the order. "Then maybe the crazy quilt?"

"Mary Elizabeth?"

"I'd like to do the crazy quilt." She bit her lip as she studied the orders. "And maybe the nine patch."

"That leaves me with the mariner's compass and a crib quilt," Lavina said, picking them up.

"Are you *allrecht* with that?" Rose Anna asked her. "You always let us choose first."

Lavina grinned. "I feel like I get the ones I'm supposed to have. And it makes for a challenge. I've only done a mariner's compass once. This will give me a chance to do another."

They spent the afternoon going through their fabric stash, sometimes arguing who got which fat quarter, but in the end they were satisfied with their choices. Taking turns at the big table they started planning their first quilt and cut their fabric. The afternoon passed quickly and Lavina regretted volunteering to make supper. She loved the start of a project.

She put macaroni on to boil for the macaroni and cheese with chunks of ham left over from Sunday's supper. It was a simple meal but warm and filling on a chilly night. The three pumpkin pies Rose Anna had made the other day had already been eaten—one had gone to David and his family. Lavina stood at the pantry looking for inspiration for dessert and wondered if David's family had enjoyed the pie. And she wondered what he was doing right now. She had taken the earthenware vase with the pussy willows he brought her up to her room and set it on her dresser. Perhaps she should have set it on the kitchen table so her family could have enjoyed it, too, but she didn't want to answer all the questions she'd get from her *schweschders*—especially Mary Elizabeth.

Jars of fruit they'd harvested from their kitchen garden and canned at the end of summer were lined up on the top shelf—bright orange peaches that had dripped with juice when peeled, plump blackberries the size of a man's thumb, delicate pears, and round little crabapples. They'd frozen a bounty of strawberries and raspberries and rhubarb. Growing and harvesting hadn't been easy, and canning in the late summer heat had been taxing, but God had been so *gut* to provide a bounty of delicious fruits—and vegetables, too—that they would eat and enjoy as winter came and snow piled up outside the house.

She chose the blackberries and decided to make a cobbler. It would bake at the same time as the macaroni dish and bring a reminder of a hot summer day when she and her *schweschders* had braved the thorns of the blackberry bushes and tried not to eat more than they put in their buckets.

Mary Elizabeth wandered into the kitchen to make herself a cup of peppermint tea and watched Lavina work as she sipped and ate a couple of cookies. She liked to watch others work, Lavina thought with a smile.

"So how is David?" she asked as Lavina drained the macaroni and poured it into a baking pan. "I hear he took you to supper at my favorite place."

Lavina raised her brows. "You've decided it's your favorite place after one time there?"

Mary Elizabeth nodded vigorously. "You're lucky you got to go there twice."

"David shouldn't have insisted," Lavina told her. "I know he doesn't have much money. But he said we always just went for coffee on our dates."

"He's right."

"How would you know?" Lavina got cheese from the refrigerator and found the metal grater. "Here, grate me two cups."

Mary Elizabeth cut a corner off the block of cheese and nibbled on it.

"You keep on eating and you won't want supper."

"That's an hour away. I'll be *hungerich.*" She began grating the cheese. "I'd remember if you'd told me you went someplace special."

"Any place is special with the right person."

Lavina set a skillet on the stove and turned the gas burner on under it. She put butter in and watched it melt and found herself remembering how it felt to talk and laugh with David last night.

"And a special place makes it even more special, *ya*?"

Lavina glanced away from the melting butter and saw her *schweschder* grinning at her. "I've never had supper by candlelight before."

"How romantic," Rose Anna said.

She'd come into the room so quietly Lavina hadn't noticed her.

"Tell us more." Rose Anna sat at the table and looked at her expectantly.

"The *Englisch* couple at the next table was obviously celebrating some special occasion." Lavina told them about the red roses, the champagne.

"We don't care about them," Mary Elizabeth said. "How was it to be there with David?"

Lavina turned her attention back to the skillet. She pulled a canister over and sprinkled several tablespoons of flour over the butter, then began whisking it.

"Where did you go?" Rose Anna asked her as she handed her a carton of milk.

"I'm right here, trying to concentrate so I don't burn this," she told her. She poured some milk into the skillet—no need to measure since she'd made the dish so often—and continued whisking until the flour and butter and milk became a smooth white sauce. Turning, she took the bowl of cheese Mary Elizabeth had grated and saw her two *schweschders* watching her.

"It was very nice," she said carefully. "But it's too early to know if we can even be friends again. He broke my trust." She touched her fingers to her trembling lips. "He broke my heart."

Lavina turned back to the skillet, stirring in the cheese a handful at a time, stirring more vigorously than she had to. "Rose Anna, butter that baking pan, would you? And Mary Elizabeth, could you get the ham from the refrigerator and cut up about two cups in bite-sized pieces for me? I need to get this in the oven so I can put together the blackberry cobbler."

She poured the macaroni into the buttered pan and then used a rubber spatula to scoop the cheese sauce out of the skillet over it. Mary Elizabeth dumped the ham into the mixture, and Lavina stirred it all together. She set it in the oven and got out a bowl to start the cobbler topping.

"Do you remember the day we picked the blackberries?" she asked them, hoping to turn their attention from the topic of her and David at supper. "I didn't think we'd bring home enough of them to make anything. Rose Anna, you ate more than Mary Elizabeth and me."

"Did not."

"Did too," said Mary Elizabeth.

And they were off, arguing amiably as they always did.

"What's all the racket?" their mother asked as she walked into the room.

"They're arguing over who ate the most blackberries the day we went picking them."

"As I remember it, all three of you came home with purple juice dripping down your chins," Linda said with a smile. "Just like when you were *kind*." She lifted the cheese covered spatula to her lips and licked it. "Mmm. This is *gut*. Can't wait for supper."

"Now look who's got something on her chin," Rose Anna cried, laughing and pointing at their *mudder*.

Lavina grabbed a paper napkin from the holder on the table to wipe her mother's chin. "What manners," she teased.

Her *dat* walked in the back door, his cheeks ruddy, bringing with him a rush of cold air. "What's so funny?" he asked, smiling at them as he hung up his hat and shrugged out of his jacket.

"*Mamm's* been licking the spatula and getting cheese all over her chin," Rose Anna said.

He reached for his *frau* and kissed her, then smacked his lips. "Right tasty," he said with a grin.

Linda's cheeks pinked and she pushed him away. "Enough of such silliness," she told him. But she was smiling as she picked up the skillet and took it to the sink to wash it.

Their parents didn't often do such in front of them, but Lavina had always felt the warmth, the love between them. She looked at Rose Anna and Mary Elizabeth, and they were smiling, too.

A gust of wind shook the kitchen window, but inside it was warm and rich with the aroma of the casserole baking. Lavina opened the jar of dark purple fruit and the scent of summer's blackberries filled the air.

12

Lavina hated running late.

She almost never ran late. As the oldest, she'd often had to help her mother get her *schweschders* ready for church and for *schul*, so she was used to getting up early and being on time.

Not today. She'd set her alarm, and it hadn't gone off so she'd overslept. In a rush to get ready to leave the house, she'd stubbed her toe on the foot of her bed, so she'd been a *boppli* and had to sit down and cry from the pain for a few minutes.

Then she was so distracted she managed to stick herself in the side as she inserted a straight pin at the waist of her dress. That led to having to find a bandage. Then, when she tried to rush through breakfast, she'd burned her mouth on her oatmeal.

It just isn't my day, she thought, then chided herself. It was the day God had given her, and it wasn't like her to not be grateful.

Since she was running late she decided to take the box of completed quilt orders by Leah's shop after the class. Before she went into the shelter she threw the buggy blanket over the box on the back seat and hurried inside.

"I'm so sorry," she told Kate when she rushed into the room.

"Relax, you're helping us," Kate said. "You're not punching in at work. Sit down and catch your breath."

So she watched Kate work on a new project, one made of the fabric the *Englisch* called camouflage. "I was working on quilts for friends of my husband who are still in the military. Usually they like patriotic themes and colors. But then one day one of them wrote my husband and said they can't take them into the field because they have to pack them in their knapsack, and it makes it hard to carry with everything they need."

Kate held up the half-sewn quilt. "But they can roll these up and tie them on the outside of the knapsack with some fabric strips I'll sew on, and they'll blend in with the rest of their uniform."

She resumed sewing. "A quilt gives them the feeling someone back home cares, and it keeps them warm on a cold night." She glanced up to see if anyone needed them to help and focused again on her work. "Did Jenny Bontrager ever tell you how she came to live here?"

"I don't know all the details." Jenny was a member of their church—she hadn't been born Amish, although her father had been Amish and he'd chosen not to join the church.

"Jenny was a television reporter who did stories overseas about children living in war zones. She was hurt in a bombing and flown back to the States." She paused to make a knot and then rethread her needle. "Her grandmother, Phoebe King, sent a quilt to her hospital room and told her to come recuperate here. So Jenny came back and met Matthew Bontrager, the boy next door to Phoebe, and now they live 'happily ever after.'"

"In a way, that quilt brought two people to your community," Kate said, looking thoughtful. "Chris Matlock, Jenny's brother-in-law, met her at a hospital up in New York. He was a soldier who'd been injured overseas. He came here after they wrote to each other, and she told him about Paradise. And he met Hannah, Jenny's sister-in-law, and now they're married."

She set the quilt down and flexed her fingers. "And when Chris came to town, my husband, Malcolm, came here, too. They knew each other although Malcolm would be the first to tell you he didn't come here because he and Chris were friends."

"I remember when he came here," Lavina said. Malcolm had been seeking revenge, blaming Chris for reporting him for a crime he'd committed.

"Just goes to show you how much a person can turn his life around when he wants to," Kate said cheerfully. "He does volunteer work with veterans now, especially those who have drug and alcohol problems. I'm so lucky that he came into my life. I was thirty-five when I met him and didn't think marriage was for me."

Some days it seemed to Lavina like everyone she knew was married, going around two-by-two like the animals on Noah's Ark. She shook her head as if to chase away the negative thought. Really, this was the second time this morning she'd found herself being negative. It wasn't like her . . .

"I think I'll walk around and see if anyone needs any help."

"Thanks. I'll confess I'm glad to be off my feet for a while. I just came off a long shift and haven't been to bed yet."

Now Lavina felt guilty. She didn't have the workload or family responsibilities Kate did and hadn't shown up on time.

She stayed a little longer so she could help the women put their project boxes up, and so Kate could leave on time.

So when she walked into Stitches in Time she found herself apologizing for the second time that day.

"Don't worry about it," Leah said. "I knew you'd be by."

She pulled the top off the box of quilt orders, admiring the work as she always did. And then she frowned. "I thought you were bringing six. There's five in the box, Lavina."

Lavina counted. Leah was right.

"I have copies of the order in the drawer here," Leah said. She pulled them from a drawer under the shop counter. "Let's see what's missing."

They found that one of the quilts that Mary Elizabeth had sewn, a wedding ring quilt, was missing.

"I remember putting it into the box last night," Lavina said, wondering what had happened. "Let me go out to the buggy and make sure it didn't fall out of the box on the way in."

But the quilt wasn't in the buggy. She returned to the shop. "I don't know what happened. I'll go home and see if I left it there."

"I'm sure you'll find it. Let me give you a check."

"Only for the five."

"I know you're good for the missing one."

"Only for the five," Lavina repeated firmly.

With a sigh, Leah wrote out the check for five. "Just give me a call so I'll know when to tell the customer she can pick it up."

"I will. And *danki*, Leah."

"You're *wilkumm*." She smiled at Lavina. "We have some new fabric out on the table here," she told her, gesturing at it.

"So I can spend the check before I leave?" Lavina joked.

But her smile was forced. What could have happened to the quilt? Her *schweschders* and *mudder* wouldn't have removed it from the box . . .

She browsed the table even though she wanted to rush home and search for the missing quilt. But she forced herself to stay calm and look over the new fabric, telling herself the quilt was undoubtedly sitting on the table where she'd packed up the orders. Maybe she'd gotten distracted and not packed it, or Mary Elizabeth had taken it out to do one last thing to it and hadn't put it back. They'd laugh about it when she got home.

Lavina found two bolts of fabric that she couldn't resist, and soon was walking out the door and on her way home.

The quilt was nowhere to be found when she got home. And Mary Elizabeth said she had not only not taken it out for a last minute stitch or whatever—she'd watched Lavina pack it the night before.

They went out to the buggy to look and shook their heads when they didn't find the quilt.

"Did you go straight to Leah's?"

"*Nee,* I was running late. I went to class first." Lavina's hand flew to her mouth. "Do you think someone took it?"

"That's the only thing I can think of."

"But why would someone take one and not the whole box?"

Mary Elizabeth shook her head. "Maybe they were hoping you wouldn't notice one was gone?"

Lavina sighed. "I'll have to let Leah know and ask if the customer can wait for us to sew another."

"I'll do it as quick as I can." Mary Elizabeth rubbed her back.

"*Nee,* I should have to do it. It's my fault it's gone."

"But the pattern's one I've done a lot. It'll go faster if I do it."

"How can someone steal?" Lavina asked her. Her stomach churned. "Who would do such a thing?"

Mary Elizabeth slid her arm around her waist. "I don't know. Maybe you should call Kate. Come on, let's get inside. It's cold out here."

David hadn't had a plan in mind when he came home. He'd just come back to help his *mudder.*

Other than doing his *dat's* chores, he wasn't certain he was really helping much. Although spring planting was months away, it required planning, ordering seeds, all manner of things. And his *dat* spent so much time in chemo, or doctor appointments, or in his room, resting or moping, he wasn't doing any of it.

The farm had been his life's work. David felt if he could get him thinking about the coming planting season, maybe it would help give him something to look forward to. Because his *mudder* had confided she was afraid he was giving up, David was worried, too. If anyone knew his *dat*, it was his *mudder.* The woman had been married to him for more than thirty years. Was she saint or martyr? he wondered.

They sat there, the three of them, eating supper and as usual, his *mudder* doing her best to look and act cheerful, while Amos glowered over his bowl of chili, one of his favorites. It wasn't spicy enough, he said. Then, when Waneta jumped up for his favorite hot sauce, he added too much, tasted it, and said it was too spicy.

So she took the bowl away and brought him a fresh one, and the complaints started again.

David felt like he was living the children's story *Goldilocks and the Three Bears*. Maybe it was time to shake things up, get his *dat's* mind off himself as he'd thought earlier . . .

"I was thinking of spring planting," he said and ignored the apprehensive look his *mudder* shot him. "I'm thinking it's time to put into effect some of those ideas I've mentioned to you in the past."

"I told you they're stupid."

He winced inwardly. It still hurt that the old man wouldn't listen to any of his suggestions. But he had come to see that it came from his *dat's* refusal to consider anything he hadn't come up with—not that David was stupid. His *dat* was a man who had to be in charge of everything in his home, on his farm.

"Well, since you can't do the planting . . ."

"Who says I can't? I'm not dead yet!" he bellowed.

Waneta covered his hand with hers. "Amos, it's not *gut* for you to get upset."

"You're not taking over my farm!" Amos shook off her hand and slammed his fist on the table, making the silverware jump. "I'm not ready to die yet!"

"Then maybe you'll start doing some of the things *Mamm* says the doctor wants you to do." He looked meaningfully at the uneaten supper sitting before his *dat*. "Like eating and getting some exercise. You can't do the planting lying in bed most of the day."

Amos turned red as a beet, and for a moment David thought he'd gone too far.

"Don't you sit at my table eating my food and tell me what I can do!" he shouted. "I'm going to do my own planting, and you're going to have to get your own farm if you want your changes, you hear me?"

"I think our neighbors two farms down can hear you," David said mildly.

"Amos, here, take a drink of water." Waneta pushed it toward him. "David's only trying to help."

Amos snorted and just glared at him. But he drank some water and the redness faded from his face. A few minutes later, he began eating and scraped the bottom of the bowl of chili, then the bowl of applesauce. He rose, announced he was going to sit in the living room and read, then left the room.

Later, after his *dat* shuffled up to bed, David went out to the barn and found the seed catalogs he knew were stored in an old battered desk there. He'd leave them on the kitchen table and see what happened.

Now if he could just come up with an idea of where to take Lavina that didn't involve going to the coffee shop. His wallet was nearly empty.

When he walked into the kitchen a few days later, his *mudder* was just finishing up the dishes. She dried a baking dish and set it on the table.

"I need to return that and two more to Lavina," she said.

David glanced at the kitchen clock. "I could do that."

"You could, could you?" she asked with a smile. "I wouldn't want to put you to any trouble."

"No bother at all."

She found a tote bag and packed it. "It would be so nice if I could put in something as a thank you. Some cookies or bread or something." She sighed.

"Everyone knows what you're going through," he told her. "Someday you'll be the one baking or cooking for others just like you've done for years."

"*Ya*," she said and she smiled at him. "*Danki* for reminding me."

David drove over to Lavina's house. Mary Elizabeth answered the door and invited him in.

"*Mamm* wanted me to return these," he told her, trying not to be obvious as he glanced around.

"Lavina's in the kitchen," she told him. "Why don't you take them in to her?" She gave him a conspiratorial smile. "You know the way."

He did indeed. He'd been invited to supper here many times when he and Lavina dated.

Lavina turned from the sink and saw him. "David!"

He held out the tote. "Bringing these back to you. *Mamm* said to say *danki*."

"Tell her she's *wilkumm*. It's the least we can do. How is your *dat*?"

"Doing a little better, I think. Can you go for a drive with me?"

She glanced at the clock. "*Ya*, if it's not a long one." She grabbed her jacket from a peg by the back door.

David hurried ahead to the truck to open her door and then, once she was inside, he got in the driver's side, turned the ignition, and got the heater started.

"So what's wrong?" she asked him before they left the driveway.

"What makes you think something's wrong?"

"When I asked you how your *dat* was you said he was a little better, but you frowned."

"I did?"

She nodded.

He backed out carefully, watching for traffic. "I really do think he's doing a little better. *Mamm* was worried that he seemed to be giving up. I noticed he was resting more and more lately. So I said I'd be happy to take care of ordering seed, planning for the spring planting. Maybe try some of those new ideas I'd mentioned to him in the past."

She gasped. "You didn't! That always caused a fight before!"

David glanced at her and grinned. "*Ya*."

"But why would you deliberately pick a fight with him?"

"It *schur* perked him up," he told her, turning down the road that led to their favorite ice cream shop. It might not be summer but he felt like ice cream. "I put the seed catalogs on the kitchen table and haven't seen them since. *Mamm* said he's been looking through them each day while I'm at work. And now he's been eating better and actually getting a little exercise."

"I always wondered which of you was the most stubborn."

"Hey, I thought you were on my side."

"I was. I am."

He pulled into the parking lot of the ice cream store. "How about splitting a banana split with me."

"*Allrecht*."

"Stay here where it's warm. I'll run in and get it."

When he returned, he had a dish in each hand. She rolled down the passenger side window and took one from him.

"I thought we were going to share. I can't eat all this," she protested.

"*Schur* you can. I always used to feel bad that we split one because you knew I was short on money."

She dipped her plastic spoon into the whipped cream. "I'm surprised you have any money left after our fancy supper out."

"I'll be fine until payday on Friday. Gas tank's full."

"Gas is expensive," she said as she spooned up a bite of banana. "It's a lot cheaper to drive a buggy."

"Well, Nellie expects a lot of apples for treats, not just oats and hay," he joked, wondering why she suddenly looked so serious.

She looked up. "That's not why you're keeping the truck. You're keeping it because you haven't made a commitment to staying."

The minute she said it, Lavina wished she could call it back. She glanced at him and saw that his hands had tightened on the steering wheel.

Silence stretched between them as the truck ate up the miles.

"You want me to give up the truck."

"I didn't say that. I said you were keeping it because you haven't made a commitment to staying."

He pulled over and looked at her. "How can I make a commitment? Any day my *dat* could ask me to leave. Then I wouldn't have a way to get to my job, same as I didn't when I left last time."

"You think he'd do that?"

He leaned back, dropping his head against the headrest. "Who knows? I don't have to tell you what a difficult man he's always been." He turned to her. "Do I?"

"*Nee*," she said finally. "You don't."

"Look, this is going to sound awful, but sometimes I wonder if the only way this situation is going to be resolved is if he dies."

"David! Don't say such a thing!"

"I didn't say I wanted it. But you know it's true. He's not going to change and decide to let me take over the farm."

Lavina stared out the window. What could she say? He was right.

"I won't leave while *Mamm* needs my help," he said quietly. "But I don't see that I have a future there."

He sat up, checked traffic, and moved back out onto the road. "I'd better take you home."

They drove home in silence. He pulled into her driveway a few minutes later and when she reached for the door handle he touched her arm.

"I'm not sorry I came back," he told her. "I don't want you to think that. If I hadn't, I'd have always wondered if I could have changed something between *Daed* and me. And you were right. *Mamm* needs the help. Hopefully *Daed* will get better."

She nodded. "I'll say a prayer for him. And you."

Turning, she slipped from the truck and went into the house.

No one was downstairs when she went inside. Grateful she didn't have to talk to anyone, she fixed a cup of tea and sat at the table to drink it. Life seemed so complicated. Somehow she'd thought it would get easier as she got older, but instead it just seemed harder, more complicated.

Rose Anna walked into the kitchen. "I didn't know you were home. Did you have a good time with David?"

"It was *allrecht.*" She gave a lot of attention to stirring a teaspoon of sugar into her tea. "I thought I'd have a cup of tea before I go up to bed."

"Did you hear Isaac Troyer and Katie Miller are getting married next week?"

Lavina closed her eyes. "Not another one. That makes three next week."

Rose Anna reached over and covered her hand. "I'm sorry."

She opened her eyes and saw the quiet sympathy in her *schweschder's* eyes. "It was hard last year going to all the weddings after David left. It should be easier by now."

"But it still hurts."

She nodded and sighed. "It's not just that. Did Mary Elizabeth tell you about the quilt being stolen?"

"*Ya.* She cut the pieces out for a new one tonight."

Now Lavina felt guilty. "She had to work while I went out for a drive. It was my fault it got stolen. I should have taken the quilts to Leah's instead of going to quilt class."

"It's not your fault it got stolen," Rose Anna said firmly. "Someone was wrong to steal."

Lavina got up and walked over to the sink to pour out the cup of tea. "I think I'll go up and start the quilt tonight."

But when she went up to the sewing room Mary Elizabeth was already there and sewing.

"Can I help?"

Mary Elizabeth stared at her. "Only if you don't blame yourself."

"I don't know if I can do that." She pulled a chair over next to her *schweschder.*

"Did you talk to Kate?"

"Not yet."

"Here, you can pin this block together for me."

Lavina took the fabric pieces and pincushion and started working. "I will when I see her later this week."

"I was thinking about it. The quilt. Seems to me someone had to know you had the quilt in the buggy that day."

She looked up in surprise. "You think so?"

Mary Elizabeth nodded. "I think most people know we don't have a lot of material things in our buggies so we can park them anywhere and go inside."

Feeling restless, Lavina set the block she'd been pinning and wandered around the room, picking up piles of fabric and setting them back down.

"Lavina, it's not here."

She turned, her arms full of fabric. "What?"

"The missing quilt."

She sighed. "I know."

Mary Elizabeth got up, walked over, and hugged her. "It's hard to accept that someone would steal from us. But it happened." She took the fabric from Lavina and placed it on the shelf.

Their *mudder* stuck her head into the room. "Working late?"

"We were," Mary Elizabeth said. "But it's time to go to bed."

"*Gut nacht.*"

They kissed their *mudder* good night, walked to the room they shared, and prepared for bed. Lavina changed into her nightgown and took the first turn in the bathroom to wash her face and brush her teeth. She was tucked under her quilt when Mary Elizabeth came out ready for bed.

"There's something I hadn't considered," she said.

"What's that?" Mary Elizabeth turned down her quilt and climbed into bed.

"It's getting colder. Maybe the person needed the quilt."

"Maybe."

Lavina turned off the battery-operated bedside lamp and stared up at the ceiling, watching the patterns the moonlight made filtering through the bare branches of the maple tree outside the window. An owl hooted and was answered by one some distance away.

"You still awake?" her *schweschder* asked sleepily a little while later.

"*Ya.*"

"Stop thinking about it and say a prayer for the person who took the quilt. Leave it up to God."

Lavina smiled. Good advice and very forgiving. Mary Elizabeth would have the work of making the quilt again, yet she'd thought to ask for forgiveness for the thief. She said a silent prayer and then found herself thinking that the person wasn't the only one she needed to forgive.

She still needed to find a way to forgive David for the past year. He was trying to make amends, even making a huge effort to renew their relationship. She needed to recognize that even if she couldn't bring herself to trust him again she should be more of a friend.

So she said another prayer. And then she rolled over and closed her eyes.

13

You're early!"

Lavina looked up with a smile. "Making up for being late last time."

"I told you not to worry about it. You're a volunteer and one we really appreciate." Kate sat and took a sip of her takeout coffee. "Starting a new quilt?"

She nodded as she pinned a quilt block then with a sigh put it down. "Someone stole a quilt from my buggy last time I came to class. A new one I was going to deliver to Leah's shop."

"Oh, no. Did you report it?"

Lavina shook her head. "It's not our way. We're just going to make another. It's my own fault for leaving it in the buggy."

"No, it's not." Kate set her cup down so hard coffee sloshed over the rim. "Don't you dare blame yourself." She frowned. "Amish quilts are worth a lot of money. It's possible someone stole it to sell it. Especially this time of year."

"Oh, you mean Christmas." Lavina picked up the block and began pinning the pieces together again.

"It won't hurt for me to ask around," Kate said, picking up her coffee. "It's possible we can find it."

"I won't prosecute," Lavina told her. "Mary Elizabeth won't either."

"And I understand. Hannah, Matthew Bontrager's sister, wouldn't years ago and I'm grateful."

Lavina knew how Malcolm had gone to seek revenge on Chris Matlock and Hannah had stepped in front of him, taking the bullet meant for Chris. Hannah had survived and forgiven Malcolm. Her refusal to prosecute had led Malcolm to seek treatment for his alcohol and drug problems and now he, like Kate, helped others in the community.

"Anyway, it may be someone is going to try to sell the quilt," Kate said.

"It could be someone who needed it to keep warm since it's getting colder."

Kate stared at her. "Even after all the years I've lived here I can still be surprised at how forgiving the Amish are."

Lavina blushed. If only Kate knew that she hadn't. "Mary Elizabeth was the one who said it. But, well, it could be true, couldn't it?"

"I suppose it's possible," Kate said with a gentle smile. "But it's been my experience that most people steal for profit, not from need." She sighed. "Police work can make you cynical about your fellow man."

Was it her imagination that Kate sounded sad? Lavina wondered.

Kate pulled a notepad from her purse and flipped it open. Muttering, she pulled a crayon, then a pacifier from her purse. Finally, she found a pen, and she began firing questions. Had Lavina seen anyone suspicious hanging around the parking lot when she came that day? What about when she returned? What did the quilt look like? What's its approximate value? She made notes and shook her head. "Not a lot to go on, but I'll see what I can do."

"Thank you."

Kate put the notepad and pen back into her purse.

"Here, give me some of the blocks and I'll help you pin them. At least it's something I can do just in case we can't locate the quilt."

"Thank you." Grateful, Lavina handed them over.

"I hope we can get it back. Making even a simple quilt takes a lot of time."

Women began filing in, getting their project boxes from the shelves and settling behind sewing machines. Kate greeted them and handed out the week's block. She and Lavina walked around the room to see if anyone wanted help. Soon the room filled with the sounds of the machines, the chatter and laughter of women enjoying the class and each other.

Ellie carried her doll and the little quilt she was making for her. She got her project box and asked her mother to help her thread a needle to sew another small block to add to the doll quilt. Ellie's mother accepted the new block and began sewing.

Lavina paused by Carrie and smiled. She was surprised to see her sewing and looking happy, not sulky.

The light on the needle arm set the ring on Carrie's left hand sparkling. Carrie glanced up and saw Lavina looking at her hand. She held it out, turning it this way and that to show off the ring. "Pretty, huh?" Then she frowned and withdrew it. "I don't guess you like jewelry much. The Amish don't wear it."

"I don't wear it, but I like to look at it when it's pretty like that."

Carrie preened. "Boyfriend gave it to me."

Was it the same boyfriend who had blackened her eye not that long ago? Lavina wondered. Then she chided herself. It was Carrie's business. She just hoped the woman wasn't going back to the man who'd abused her.

Carrie bent back over her sewing.

"How are you doing, Carrie?" Kate asked as she came to stand near them. "Enjoying the class a little more?"

"It's okay," she said with a shrug. "I think I'll go take a break." She got up and left the room.

Kate jerked her head toward the back of the room. Lavina followed her. "What was that all about?"

"I don't know. She was showing me her new ring."

"Did she say who gave it to her?"

"Her boyfriend."

Kate frowned. "I hope it's not . . ." she trailed off, then shook her head as if to clear it. "I'll see if I can talk to her later."

They returned to their chairs at the front of the room and continued to work on pinning blocks.

When she returned home Mary Elizabeth was happy to take the blocks from her. "This will speed things up."

"Kate helped me. She also asked me a lot of questions about the quilt. She's hoping she can find it. I told her we wouldn't prosecute the person who stole it if she finds him. We'd just like to get the quilt back."

Mary Elizabeth nodded. "*Gut*. But if she finds the quilt it almost seems like she'd find the person, don't you think? If the thief took it to a local shop to sell it, the shop owner would know who brought it in."

"*Ya*. So then finding the quilt isn't the best thing." She sighed and rubbed her forehead. Thinking about it was giving her a headache.

"Let's go get some lunch. *Mamm* and Rose Anna are over at Waneta's house helping her clean. I told them we'd make supper for tonight."

Lavina's headache faded as she ate her sandwich and drank a cup of hot chocolate. The house was quiet with just the two of them here. She cleared the table and washed up the few dishes. "Let's get back to work."

"Slave driver," Mary Elizabeth pretended to complain as she slung her arm around Lavina's waist and they started up the stairs.

David couldn't help noticing his *dat* was in a *gut* mood at supper.

The man ate the way he used to after a hard day in the fields. His color was better, and he actually smiled once at his *fraa*.

He glared at David when he saw him watching him and dug a piece of paper from a pocket. "Made out the seed order today!"

"*Gut*!"

"*Ya!*" He put the paper down on the table and thumped it with his fist. "Gonna put the seeds in the ground myself; you wait and see if I don't."

"Nothing would make me happier," David told him sincerely.

His *dat* stared at him in utter shock. "You're just saying that."

"I mean it."

"I told you, Amos." His *mudder* smiled at him fondly. "He cares more about you than inheriting the farm."

He harrumphed but stopped glaring and returned his attention to his food.

Silence reigned as the three of them ate supper. When they finished, his *mudder* rose and went to fetch apple dumplings that she'd pulled from the oven just before they started eating.

"David, would you get the ice cream?"

Amos watched as she placed a dumpling in a bowl then added a scoop of ice cream to it. He dug into his without waiting for her to finish serving David and herself. She glanced over at David and smiled as she put two scoops of ice cream on his.

Amos looked up and frowned. "Why'd you give him two scoops? You only gave me one."

"Because he loves you," she said simply.

He glared at David and then continued eating.

David bit the inside of his cheek to keep from grinning.

They'd no sooner finished supper when there was a knock on the door. It was Mark, David's old friend from *schul*. "If Mohammed won't come to the mountain," he said.

He stepped forward and hugged David when he hesitated at the door, unsure how to react. "I thought I'd come to see you. You haven't been by since you came back."

Waneta appeared in the doorway. "Mark. *Wilkumm.* I have a fresh pot of coffee on if you'd like a cup."

"I would, *danki*. Is that one of your apple pies I'd be smelling?"

"He's got timing like David for food," Amos grumbled as he shuffled into the room and sat in his recliner.

"*Gut-n-owed*, Amos," Mark said cheerfully. "It's *gut* to see you doing well."

"Better than some expect," he muttered and snapped open *The Budget* newspaper.

Mark grinned at David as he shed his jacket and hat and hung them on hooks by the back door. He took a seat at the kitchen table. "How have you been?"

"I'm sorry I haven't been by."

Mark's eyes widened in appreciation as Waneta set an apple dumpling before him. "*Danki*, Waneta. I used to love these when I came to supper here."

"I remember." She patted his shoulder and looked at David. "Get him some ice cream."

"Two scoops?" he asked as he brought the container to the table.

She nodded. "Two scoops."

Mark looked from one to the other. "Huh?"

David shrugged as he scooped out the ice cream. "I'm sorry I haven't paid you a visit. I wasn't sure if you'd want to see me."

"Why wouldn't I?" Mark smiled at Waneta as she set a mug of coffee before him.

He took a bite of the dumpling, closed his eyes, and sighed.

Waneta chuckled. "Guess you'll be by more often now that you remember my dumplings."

"I never forgot them," he told her and gave her a mischievous grin.

She left them, joining Amos in the living room. David watched his friend eating the dessert, acting as if the past year hadn't happened, and he'd dropped by looking for one of Waneta's desserts after he'd finished supper at his own home. No one baked like Waneta, he always told her. He'd then turn to David and warn him that he'd deny saying it, if he ever told his *mudder.*

Could it be this easy? David wondered. Could they still be friends even though he'd never told Mark that he was leaving and had never contacted him this past year?

Mark glanced up and saw him staring. He smiled. "I missed you."

David felt a lump rise in his throat. "I missed you, too," he told him gruffly.

Suddenly restless, he got up. "Let's go for a walk."

"A little chilly for a walk."

"Did you turn into a wimp while I was gone?"

Mark chuckled as they pulled on jackets and hats. They stepped outside, and when they were a distance from the house David turned to him. "I just didn't feel I could talk about my *dat* when I was sitting in his house."

"I understand. What's going on?"

David headed toward a nearby field. "You know he's getting treatment for cancer?"

Mark nodded. "How's he doing? He hasn't been in church much lately."

"He wasn't doing so well when I first came back, but the past few days he's looking a little better. I kind of egged him into ordering seed for the spring planting. I knew he wouldn't want me doing it since he's always said my ideas about doing things differently with the crops are crazy."

"So how is he treating you? I know you left because he was so difficult," Mark said. "I think everyone knows that."

"He hasn't changed."

"That's rough. I'm sorry."

A flock of blackbirds flew over heading south. The sky was gray and heavy with rain clouds, some of them glowing orange in the distance. It would be turning cooler tomorrow.

The birds reminded David of the bishop in his severe black, his coat flapping in the wind the night he'd shown up at the door.

"So I hear that you're seeing Lavina again."

"Amish grapevine's working as well as always, huh?"

Mark chuckled. "*Ya.* How's it going?"

David hesitated. "She hasn't forgiven me yet for leaving," he said carefully. "I hurt her a lot."

A cold raindrop plopped on his forehead. "We'd better head back in."

They made it to the back porch before the rain pelted down.

The kitchen was warm and still filled with the wonderful scent of baked apples. His *mudder* had left a percolator on the stove.

"Coffee?"

Mark nodded and stole a glance at the pan that held several dumplings.

"I don't suppose . . ." he said.

"*Schur.*" David found a plate and served them both. "We're growing boys after all."

Mark patted his rounded stomach. "Some of us more than others. My Hannah's quite a cook. You remember, Hannah Miller. That's why I came by. I wanted to invite you to the wedding. We're getting married next Friday."

"That's *wunderbaar*!" David reached over to shake his friend's hand.

"You'll come, won't you?"

David hesitated.

"Lavina's going to be there."

Mark looked so eager David hated to turn him down. Weddings were all day affairs in the Amish church. It might be impossible to avoid the bishop. If the bishop had something to say to him, he'd just have to excuse himself and leave.

"*Schur,*" he said. "I'd love to."

His *mudder* walked into the room a few minutes later and smiled when she saw them eating the dumplings. "Your *dat* said I'd better hide these or he wouldn't be able to have one later before he went to bed. He knew, didn't he?"

Mark looked shamefaced, but David just grinned. "We're growing boys, *Mamm*."

She just chuckled. "*Ya*. For *schur*."

"I can do this, I can do this, I can do this, I can do this," Lavina chanted in her mind as she sat in the back seat of the family buggy. After all, she'd attended a number of weddings last year after David left and she'd survived.

"Lavina, are you *allrecht*?" Rose Anna called over her shoulder from the front seat. It was her turn to drive.

"I'm fine." Lavina smoothed the skirt of her best dress, a dark blue one she wore to church this time of year.

Rose Anna took her eyes off the road and glanced back at her.

"You look tense."

"I'm not."

"You do look a little tense." Mary Elizabeth leaned over the seat to study her.

"It should be easier by now," she said, staring straight ahead. "After all, it's been a year since I thought I was getting married."

"Who's to say how long it should take to get over things? Besides, I don't think any of us are in the mood to attend a wedding. We all thought we'd be married by this time, didn't we?" Rose Anna said thoughtfully.

"Three old *maedels*," Mary Elizabeth chimed in glumly.

Lavina rolled her eyes. "Oh please, don't start that! We're in our twenties!"

Mary Elizabeth slumped back in her seat. "I feel like an old *maedel*."

"We just have to find different men," Rose Anna said. "At least you and I do, Mary Elizabeth. David's back for Lavina."

"I wouldn't say that."

Two heads swiveled to look at her. "What?" they cried in unison.

"Neither of you should expect I can just welcome him with open arms," she told them with more tartness than she should have. "I don't want to be hurt again."

"I thought you were happier after the two of you went out to supper?"

She had been . . . and then the next day the same old doubts had crept back in. She sighed.

"Maybe we could skip the wedding," Rose Anna offered hopefully.

They looked at each other and finally shook their heads. "We can't do that," Mary Elizabeth said before Lavina could. "We can't miss Hannah's wedding. It wouldn't be fair to her."

So they continued riding to the wedding. The day was gray and overcast, matching Lavina's mood. When they pulled into the driveway of Hannah's home, she sat up straight and pasted a smile on her face. Amish weddings were daylong events. She just hoped she could get through it.

And then she saw David talking with another man as they stood outside the barn with several others helping unhitch horses and lead them into the barn. Disconcerted, she stared at him. It was the first wedding he'd attended since a month before he'd left a year ago.

"Oh my," she heard Rose Anna say under her breath. "Look who's here."

Mary Elizabeth glanced over her shoulder. "I wonder what this means?"

"His friend Mark is marrying Hannah, remember?" She just hadn't expected that he'd be here. She got out of the buggy as soon as it stopped and started unhitching the horse.

"*Guder mariye*," David said in his deep, rich voice. "Let me help you."

"I can manage."

"Don't want to get that pretty dress dirty," he told her easily, laying his big hand over hers on the bridle.

His touch seemed to burn. She withdrew her hand quickly and stepped back. "*Danki*."

She watched him lead the horse into the barn and turned to her *schweschders*. "I think I'll go inside."

Rose Anna held out the gaily wrapped present in her hands. "Here, you can take this in."

"*Danki*." Lavina clutched the gift and hurried into the house.

The bride's home was warm and fragrant with the scents of the food that had been prepared for the wedding. Lavina went to take off her jacket. She found a seat in the section set aside for the women and waited for her *schweschders to* join her.

"Beautiful day for a wedding," said a familiar voice.

Lavina turned. "Kate!" She'd forgotten that Kate might be here.

"So I did some asking around," she said in a low voice. "Guy came into a quilt shop just outside town, looking Amish, wanted to sell a quilt like the one that was stolen. Didn't like leaving it on commission, but that's the way the shop operates. I have his phone number."

Lavina's eyes widened. "Really? What are you going to do now?"

"I'm having the shop owner call him and tell him he sold it. He'll have him come in the shop on Tuesday morning and I'll be there."

"I don't want him arrested."

"I know that." She glanced up and smiled as Rose Anna and Mary Elizabeth took seats next to her. "Shop owner wasn't surprised I came in to ask questions. Said he felt something was suspicious about the man."

"Why?"

"The man wore Amish clothes but he had a mustache. That was a dead giveaway he wasn't Amish."

Lavina saw David walk into the room and watched as he looked around. The minute he spotted her he smiled that slow, warm smile of his that stirred her inside. The voices, the movements of the people around them faded away as they stared at each other. What was it about this man that she couldn't seem to pull herself away from?

"So that's the way it is," Kate murmured.

"Hmm? What?" Lavina pulled her attention from David. "Did you say something?"

"Just noticed David Stoltzfus walked in," Kate said, brushing a piece of lint from the skirt of her dress. "Haven't seen him in quite a while. At least, not here in the community."

"He's back for a while," she told her, trying to sound neutral. "His father's ill."

"I heard."

Lavina hated saying "for a while," but it was better for her not to get her hopes up that he'd stay.

As church members settled into their seats Lavina wondered what David's attendance at the wedding really meant. Was he here merely to see his friend get married, or was he thinking of joining the church?

No, she couldn't think about him joining the church. That was just wishful thinking.

Or was it? She sneaked a cautious look over now and then, and she saw David chatting with other men, seemingly at ease.

Then there was a rustle of alertness in the assemblage and people turning. Hannah and Mark were walking together to the front of the room where the ministers stood.

Hannah glowed in a dress the color of pale blue spring violets that brought out the color of her eyes. Mark looked solemn and just a little nervous, dressed in his Sunday best white shirt and somber black jacket and trousers.

And the wedding began.

The assemblage stood and sang, and when Lavina sneaked a glance she saw that David sang without looking at the words in the hymnal. He remembered, she thought, secretly pleased. Maybe church still meant something to him. Well, it always had, but he and the bishop had been at odds at times because David had gone to him in an effort to get him to intercede in the family discord, and it had backfired. The bishop had solidly aligned himself with David's *dat* and caused more problems when Amos felt David shouldn't have taken their problems to the bishop. She sighed.

"You okay?" Kate whispered.

Embarrassed that she'd made a sound, Lavina nodded quickly.

The ceremony was long and quietly joyful. Hannah seemed to glow with happiness as she stood with Mark and was joined in matrimony. He gazed at her adoringly if a little shyly. Mark had always been a quiet, introverted boy at *schul*, and Hannah a little more outgoing.

Passages from the Bible were read, one of the ministers spoke personally about marriage and its joys and sorrows and challenges, and then there was more singing. Lavina felt her spirits lift as the harmony of the familiar hymns filled the room.

As the last hymn concluded and the last notes faded away, something made her glance over at David in the men's section, and she caught him watching her. He smiled. She smiled back and then had to hide her chuckle when Marlon, a *schul* friend of theirs, grasped the hem of his jacket and tugged it to warn him it was time to sit.

"Beautiful wedding," Kate said after the ceremony concluded. She brushed away a tear and looked embarrassed. "I always cry at weddings."

"Ours must seem very different from *Englisch* weddings. I know *Englisch* weddings have flowers, music, fancy dresses."

Kate shrugged. "Sometimes people get so caught up in those things they forget what's important. I loved the simplicity of the wedding today. Hannah and Mark look very happy."

Lavina glanced around, then leaned closer to whisper, "I bet your weddings aren't as long."

"Well, I went to a Catholic wedding once that was almost as long as this one today."

"Are you staying for the reception? It's even longer than the wedding. There'll be two meals served."

"I can only stay a little while. I have to work for a couple of hours."

"Let's get my sisters and we'll sit together."

"I'd love to."

Tables were loaded with food. Lavina was surprised they didn't collapse under the weight. Baked chicken with *roasht* was a wedding staple, and here in Pennsylvania, creamed celery was a must. Weddings were scheduled after the harvest was in, so the tables at receptions reflected the bounty of it. Lavina filled her plate with mashed potatoes and gravy, sweet potatoes, butternut squash, green beans, and corn.

"You don't like chicken and *roasht*?" Kate asked as she helped herself to big portions of both.

"By the time we get a few weeks into the wedding season, and we have it a couple of times a week, it gets a little old," Lavina whispered. "*Daed* asks for shrimp for our holiday dinner."

"I never get tired of *roasht*," Kate said. "I'll be spending some extra time at the gym after today."

"Save room for dessert," Rose Anna told her.

Kate sighed. "I can't. I really need to get to work."

Lavina stood. "Tell me what you want, and I'll make a plate for you to take with you. The cake won't be cut for a while but there are plenty of other things."

"I know. Too many!"

"Maybe a small piece of everything?" Lavina said, grinning at her. She assembled a plate with apple pie and pumpkin bars, Fannie Zook's famous fudge cookies, and homemade candy.

Then, when she ran out of room she grabbed a second plate and filled it. It seemed only fair that Kate's *mann* should have some treats since he hadn't been able to attend. She felt someone staring at her and when she looked up, saw that David was watching her from the other side of the room.

"I don't know if I can carry all this to the car," Kate pretended to complain when she returned to their table.

"I'll carry one of the plates out to your car," Lavina told her. "I could use some fresh air."

"I'll be the envy of every cop in the station," Kate said when they put the plates in the back seat of her car. "I'd better put the plate for Malcolm in the trunk, or someone will see it and try to guilt me into giving them some." She turned to Lavina. "Thank you for all the goodies. I hope no one minded your being so generous."

"We love to feed people. You know that."

Kate studied her. "Weddings are still hard, aren't they?" she asked as she pulled on her jacket. Her eyes were kind.

"Do you know everything about everybody?" Lavina asked her, trying to keep her tone light.

"I know what happened to you last year. I'm sorry." She started to say something and then seemed to change her mind.

"I don't know if I'll get back together with him," Lavina told her. She didn't mind telling her because she hadn't pried as some had. "He hurt me, and I'm afraid to trust."

Kate touched her hand. "Trust your heart. You'll know what to do."

Lavina nodded. "Thank you."

They walked to Kate's car. Kate put the bag with the food on the front seat and turned to thank her again. "I hope you have a good time."

"I will."

She watched the car drive away and then turned to go back into the house.

And saw David standing on the porch watching her.

14

David watched Lavina leave the house with Kate. He wondered if she was getting a ride home.

He hoped not. He wanted a chance to talk to her, maybe see if she'd go for a ride with him after the wedding.

But as he stood on the porch he was relieved to see that she didn't leave with Kate. He waited, studying her face as she climbed the porch steps. "So your guard went home?"

"Guard?"

"Kate sat with you all through the meal."

"She wasn't guarding me. She's a friend of mine and Hannah's."

"I was joking."

"Oh."

She seemed subdued. He'd noticed a forced gaiety as she sat with Kate and her *schweschders*. And while she pushed the food around on her plate, he hadn't seen her eat much. "Lavina, are you *allrecht*?"

"*Ya. Schur.* Why?"

He stared at his shoes, then looked up at her. "I wondered if it was hard for you to attend the wedding since—" he broke off.

"Since you left when I thought we were getting married?"

He winced. "*Ya.*"

"It was harder last year." Then she closed her eyes and shook her head. "I'm sorry. I don't mean to sound bitter."

David shrugged. "I don't blame you."

A cool wind swept briskly across the porch. She shivered.

"We should go in," he said, but he made no move to do so. "Lavina, could we go for a ride after the wedding and talk?"

She hesitated and then, apparently feeling bad because of the way she'd said what she did, she nodded. "Maybe after. Now I have to go in and take my turn helping in the kitchen."

David opened the door and she walked inside, left her jacket in the bedroom, and joined the other women working in the kitchen. He heard a lot of chattering and laughing as he walked past the room and back to where people were sitting and eating. Hannah and Mark sat at the *eck*, the corner of the biggest table, and received good wishes from their guests. He'd wait and talk to them once things settled down.

The first group of attendees had eaten, and now a new group was taking their place. He nodded as someone would pass by and say hello or ask about his *dat*. Although he'd been away a year, he'd been warmly welcomed back to this community where he had attended Sunday services and weddings and funerals with them from the time he'd been born. He hadn't attended services since he'd moved back home so that he could be there if his *dat* needed him while his *mudder* got out for worship and for the company she needed.

So today he was feeling a little at sea, a bit disconnected, moving like a ghost among them. Physically close and yet as distant as if he hung in a separate world from them. Well, it was to be expected, he told himself. He *had* been in another world—the *Englisch* world—so different from this world. Some Amish worked by day with the *Englisch*, but he'd torn himself totally away from his community and even lived in a small apartment over an *Englischer's* home. He'd cut his hair in the *Englisch* style. Even bought a truck.

It was still an adjustment coming home, and here, in the midst of the reception after one of the most important religious ceremonies in their church, he was mingling with people who had been important to him all his life and he'd severed himself from.

Looking around, he suddenly felt a lump form in his throat. Here was home. It wasn't just the wooden frame structure where he lived with his parents. It was his church community. He caught a movement and saw Lavina watching him from across the room, a puzzled expression on her face.

Emotions tangled in him. He'd missed all this more than he had thought. Convinced there was no future for him in his world, he'd fled to the *Englisch* world. And now he realized just how much in exile he'd been.

Suddenly the room felt too small, too full of people. He had to get out, get some air.

He rushed out, bumping into someone as he rushed down the hallway.

"Sorry," he said, not looking back.

He found his jacket and pulled it on as he pushed out the front door. The air was crisp and cold. He dragged in a lungful, then another and felt better. Still, he didn't feel ready to go back inside.

The women of the church were busy inside the house serving, washing up, entertaining *kinner,* but once the men had set up tables after the ceremony was over, they didn't have much to do. He saw men milling around the barn, talking, taking a break. He joined them in the barn, making himself useful watering the horses.

After a time he heard singing coming from the house. The sound of the hymns he'd sung since he was a *kind* soothed his troubled spirit.

He made himself go back into the house, spoke to the happy couple and joined in the singing. After a time he had a piece of wedding cake, but it tasted too sweet, and he looked around carefully for a way to set it aside mostly uneaten.

Lavina and her *schweschders* finished their turn in the kitchen and joined in the festivities. He watched Rose Anna flirt a little shyly with a young man and wondered if she'd given up on waiting for John.

The supper meal was served and although everyone had enjoyed a hearty lunch, most found an appetite for this one too.

David wondered how soon he could persuade Lavina to leave with him.

Finally, she approached him. He could see something was wrong. Her face was pale and she rubbed her fingers at one temple.

"Rose Anna's going to drive me home. I have a headache."

"I'll take you—" he began but she shook her head, and he could see the movement hurt. "*Nee*. We can talk tomorrow if you want."

"Lavina, let me take you. We don't have to talk. And this way, Rose Anna doesn't have to leave the wedding."

She hesitated, looked at her *schweschder* and then sighed. "*Allrecht*."

"Warm enough?"

Lavina stroked her hand over the blanket he'd insisted on spreading over her lap after she climbed into the buggy. Dusk was falling and the air was chilly.

"I'm fine, *danki*." She looked at him. "It was kind of you to do this so Rose Anna could stay. Are you going back?" The reception would last until ten or so.

He shook his head. "I thought I'd see if *Mamm* wants to go for a while, and I'll sit with *Daed*. I offered earlier, but she said she wasn't feeling well and wanted to stay home with him."

"I hope it's nothing serious."

"I don't think so. She gets tired running around taking care of him."

Lavina stared at her hands folded atop the blanket. "Were you worrying about her earlier? At the wedding? You looked like something was wrong before you went outside."

He'd promised her they didn't have to talk, but she was the one asking questions.

"*Nee.* I was thinking how much I missed being here, being in church with everyone. I didn't leave because I wanted to leave that part of my life." His fingers clenched on the reins.

"I know you didn't."

"You didn't look happy at the wedding. I'm sorry that I made it difficult for you."

She glanced at him so sharply it sent a wave of pain across her forehead. "You didn't make it hard because you were there."

"I didn't think I made it hard today. I meant it has to make you think about how we didn't get married when you go to a wedding."

She sighed. "It does."

"Lavina—"

Sirens blared behind them. David glanced over his shoulder then guided the buggy to the side of the road so a fire engine, then an ambulance could rush past. He checked for traffic and pulled back onto the road.

"They're turning down our road," she murmured.

"I see that." He urged more speed from his horse, and soon they were turning down the road to their houses.

Lavina's hand flew to her lips. "David, they're stopping at your house!"

He parked behind the trucks and was out of the buggy the moment the wheels came to a stop. She climbed out and followed him inside.

Paramedics were settling David's *dat* onto a stretcher. His *mudder* stood to the side, wringing her hands.

Lavina went to her and put her arms around the woman's waist. "What happened?"

"He's having chest pain," she said, looking worried. "I called the doctor and he said to call 9-1-1."

"It's probably just heartburn," his *dat* said, glaring at David. "No need to be making such a fuss."

"Good idea to get it checked out," one of the paramedics told him as he wrapped a blood pressure cuff around his arm.

"Had chili for supper," Amos grumbled.

"You've had my chili many times, even doused it with hot sauce and not had heartburn," she told him. "I'll get my jacket."

One paramedic told the other one what the blood pressure reading was and he noted it on a tablet. He looked up. "A bit high. Let's get you to the hospital and let the doctor look you over."

"I'll be right behind you," David told his *mudder.* She nodded and hurried after the paramedics pushing the gurney to the waiting ambulance.

David locked up the house and they hurried back to the buggy. "I'm taking you home, and then I'll follow the ambulance to the hospital."

"Wait," she said. "Take your truck to the hospital. It'll be faster. I'll put the horse and buggy up."

When he hesitated, she got into the driver's side of the buggy. "Go."

"I don't like you walking in the dark."

"It's not quite dark yet. And it's a short distance. Now go. Arguing with me is wasting time."

"*Allrecht,*" he said. He pulled out his keys and started for his truck.

"I'll say a prayer for your *dat.*"

"*Danki.* And Lavina?"

"*Ya?*"

"I hope you feel better."

"*Danki*. Let me know how your *dat* is."

"I will."

Lavina made quick work of unhitching Nellie, giving her water and feed, then hurried home. She let herself into her house and wandered into the kitchen. After she shed her jacket and bonnet and set her purse on a counter she went straight to the cabinet where they kept a bottle of aspirin. She put the kettle on, made a cup of tea and carried it up to bed. It felt *gut* to tuck herself in early. It was a relief to relax, be alone, and not pretend that everything was *allrecht* like she'd had to do at the wedding and reception.

Two hours later she heard her family come home. Her *mudder* came in to check on her. A little while later Rose Anna peeked in as well. Lavina moved over so Rose Anna could sit on her bed.

"Headache better?" she asked as she sat.

She nodded.

"So how did it go with David? Did he talk you into going for a ride?"

"*Nee*." She told Rose Anna about what had happened to David's *dat*. She glanced at the clock on her bedside table and wondered how he was doing.

"I'll say a prayer for him."

"Did you have a *gut* time talking with Isaac Miller after I left?"

Rose Anna frowned as she unpinned her *kapp*. "He's a nice man, but he's no Sam."

Lavina knew what she meant. There hadn't been any man she'd been interested in after David left—even after so much time passed and she'd come to realize he wasn't coming back. It was the same for Mary Elizabeth and Rose Anna. They hadn't moved on and found anyone else, either.

"Well, I'm going to bed. *Gut nacht*." She bent and hugged Lavina. "Sweet dreams."

She reached over and turned off the battery-operated lamp and lay back. But sleep was a long time coming, and when it did, it was filled with confusing dreams. She dreamed of walking down the aisle with a man whose face she couldn't see until they reached the minister and when she turned to look at him he wasn't David but a stranger she'd never met.

She woke with tears on her cheeks.

David drove as fast as the speed limit allowed. He wasn't going to risk his life—or, more importantly, someone else's—speeding. As he followed the distant lights of the ambulance, he prayed that his *dat's* chest pain was, indeed, the heartburn he claimed it was and not a heart attack.

He knew chemotherapy weakened a person's body and had other dangerous side effects such as heart attacks. He and his *mudder* had sat in the kitchen late that night when he'd come home and found her weeping. She'd talked about her fears in a halting voice, and he'd come to understand the consequences of treatment that some described as poisoning the bad cells and risking the good ones.

As he drove he asked himself if pushing his *dat* to rise above his inertia, his bouts of tiredness and depression, might have brought on this new problem.

The ambulance turned into the emergency entrance. David found a parking place and ran inside. He spent ten nerve-wracking minutes in the waiting room until he was allowed back to the cubicle where his *mudder* sat by herself.

"David! I'm so glad you're here!" she cried when he stepped into the room.

"Where's *Daed*?"

"They've taken him for some tests." Her knuckles were white as she clutched her purse.

He pulled a plastic chair up to sit beside her. "*Daed's* tough. I'm sure he's *allrecht*."

But twenty minutes passed and he didn't return to the room. David checked with a nurse and found that his *dat* was nearly finished with testing and would be returned shortly. He passed on the news to his *mudder* and went to get her some coffee.

When he returned with the coffee he could hear his *dat's* voice before he got halfway down the hallway. He stepped inside the room, and his *dat* looked up with a triumphant expression.

"It's just as I said," he told David. "Heartburn. They've given me some medicine, and I can go home as soon as the doctor discharges me."

"Thank *Gott*," his *mudder* said fervently. "Let's get you dressed then." She picked up the plastic bag his clothes had been stored in and handed it to him.

"Whole lot of fussing for nothing," he snapped at her. "You should have listened to me. Now we have another bill to pay."

"I did what I thought was best," she said, her lips trembling. "What if it'd been your heart? Now stop yelling at me."

She swayed and if David hadn't grabbed her arm, she would have slumped to the floor. He guided her into a chair. "*Mamm*! What's wrong?"

"Just dizzy for a minute," she told him. "Got up too quickly, that's all."

But she looked ashen. He turned to his *dat*. "Press the call button for the nurse."

"I'll be *allrecht* in a minute."

But when she stood she swayed again. David grabbed her arm. "What's wrong?"

"Just a little lightheaded," she said.

"Stay put." He looked up as a nurse came in the room. "Can you take a look at my mother? She nearly passed out just now."

"What seems to be the problem?" the nurse asked her.

"I must have stood up too quickly." She shrugged. "I feel better now."

"Do you have high blood pressure?"

She nodded.

David raised his eyebrows. This was the first he'd heard she had high blood pressure. He watched as the woman wrapped a blood pressure cuff on his *mudder's* arm and frowned as she noted the numbers.

She turned to David. "Make sure she doesn't get up. I'm going to get the doctor in here."

"Now look what a fuss you've made about this," she told David. "So it's up a bit. There was no need to call a nurse in here. I can just take my pill when I get home."

David glanced at his *dat*. The man hadn't said a word since the nurse had come in and taken his *fraa's* blood pressure. He finished getting dressed and slid off the gurney.

"Waneta, *kumm*, sit here," he said gruffly, patting the gurney. He reached for her arm, and she let him guide her to sit on it.

The same doctor who'd seen Amos walked in. "So, I hear I have another patient?"

David and his *dat* stood outside while the doctor examined Waneta.

"You gonna drink that?" Amos gestured to the cup in David's hand.

He handed him the coffee he'd meant for his *mudder*. "Probably cold by now. I'll get you some after we find out how *Mamm* is."

"This'll do." Amos drank the coffee.

"I didn't know she had a problem with high blood pressure."

"Happens sometimes when you get older."

David started to turn, to snap that he shouldn't take it lightly, but he saw the worried expression on his face. "You being sick has been hard on her," he said quietly.

"You blaming me for getting sick?"

He took the cup his *dat* was crushing in his hands. "*Nee*. I'm just saying she's worried about you more than you know."

"Well, you don't know how she worried over you and your *bruders* when you left," Amos snapped.

He winced inwardly, and to keep himself from responding he walked to a nearby wastepaper basket and dumped the cup.

"We can't let her hear us arguing."

To his surprise, his *dat* nodded.

The doctor came out. "Her pressure's high. I'm giving her something, and we want to keep her here a little while until it goes down."

"Can we go in now?"

"Sure."

"*Daed*?"

Amos turned.

"You want me to take you home and then I'll come back and sit with *Mamm*?"

"*Nee.*"

"Fine. Then I'm staying."

So they both went in, both sat with her, until the doctor was satisfied with the blood pressure readings.

Finally, with both of his parents clutching discharge papers in their hands, David went to get his truck and pulled it up at the emergency entrance.

Amos looked at the vehicle skeptically as David rounded the hood and opened the passenger door. "You came in this?"

"It was faster than the buggy." David held out a hand to his *mudder.* Now it was she who looked skeptically at the truck.

"I don't know if I can climb up in there."

"I'll help."

"I'll help," Amos told her.

With a hand from each of them Waneta made it up into the front seat of the truck. But when David turned to Amos, his *dat* shook his head. "I can make it myself."

So David watched, ready to give him a boost if needed, then, when help wasn't necessary, closed the door and got back into the driver's seat. He fastened his seat belt and once they were safely belted in, he pulled out of the parking lot and headed home.

He'd thought he was nervous when he took his test to get a driver's license . . . when he drove the buggy for the first time after his *dat* handed him the reins. But it was nothing compared to having the man sitting in his truck observing him driving it.

He focused on watching the speed limit and getting them home safely and spared only a quick glance over at him when they passed under a streetlight. His *dat's* expression was grim.

His *mudder*, tuned as always to the moods of her family, patted David's arm. "You can really see the road from up here, can't you?"

Compared to the view from a buggy or the van they occasionally took that was driven by an *Englischer*, David guessed that was true.

"How long have you had it?" she asked brightly.

"Just a couple of months. It took me that long to save for it. It's used. I couldn't afford a new one."

He heard a noise—a snort?—from his *dat* but ignored it. No way was he going to get into an argument in front of his *mudder*.

"Is it fun to drive?" she asked him.

"It's *allrecht*. It makes it easier to get to my job. And the boss gets me to deliver for him sometimes so . . ." He shrugged.

Finally, he pulled into the driveway and shut off the engine. "We're home."

His *mudder* sighed.

He glanced at her. "Feels pretty *gut* to be home, huh?"

"Feels really *gut*," she agreed.

"Come on, Waneta," Amos said, sliding from the truck and holding out a hand to help her. "Cold out here. I'm a little hungry."

"No more chili for you tonight," she told him sternly.

"I was thinking about some hot coffee and a piece of that custard pie you baked today."

"Coffee and pie it is." She stepped out of the truck and turned back to David. "Coming, *sohn*?"

"In a minute, *Mamm*. In a minute."

"Don't be long. It's cold out here."

He nodded and watched them climb the stairs and go into the house, then, exhausted from the tension of the evening, he leaned forward and rested his forehead on the steering wheel.

People said life could take an unexpected turn. He'd always thought he knew what they meant. But after the last few hours, watching both of his parents suffer a health scare, he realized he hadn't known what people meant at all.

15

Lavina walked into the quilting classroom and smiled at Kate. "Good morning!"

Kate looked up and returned her smile. She sat at a front table sewing on one of the quilts with camouflage printed material she was making for soldiers.

Lavina set her tote bag and purse down on the table next to a big box. "What's this? Material for the class?"

"Nope. Something for you. Well, for you to give to Mary Elizabeth."

Curious, Lavina lifted the lid and saw the quilt that had been stolen.

"You found it!" she exclaimed, and she beamed at Kate. Then her smile faded. "You didn't arrest the person who took it?"

Kate shook her head. "Let's just say the person returned it. There's a note in the box."

She picked up the sheet of paper. It was a short note apologizing for the theft. "You made him—her?—write it?"

"I strongly suggested he'd want to do it since you weren't pressing charges. He was happy to do it." Kate's tone was matter-of-fact, but she couldn't hold back a grin.

"I wonder if that idea came from you being a police officer or a mom?"

She laughed. "Probably both."

Lavina tucked the note back in the box and replaced the lid. "This is wonderful. Mary Elizabeth will be so happy. I'll take the quilt by Leah's on my way home so the customer who ordered it still gets it in plenty of time to give it for Christmas."

Relieved, she sat. No more extra hours sewing the new one on top of their already busy schedule. And it felt *gut* that the person had apologized.

"Malcolm said to say thank you for the food you sent home from the wedding."

"I'm glad he enjoyed it. But you know I didn't do anything but plate up food others cooked."

"It's the thought that counts."

Lavina drew the quilt she was sewing from her tote and threaded a needle.

"I thought about you after I left. How we talked about it still being hard to attend a wedding."

She stared at Kate, dismayed. "I hope it didn't show—"

Kate touched her hand. "No, you did a good job of looking like you were having a good time. I hope that you were able to more after I left."

"Actually, I went home early with a headache. But I'm kind of glad I left when I did." She told her what had happened when David gave her a ride and they saw the emergency vehicles at his house.

"Amos is fine. David left a message on our phone answering machine that his father kept telling everyone it was heartburn but no one would listen."

"Can't be too careful," Kate said as she made a knot and clipped the thread. "Always best to get it checked out. First responders would rather people called and it ended up being something like heartburn than risk it being a heart attack."

Lavina didn't tell her how Waneta had gotten sick in the emergency room and had to stay for a while because she didn't feel she should share such.

"So, speaking of Christmas, what are you making for gifts?"

Women started filing in. They smiled and greeted them as they got their project boxes and took their seats.

"I knit sweaters for Rose Anna and my parents, but I don't have anything yet for Mary Elizabeth," she told Kate. "I was thinking we could come up with a couple of simple things the women could sew for gifts since they don't have much money."

"That sounds like a good idea."

"A friend of mine makes little patchwork hearts filled with potpourri that she sells at the store she and her husband own. Something like that. Maybe a simple fabric ornament for a tree or an embroidered saying we could get some inexpensive frames for. What do you think?"

"I think that's a great idea."

"Maybe you could come up with some suggestions."

"Sure. I'll look around in Leah's shop, maybe pick up some supplies."

"I don't want you to spend your own money. I have some donations from friends and coworkers I can give you."

"Let's see what I come up with."

"Okay. If you promise to let me reimburse you," Kate repeated.

"Promise."

Pearl appeared in the doorway a little later and signaled to Kate.

Kate stood immediately. "I'll be right back."

She didn't return for nearly twenty minutes, and when she did she was frowning.

"Something wrong?"

She sighed. "Carrie's been hurt. Apparently she's been seeing her boyfriend."

Lavina bit her lip. "I wondered if the man I saw her with one day gave her a ring. I almost didn't mention it to you that day."

"I saw it. Remember?"

"I figured you would. I mean, I guess you have to be observant in your line of work."

Kate grinned. "Yeah. Especially if you want to make detective."

"You do?"

She nodded. "Chief of police, too. But let's not let that get around. Best to keep quiet about that sort of thing. You know how gossip can be a problem in a small community."

"How well I know." The Amish led very private lives, but nothing traveled faster than news on the Amish grapevine.

Kate looked at her. "You and Mary Elizabeth may be getting another apology."

"Oh?"

She leaned closer. "I didn't think it was a coincidence that the quilt got stolen here and Carrie was wearing a sparkler, if you know what I mean."

Shocked, Lavina stared at her. "You're not saying she stole it. She couldn't have. She was in class with us that day." Then she paused, thinking. "The boyfriend did it."

Kate nodded. "That's some great deductive thinking there."

Lavina blushed. "I wouldn't have thought of it if you hadn't brought up Carrie and the boyfriend."

"Well, like I said, she may come to you at some point and apologize. She feels responsible for him taking it. I don't believe it's her fault at all, and I told her so. I think she said something about the class and quilts, and he got to thinking he could make a fast buck." She sighed. "She paid a price for an innocent conversation. I just found out that he hit her after I talked with him."

Lavina's hand flew to her throat. "Oh, no!"

"Two of my fellow officers are on the way to see him now, and this time a note of apology isn't going to keep him out of trouble. This time she's agreed to press charges. She never would in the past."

Lavina was glad the class came to an end a short time later. The news that Carrie had been hurt dimmed some of the pleasure in having the quilt returned. Her spirits lifted when she parked in the lot behind Stitches in Time and got out of the buggy with the boxed quilt under her arm.

The front display window caught her attention as she walked past it. The colorful, creative work of Leah's *grossdochders* was artfully arranged: woven throws and totes by Mary Katherine, cozy quilts by Naomi, and whimsical, warm knitted caps for babies by Anna. Leah's charming little Amish dolls sat before the orange cellophane flames of a little fireplace. Leah had a reputation for encouraging creativity not only in her *grossdochders* but also in her part-time employees. There were rag baskets by Emma, and decorative pillows for children in the shape of gingerbread cookies made by Rachel Ann, who divided her skills and time between the shop and a local Amish bakery.

Surely she'd find some inspiration here for some gifts the women at the shelter could make for Christmas. Hopefully, she wouldn't also walk out with more new fabric to add to the ever-growing fabric stash in the sewing room at home. Her *dat* often teased that his *dochders* and *fraa* had nearly enough fabric to start their own store.

David felt a little uneasy leaving his parents the next morning, but his *mudder* assured him she was feeling fine and had taken her blood pressure medication on time. His *dat* obviously had recovered from his bout with heartburn, as he was plowing through a hearty breakfast of bacon, *dippy* eggs, and biscuits.

This must be what it felt like to be a parent, he couldn't help thinking as he got into his truck and headed for work. He wanted to stay and watch over them to make sure they were *allrecht*, which was ridiculous. They weren't *kinner*—they were adults who'd managed to raise three boys and run a farm.

But he worried.

Later, he'd give his *bruders* a call and let them know what had happened last night. They deserved to know.

He sat with Bill at lunch. Bill eyed David's sandwich and for once didn't try to trade him something for it.

"That doesn't look like the kind of lunch you usually bring. Maybe I should offer you some of mine." He bit into his ham and cheese sandwich.

"I wouldn't let *Mamm* pack my lunch last night." He told Bill what had happened.

"Man, sorry to hear that. Anything I can do?"

David shook his head. "No, thanks. Everything was fine this morning. You should have seen the breakfast my father was putting away this morning. They looked better than ever."

"We never think about our parents getting old and needing you to worry about them, do we?"

"I sure didn't use to. Especially not my dad. He's always been too . . ." he searched for the right word.

"Too ornery to get sick?" Bill finished for him.

David chuckled. "Yeah. But even he can get something like cancer that he has to fight. No one's immune."

He finished his tuna salad sandwich and pulled out a plastic baggie of oatmeal raisin cookies. When he saw Bill's eyes light up he held out the baggie.

"Love your mom's cookies," Bill said as he bit into one.

"You're welcome to come to supper one night."

"Not sure I want to beard the dragon in his lair." Bill popped the last of the cookie into his mouth and reached for another.

"Chicken."

"Yup," Bill responded cheerfully. He glanced at the clock. "Let's go take care of our deliveries, get out of here for a while."

"You'd have enjoyed being along for the ride home last night," he told Bill as they headed out of the parking lot. "I was with Lavina when we saw the ambulance outside my house. She convinced me it would be faster to take my truck than follow it to the hospital in the buggy. So when my parents were ready to go home, I drove us in the truck."

"What a ride that must have been. You and your old man in this *Englisch* truck. I'm surprised he hasn't made you get rid of it."

David's grin faded. "No, I think he's still hoping I'll get in it one day and do a wheelie as I leave the driveway."

"Sorry." He stared at the road ahead. "I always wondered why the Amish can't have cars. I mean, is it because they really want to keep those old-fashioned buggies—no insult intended—or is it something else?"

"Think about it: when you have a buggy you can't take off in a hurry when you're mad," David told him. "And you can't go very far. So it keeps you near to home to work things out."

"I hadn't thought about it that way. There's no keeping up with the Joneses either."

"I don't know anyone named Jones."

Bill chuckled and slapped him on the shoulder. "It's an *Englisch* expression. It means people think they have to have what their neighbors have—actually, they always want to have something better so they can feel superior. So then the people who live next to them try to have even more. And it's like it becomes a vicious circle—everyone wanting more, more."

He glanced at David. "Not a good attitude at all. It's one of the reasons we buy new cars and trucks each year and spend too much money on everything. Bigger houses, flashier clothes. You name it."

"Your truck is several years old."

"Yeah, well I'm trying to be less materialistic. Plus I'm saving up. I'd like to go into business for myself one day."

"That would be good. You have a head for business. I think you'd do well."

"Thanks. Maybe if I do and you aren't running your own farm then you'll work with me. We could be partners."

"I don't have much money saved."

"Me either." He laughed. "We're a pair, aren't we? Hey, speaking of pairs, have you talked to your brothers about what happened to your parents last night?"

"I'm calling them after work. I kind of doubt it'll change anything. Neither of them was interested in coming home when I did. But I still need to tell them."

He wasn't surprised when he talked to Sam and John later when he got home. They were sorry to hear that their *mudder* had had a crisis with her blood pressure, but they had no sympathy for their *dat*.

"Don't let him drag you down again," John, the youngest, said bluntly, sounding more like an *Englischer* than an Amish man.

David could hear loud music and someone singing along with it in the background. He wondered just how much his *bruder* was enjoying living in the *Englisch* world.

His *mudder's* color was better, he noted when he sat down at the supper table. His *dat's*, too. She seemed happy to be in her own kitchen.

They gave thanks for the meal, and David took two thick slices of meatloaf. "My favorite."

"I know." His *mudder* smiled.

"Maybe there'll be some left, and I can take a meatloaf sandwich to work tomorrow."

"Maybe."

His *dat* grunted and served himself another slice

"Bill talked me out of several of your oatmeal raisin cookies today," he told his *mudder*.

"You should invite him to supper some time."

"I did." He slid his glance over at his *dat* who was absorbed in his meal.

She frowned, obviously getting his unspoken message. "I made chocolate chip cookies today. You'll have to take him some tomorrow."

"I will."

His *dat* finished his meal and decided he was too full for dessert. He shuffled off to read *The Budget* in the living room.

"How was the wedding yesterday? You came home early."

David helped himself to more mashed potatoes. "Lavina had a headache, and I offered to take her home so her *schweschders* could stay."

"That was nice of you."

"Least I could do. It didn't look like she was having a very good time. I figure I'm responsible for that. We'd have been married by now if I hadn't left."

"That's what I guessed." She leaned back in her chair and studied him as he ate. "She came to visit me every week while you were gone. I like her a lot."

"Me, too," he said with a grin as he set his fork down. "I think after I help you with the dishes I should go see if the headache she had yesterday is gone."

"I think that's a *gut* idea. And if you need an excuse, you can take back the casserole dish she brought over last week."

"I don't need an excuse," he told her.

What he did take was the buggy.

Lavina opened the front door and found David standing on the porch.

"I wanted to see if you were feeling better."

She nodded. "I'm fine. Do you want to come in?"

He shook his head. "I thought I'd see if you'd like to go for a ride."

"*Schur.* Let me get my jacket."

"So how is your *dat*?" she asked the minute she got into the buggy. "I listened to the message you left on the machine."

"He's fine. It was heartburn, just like he'd insisted. He started to give us a hard time for making him get checked out, and then *Mamm* got sick and we had to stay for a while. I didn't even know she had high blood pressure."

"Your *dat's* cancer therapy has been rough on her."

"I know."

"She's *allrecht* now?"

He nodded. "I brought them home last night."

It took her a minute and then she stared at him. "Do you mean you drove them home in your truck? Oh, I'd have loved to be a fly on the windshield listening to what your *dat* said."

So he told her about his *dat's* reaction. "I'm glad you insisted I take the truck. I got there quicker. Anyway, I wanted to talk to you."

"*Allrecht*."

"Yesterday, I told you that I'd missed church, the people here. I wanted to say more but you weren't feeling well."

She nodded. "Go on."

"I'm staying, Lavina. No matter what happens. Whether *Daed* lives or dies." He took a deep breath. "And whether you'll give me that second chance I want, or not."

She blinked. "Well, that was blunt. The last part, I mean."

He pulled over on the shoulder of the road and took her hands in his. "I'm laying it on the line with you. I want to be with you and make it up to you, all you've been through. I think we can have the future together we talked about once."

He looked down at their joined hands. "And if *Daed* lives through this and goes on to farm for years to come as I hope he will, that's fine. I'll figure out some way to get my own farm one day."

"You make it sound so easy."

"It won't be. But it's harder to think about a future, Lavina. Can we see if we can make a future together?" He squeezed her hands. "I know you're afraid to trust your heart to me again. I promise you, I won't hurt you again."

"You can't promise me that."

"You're right. I'll probably mess up. But we can work it out because I'm not going anywhere. I'm not running away from my problems—and you—again. I promise."

He saw the doubt on her face. "Look, I want us to get married, but we don't have to decide that now. I wasn't finished with the classes to join the church before I left, so there's no way the bishop will let us talk to him about getting married now anyway. So we take it slow, date, enjoy getting to know each other again. I save to buy us our own place."

She took a deep breath, then another, and then she nodded slowly. "*Allrecht*."

David glanced around and then he gave her a quick, fervent kiss. He picked up the reins, spoke to Nellie, and got the buggy back on the road.

"So where are we going for our first official date?" he asked her.

"Dinner at that fancy restaurant wasn't a date?"

"I guess it could be," he allowed, in too good a mood to disagree.

"Let's go to our favorite place."

He didn't need to ask where that was. And he was grateful that she wanted to go there, since going the first time after he'd returned hadn't been the most successful.

They found their favorite table empty and grabbed it. David bought hot chocolate and a slice of pumpkin bread and the apple tart for Lavina.

They sat drinking their hot chocolate and talking until they were told the shop was closing.

"Just like old times," she said, grinning at him as they walked out. "There's just one thing that would make things perfect."

"What's that?" he asked her as he helped her into the buggy.

"If your *bruders* would come home to Paradise."

He got into the driver's side and turned to her. "Lavina, I don't think that's going to happen. I talked to both of them yesterday and told them about *Mamm* and *Daed*. I was hoping they might say something about coming back. But they weren't interested."

Disappointment swept over her face. "I think Mary Elizabeth and Rose Anna have been hoping they would since you came back."

"Maybe if our *dat* had showed any signs of changing," David said. "I couldn't lie to them about the way he was when I came back. What good would that have done? If they had given up their apartment and come back and found out he was just as miserable as ever, they'd be furious with me, and they'd be right."

She sighed. "You're right. It's such a shame he has to be the way he is. You know, sometimes when people go through things like cancer it changes how they look at things. They try to show their families that they appreciate them, love them."

"You're talking about Marvin King. But he was never like my *dat.* He was a loving, caring man before he got sick with cancer."

"True."

"Why do you suppose God gives us the family we have?"

"That's a strange question."

"You never asked yourself that?"

David pondered that as the buggy rolled down the country road. The moon was only a sliver of a moon filtering through the bare tree branches beside the road, so it was dark and mysterious.

"You're nothing like him, thank goodness," she was saying. "I watched you for a long time wondering if you'd turn hard and bitter with the way he treated you."

Surprised, he turned and stared at her. "You did?"

She nodded. "But you didn't."

"Then I worried that we'd have a marriage like your parents." She shivered. "But I'd never allow you to talk to me the way he does."

"I had no idea you worried about something like that."

But he had wondered if all marriages were like theirs, until he spent more time at Lavina's house and seen that her parents had an entirely different relationship. Visits to the homes of his male friends had shown warm, loving parents and that reassured him as well.

The band of his hat suddenly seemed too tight. He took it off, set it on the seat between them and ran a hand through his hair.

"Now are *you* getting a headache?"

He glanced at her and chuckled. "A bit of one. I don't know how all this is going to work out."

He fell silent, wishing he could figure out a solution. "We've talked about pooling our money and buying a farm together, my *bruders* and me. But with the land prices in Lancaster County . . . well, we just can't save fast enough. Prices are sky high and going higher."

"God's got a plan for us," she said slowly. "I figure it's a lot like this road. We can see just a little ahead but not all the way home. But maybe all we need is to see just a little ahead. I mean, we have to trust."

She found herself remembering what Leah had said: "We live by faith not by sight."

Leaning back in her seat, she pulled the buggy blanket up. "I wonder what would have happened if I'd trusted God more last year. I listened to you being so upset with your *dat,* but I kept planning how it would be when we got married. I decided we'd still be married even when things were falling apart. I should have listened and been open to things changing."

He reached over and grasped her hand. "We both learned a lot, *ya?*" He sighed. "A year seems so far away."

"It'll go quickly now that you're here and we're seeing each other," she said. "And the time would pass the same if we were waiting for something or not," she reminded him.

"True." He raised her hand and kissed her knuckles, grinning when she looked surprised. It showed him he didn't make romantic gestures often enough. Public displays of affection were discouraged in their community but in private, at times like this, when no one could see, he could make them.

Reluctantly, he turned in the direction of home and dropped her off at her house before pulling into his drive and putting the horse and buggy up for the night.

"We had a good ride for the day, didn't we?" he asked Nellie as he led her into her stall. "I'm so happy to be with both of you again. Well, happier to be with her but you understand." He rubbed her nose and latched the stall gate.

Inside, he found his *dat* dozing in his recliner, *The Budget* newspaper spread over his stomach. His *mudder* looked up with a smile. Her fingers were busily knitting a baby blanket.

"For the new Miller *boppli*," she explained when she saw him glance at it. "Did you have a *gut* evening?"

He nodded. "I called Sam and John. They said they hoped you were both feeling better." It was mostly the truth. They cared about her even if they hadn't said it quite that way. But he couldn't say they said the same about their *dat*. That would be lying.

"That was very nice of you to call them." She gathered up her knitting and tucked it into the basket beside her chair. "Time for me to get to bed."

"*Gut nacht.*" He escaped before she woke his *dat*.

He heard her chuckle as he left the room. She knew what he was doing.

16

Lavina and Mary Elizabeth worked quickly to hitch up the buggy. Together they made fast work of it.

"It's definitely getting cooler," Mary Elizabeth said as she jumped into the buggy. She shivered and pulled the buggy blanket over her lap. "Do you need a blanket?"

Lavina shook her head. "I'm fine."

"Wonder if we're going to have a cold winter."

"Winter's always cold, silly."

"*Nee*, I mean are we going to have a record cold one like we had two winters ago?"

"I don't know. Check *Daed's* almanac."

Mary Elizabeth took a deep breath. "It might be a little cold, but it feels gut to be out of the house. I'm so happy that the quilt was found so I don't have to replace it quickly."

"Me, too."

"Look, there's a patch of frost on the ground," Mary Elizabeth said as they approached the road. She shivered again.

"I can't wait for the first snow."

"I can. I don't like cold weather." She looked over. "Tell me why you're in such a *gut* mood this morning."

"I am?" But Lavina could feel herself smiling.

"You are! C'mon, tell me!" Mary Elizabeth bounced on the seat.

"Calm down. You'll scare Daisy." She glanced at Mary Elizabeth. "I'll tell you if you promise you won't tell anyone else."

"I promise."

Lavina bit her lip. Such things were kept private, but she knew Mary Elizabeth would keep it a secret. Rose Anna, on the other hand . . . couldn't keep a secret for five minutes.

"David and I are dating again."

Mary Elizabeth let out a whoop, startling their horse. "That's fantastic! Oh, I'm so happy!"

"Remember, you promised."

"I know, I know. Oh, I just felt this would happen."

"Then you knew more than I did."

She pulled to the side of the road to allow a car to pass. After she checked for traffic, she pulled back onto the road.

"You know I told you that when we got home there was an ambulance at David's house, and his *dat* had to go to the hospital? Well, he's *allrecht;* he just had heartburn, not the heart attack they feared. But his *mudder* got sick while she was there with him."

"Oh my, what happened?"

"David said her blood pressure spiked because of the stress. She has to watch it more carefully. He seems worried about her. But we've been talking, and I think David's been doing a lot of thinking. He said attending the wedding made him realize how much he missed church and everyone. And I think he sees his parents are getting older and he should be here. He says he's staying no matter what happens. He's hoping his *dat* will beat the cancer and be around for a long time."

She glanced at Mary Elizabeth. "He hopes one day he can find a way to buy his own farm."

"That's not going to be easy."

Lavina bit her lip. "*Nee*. Look, I don't know if I should say anything about this, get your hopes up. He said he's going to try to talk to his *bruders* about buying a farm together."

Mary Elizabeth's hand flew to her lips. "That would be *wunderbaar.*" Then she dropped her hand and her shoulders slumped.

"How can that happen? You know land is as dear as gold in this county. And none of the *bruders* is working a job that pays much."

Lavina nodded. "I know. So you know what it's going to take?"

"What?"

She smiled slowly. "A miracle."

"You say that like it's so easy."

"It is. I'm not the One who has to make it happen." She turned to smile at Mary Elizabeth. "Right?"

"You're right," Mary Elizabeth's smile bloomed slowly. "You're right."

They rode along in silence for a few blocks.

"It would be . . . beyond *wunderbaar* if Sam and John came home and the *bruders* worked a farm together again."

"It would."

Mary Elizabeth's lips trembled. "I've missed Sam so much. Rose Anna's missed John."

"I know."

She looked over. "Of course. You had longer to grieve than we did. David left first. Sam and John stayed for several months before they couldn't stand it and left the farm."

"I don't think Rose Anna is ready for us to talk about this yet," Lavina said carefully. "I don't want to get her hopes up."

"I agree."

"So we pray for this without Rose Anna?"

Mary Elizabeth nodded. "*Allrecht.*"

Lavina pulled into the parking lot behind the shelter. "*Kumm*, let's go have fun."

"What's in all these bags?" Mary Elizabeth asked as she helped carry two of them into the shelter.

"You'll see."

Kate looked up as they walked into the classroom. "Looks like someone went shopping."

Lavina grinned. "I got some ideas when I went to Leah's shop, and well, they were having a sale, and when I told her what I was buying for she gave me this discount . . . "

"So you couldn't resist . . ." Kate said, chuckling.

"The ladies can make some quilted hearts, or Christmas tree ornaments, or some microwave or oven potholders. Or look how cute this little basket is made of rags that you roll and then build the shape. Emma makes them for Stitches in Time." She pulled one of Rachel Ann's gingerbread cookie shaped pillows out of the bag. "These don't take much time at all and they're so cute for kids, don't you think?"

"I've never seen you so excited," Kate said, grinning.

"It's not just the gifts or Christmas," Mary Elizabeth told her.

"You promised!" Lavina cried. "You're as bad as Rose Anna. Actually, I don't think that was five minutes."

"What's going on?" Kate looked from one to the other.

"David and I are dating again. But Mary Elizabeth promised to keep it a secret."

"Oh, that's wonderful! Congratulations!"

"Thank you." Lavina felt herself beaming.

Kate held up her hand. "I swear, I won't tell anyone. Not even my husband. You've got my word of honor."

She looked past Lavina. "I think someone would like to talk to you," she murmured.

Lavina turned and saw Carrie standing hesitantly in the doorway. "I'll be right back."

"Can we talk for a minute?" Carrie asked her when she got to the back of the room. Her eyes were a little red and puffy like she'd been crying, and one of them had a faint purple bruise around it.

"Sure."

"I wanted to apologize to you for what happened to your quilt. I never thought talking to Ed would lead to him stealing it."

"It's not your fault. He's the one who did it. Are you all right?"

Carrie touched a finger to the corner of one eye. "That's the last time that man is ever going to hit me."

She sniffed and raised her chin. "Anyway, I just wanted to say I'm sorry and I'm glad you got the quilt back."

"Thanks. Are you going to stay and sew today?"

"I don't think so." She stepped out of the way as women began filing in.

"Please stay," Lavina said, holding out her hand. "I got some great material and crafts and things for us to make Christmas gifts."

"I don't have anyone to make anything for."

"Then let's make some for people who don't have what we have."

"What do I have?" Carrie asked, sounding bitter.

"You have a place to live where people care about you," Lavina said gently. "Friends. A chance to make a new, better life for yourself."

The tears started again. Lavina put her arm around her and led her to a chair. "Stay. We'll have some fun."

Carrie pulled a tissue from the pocket of her worn jeans. "I'm not making a potholder. We had to make those in home ec class."

Lavina laughed. "You don't have to make a potholder."

David found himself looking at his surroundings in a different way since his talk with Lavina.

He had to admit that he'd been like a horse with blinders on all his life—looking straight ahead, never to the right or left, totally focused on what was straight ahead. And that focus was on the family farm. All the time that he and his *bruders* weren't getting along with their *dat,* somehow it hadn't sunk in that it wouldn't be theirs one day in the future.

That was the way things were here. A family built together, whether it was a farm or a business, then the *kinner* took over and the parents moved into the *dawdi haus* at the rear of the family home. And when it was time, if the parents needed caring for, the *kinner* did it. They took care of their own, the Amish did.

But then things had become unbearable and David had had to leave. The farm, his beloved farm, had been left behind along with a *dat* he'd never gotten along with, a *mudder* he'd loved but who'd been put in the middle, and because of the way she'd been raised, stood with her *mann* and watched her sons leave one by one.

David hadn't been able to think of finding his own farm then—not only was he caught up in the emotion of leaving the only home he'd ever known, he barely had enough to rent a room in the home of an elderly widow distantly related to his friend, Bill.

Now, as he drove to work, he found himself looking at the land he passed with new eyes. The land hadn't changed in price overnight but something in him had. For the first time in a long, long time he had hope. He and Lavina were together again and he could envision a future with her. They couldn't get married until next fall but they'd be together, dating, planning their future.

The two of them had been given a second chance and with that second chance . . . well surely there would be some place for them to have a home, however small it was. Many Amish homes were big, but that often came years after a newly married couple moved into them. They moved into a small house and as their family grew, they added on. And on.

Surely there was some small place they could start and build on. A verse from the Bible came to him. *In My Father's house are many mansions; if it were not so, I would have told you. I go to prepare a place for you* (John 14:2).

He didn't know what God's plan was for him, for Lavina. But surely there was some small patch of land, a small house, where he could farm, where he could start a family.

He had to believe.

For now it was *gut* to do an honest day's work, go home, get cleaned up, and eat supper with his parents, or go to eat at Lavina's house where her parents and her *schweschders* welcomed him and made him feel part of the family again.

He and Lavina had always enjoyed being together inexpensively—drives in the buggy cost only some horse feed, after all, and they loved having an occasional coffee and baked treat at their favorite place. Sometimes they just took along a thermos of coffee and something Lavina baked. Being together, talking, discovering each other again was all the entertainment they needed.

David told her about his time in the *Englisch* world when he'd rented the little room, and she told him how she'd begun volunteering teaching the quilting class with Kate. It was at a shelter for abused women and their children in a hidden location. That was why the day he'd wanted to help her and Mary Elizabeth deliver the bed they were donating, they hadn't allowed him to go there with them.

As she talked he saw a side of her he hadn't before. Before he'd left, she'd been a bit shy, introverted, and while experienced in quilting, she hadn't acted as confident of her skills as she did now.

"You're really enjoying teaching the class."

"Well, I'm not so much teaching as helping," she said modestly. "But *ya*, I'm enjoying it. I like helping. A lot of these ladies don't have any confidence, any skills. Kate's class is helping them with both. And it's nice to see them making friends with each other after not having any for so long. Their husbands and boyfriends kept them from having friends as a way of isolating them and controlling them."

That concept was new to him, but he listened and tried to understand what she was saying. Mary Elizabeth had even joined her a couple of times.

"What did you do while you were gone last year? In your spare time, I mean?"

He shrugged. "Nothing interesting. Watched a lot of television. Sports, mostly. The landlady had a little television in the room I rented. Read. Brooded."

"You're good at brooding."

He glanced at her and saw her grin. "Oh, you think you're funny."

"It's true. You know it's true."

David turned back to look at the road. Then he couldn't help chuckling. "You're right. Well, it used to be true. I don't think I brood much anymore."

"Maybe not."

"I should stop by my landlady's house one day after work," he said. "She was very nice to me. I sometimes raked her yard or shoveled her walk so she wouldn't have to do it. So she'd invite me to supper once in a while. She reminded me of my *grossmudder*."

He fell silent. One of the things that grieved him still was that his *grossmudder*—his *dat*'s *mudder*—had died while he was gone.

A few minutes later he pulled up in his drive and turned to her.

"Ready?"

"*Schur*."

He got out, opened her door, and held her hand, giving it a squeeze for reassurance as they climbed the steps to the front door.

"Remember, no telling them about our plans. You promised." She tried to withdraw her hand from his.

"I promise." Reluctantly he let go of her hand and they went inside.

She'd been in his house many times over the years, been invited to supper many times, until tensions had run so high that he hadn't wanted to expose her to it.

His *mudder* stood stirring something in a pot on the stove. His *dat* already sat in his chair at the head of the table. David hid a grin as he reached over and pinched off a corner of a piece of cornbread and popped it into his mouth.

Waneta turned from the stove and gave her a big smile. "*Wilkumm*! So glad you could have supper with us tonight. Isn't it nice, Amos?"

He mumbled a greeting that had his *fraa* narrowing her eyes and glancing at the food already sitting on the table. "Amos, are you getting into the cornbread?"

He shook his head, but didn't say anything, his cheeks obviously full of cornbread. He nodded at Lavina and continued munching.

David pulled out a chair for Lavina and earned an approving nod from his *mudder*.

"Something smells delicious," Lavina said.

"I made stuffed pork chops and scalloped potatoes. One of Amos's favorites. Hope you like pork chops."

"Love them."

Waneta set the platter on the table and seated herself. "I had the time to cook today, but tomorrow we'll be spending much of the day at the hospital."

David saw his *dat* frown, but after the meal was blessed, he forked up a chop and passed the platter to David.

The atmosphere was different than the last time. Amos sat eating his supper, and while he didn't contribute much to the conversation, he didn't sit glowering at David as he had in the past. Waneta asked Lavina about her family, the quilting class, about Leah and her shop.

"Been a while since I got there," she said. "Since I shopped."

"I'd be happy to pick up anything you need," Lavina offered.

"I'd just like to go and look at some new fabric."

"Why don't I pick you up and we'll go tomorrow?"

Waneta passed her the dish of applesauce for her pork chop. "Amos and I have to go to the hospital for his PET scan tomorrow."

Amos looked up. "You don't have to go. I can go by myself."

"But I want to go."

He got up and slammed his chair against the table. "I don't have to be taken like I'm a *kind*!" he snapped. "Go do something you want to do!"

"But I want to go!" she cried.

But she spoke to his retreating back. He stomped upstairs, and they heard his footsteps stop and then the bed creaked as he sat down on it.

"I'm sorry," she said to Lavina. "He's just nervous about the test." She put her napkin down and rose. "I'm going to go up and talk to him."

"*Mamm*, eat your supper."

She patted his hand. "You keep Lavina company. I'll be right back."

Lavina couldn't help wincing as she listened to the argument upstairs.

"I'm sorry," David said quietly.

She looked at David. "It's not your fault."

"Finish your supper and I'll take you home."

"What's a PET scan?"

"Some fancy test to see if the chemo has done its work."

"No wonder he's worried."

"He doesn't need to take it out on her. She's worried too."

"Still—" she began.

Distracted, he waved his hand as he listened to the argument. "Eat your supper, Lavina."

Now who was treating who like a *kind?* she wanted to ask. She pushed the food around on her plate, but it was hard to eat when they could hear the older couple yelling at each other.

Finally, she got up, scraped the food from her plate into the garbage, and set her plate in the sink. She stood there, uncertain of her next move.

Amos was accusing Waneta of treating him like a *kind* one minute, a sick old man the next.

Waneta urged him to calm down, saying it wasn't good for him to get so upset. She urged him to take a pill, to go down and finish his supper. To apologize to Lavina for his temper. He just shouted to her that it was his *haus* and he wasn't apologizing to anyone.

Nothing worked. Again she urged him to take a pill, and they heard a glass break. David jumped to his feet.

"I told you before, I will *not* be an old lady cowering in the corner while you rant at me!" she shouted, and then they heard her descend the stairs.

"I heard something break."

"It's *allrecht, sohn*, just a plastic glass. I keep one at his bedside table if he needs water in the middle of the night. But it's plastic so there's no worry of him dropping it and getting glass all over the floor."

She resumed her place at the table. "I'm sorry, Lavina. I was hoping Amos would behave better tonight. He's worried about the test."

"You always make excuses for him."

"David! Don't talk to your *mudder* that way."

"It's true." His hand clenched into a fist. "Maybe if you'd stood up to him before."

She cut a bite of pork chop. "I just did."

"Too little, too late."

Lavina couldn't believe what she was just hearing. But when she opened her mouth to say something Waneta waved her hand. "Let him talk. He doesn't understand a wife is supposed to submit to her husband, to—"

"I can't listen to this." David stood, picked up his plate, and dumped it in the sink.

"David, you're being rude to your *mudder*!"

"Some things have to be said."

Waneta sat there, pale, her eyes fixed on her plate. "You've never understood the relationship I have with your *dat*." She lifted her gaze. "The bishop tried to explain the role of men and women in marriage, but you wouldn't listen—"

"Of course I wouldn't. He was full of hogwash!"

The butterflies that had flitted around in Lavina's stomach on the way to supper tonight felt like they'd turned into elephants. Maybe it would be best if she went home so the two of them could talk. But before she could say anything, David was talking.

"I can't sit and listen to him treating you like this," David said in a low voice.

"He's gotten better," Waneta insisted. "It's just that he's sick. He's worried about tomorrow."

David grabbed an apple from the bowl on the counter. "I'm going to check on Nellie."

He snatched his jacket from a peg near the back door and walked out. The door slammed behind him.

"He's just going to go out to the barn and cool off," Waneta told her reassuringly. "I have some chocolate cake for dessert. Would you like some with a cup of coffee?"

She shook her head. "I'm sorry, I'm full." She was glad she'd gotten rid of the food left on her plate so that Waneta didn't know how little she'd eaten.

"I think I've had enough, too."

Lavina wondered whether she simply meant that she'd eaten enough or she'd had enough of the turmoil. Considering that she hadn't eaten much more than Lavina, she thought it was the latter.

"Let me help you wash up."

Together they packed up the leftovers. "These will come in handy tomorrow when we come home from the hospital," Waneta said as she put the Tupperware containers in the refrigerator.

They stood at the sink, and Waneta washed the dishes, and Lavina dried them and put them in the cupboard. They talked quietly as they worked. Lavina had always liked Waneta and she felt the older woman liked her as well. Undoubtedly, she'd figured out that her *sohn* and Lavina had been close to getting married, but like most Amish parents, didn't pry. The only time Waneta had alluded to their relationship had been when she'd asked Lavina if she'd heard from David while he was gone . . . when she'd begged her to find him and ask him to come home because his father was ill.

And that had changed so much.

Waneta glanced at the stairs as if expecting her *mann* to come down, and then she glanced out at the barn looking for her *sohn*. She sighed.

"I think the two of them have been at odds since David was a boy," she said as she handed Lavina a freshly washed dish. "I'm not so sure they even know what they started fighting over any more."

"David wants his *dat's* approval," Lavina said. "He wants his ideas about the farm to be considered."

"They had a fuss about spring planting a while back," Waneta told her. She stared out the window, looking thoughtful. "But this time David was trying to goad Amos into thinking about something in the future, something beyond this depressing chemotherapy."

She stopped, put her hands on the lip of the sink. "We're all so worried about the scan tomorrow."

Lavina took her hand, led her over to the table. "Let's sit down and pray."

So they sat and prayed, Waneta's thin, worn hand in Lavina's, and did what women did everywhere when faced with problems they couldn't solve.

When they finished, Waneta looked around the kitchen. "If you'll excuse me, I'll go check on Amos." She gave Lavina a mischievous smile. "Maybe you'd like to go check on David."

Lavina glanced out at the barn. Then she looked at Waneta. She frowned. As much as she wanted to soothe the David about the scene at the supper table, she couldn't help thinking about what he'd said to his *mudder*, about how Waneta always made excuses about his *dat*. Was she any different when she urged him to keep trying to get along with the older man? Was she like David's *mudder*?

Tonight she'd been so optimistic the four of them could share a family supper, and look at what had happened. Maybe she and David had both been too optimistic.

She walked over to pluck her jacket off the peg by the door, and as she pulled it on she felt an uncomfortable thought wash over her. She thought about how she'd once worried about her and David ending up having the kind of relationship his parents had, instead of the kind her parents had. The one he'd seen them have all his life was so rigid, so unhappy. Tonight, when his dat had stomped upstairs and she'd said something, David had spoken harshly to her without a thought, telling her to eat her supper. She didn't like it, didn't like it one bit.

She hesitated at the door, feeling cold even though she hadn't opened the door to the outside.

Then she found herself turning and walking toward the front door. The more steps she took, the more steps she took until she had the doorknob in her hand, and she was opening the door and walking outside.

The cool air hit her. The temperature had dropped at least ten degrees—maybe more—since they came here tonight. It felt good after the warmth of the kitchen that had started to feel oppressive. She descended the steps quickly and began to run toward her house faster and faster. All she wanted was to get home where people loved each other, and there was no tension, no fear about what the future could bring.

Home.

She hurried into the house, shut the door behind her.

Her parents looked up from their chairs in the living room. "Lavina! You're home early. Everything *allrecht*?"

Her *dat* frowned and looked at her over the tops of his reading glasses. "Have you been running?"

"Just a little cold out," she said. Which was true. "Just wanted to stay warm."

"Why don't you go fix yourself a cup of tea and warm up?" her mother said. "I'll join you."

"I think I'll just go on up to bed. I'm kind of tired."

"*Gut nacht*, then."

Her father tapped his cheek. It was their little game, one he'd started since she was a little girl. She smiled and kissed his cheek, and he hugged her. She did the same with her *mudder.*

Feeling loved, secure, she went upstairs and got ready for bed. As she lay there tucked under her quilt, she wondered if David could truly be a loving *mann* when he hadn't known love from both his parents.

It was a disturbing thought.

17

David watched Nellie munch the apple he'd brought her.

If only his life could be as simple as hers. He leaned against the stall and felt some of the tension drain out of him.

He'd been so naïve to think they'd have a nice, quiet supper with Lavina joining them. Since when had his *dat* ever thought he had to behave just because company was in the *haus*. He'd even said he could do what he wanted in his own *haus* as he'd stomped upstairs.

Well, his anxiety over the big test tomorrow didn't excuse his behavior. Nothing did. And he was going to tell him that when he went inside.

Just as soon as he cooled off a little. He walked to the doorway of the barn and looked toward the house. He could see his *mudder* and Lavina framed in the kitchen window as they washed dishes. They were talking so easily, these two women he loved. Too bad his *dat* couldn't be more like his *mudder.*

"Can you imagine that?" he asked, walking back to Nellie. "Can you imagine *Daed* being more like *Mamm?*" he chuckled.

Nellie picked up on his mood and shook her head and neighed. David hugged her neck and absorbed the quiet comfort of the horse.

He lingered, puttering around the barn for a time. Finally he turned to Nellie. "I have to go in. I hope Lavina isn't too upset."

But when he got inside the kitchen was empty. The supper table had been cleared, dishes washed and put away, and the counters scrubbed.

He couldn't have been gone that long. Baffled, he walked to the front door and looked out but didn't see Lavina. He returned to the kitchen, poured himself a cup of coffee, and sat down at the table.

A few minutes later his *mudder* descended the stairs and walked into the room.

"Did you take Lavina home?"

He shook his head. "I just came in and there was no one here."

She swatted his shoulder. "I had to go up and check on your *dat*. I thought you'd be right in from the barn. She must have walked home. Shame on you!"

"It's not my fault!" he said, rubbing his shoulder. "I didn't know you weren't still with her."

"She was your guest, David! What kind of *sohn* did I raise? Where are your manners?"

He glanced at the window. It had grown dark. He stood, snatched his jacket and hat and started for the door.

"I'm going to make sure she got home safe."

"Too little, too late," he heard her mutter behind him.

David smashed his hat on his head and slammed out the front door.

He didn't bother taking the truck since it was a short walk. When he knocked on Lavina's front door her *dat* opened it and stared at him in surprise. "David!"

"*Gut-n-owed*. Is Lavina home?"

"She's gone up to bed."

"Oh. Uh. *Allrecht*." What else could he say? "*Danki*."

Lavina's *mudder* came to the door. "I'll tell her you came by when she gets up in the morning."

"*Danki*."

He turned and walked back down to the road. Glancing up, he saw the light on in her bedroom. More than once he'd thrown a handful of gravel at her window and she'd come down to sit on the porch and talk to him late, after he'd had a fight with his *dat*. It hadn't mattered how late, how warm or cold the night, they'd sat in rockers on the porch and talked.

Somehow he didn't think she wanted to talk to him tonight.

So he walked home, his steps slower this time. He let himself back into the house and found his *mudder* in the kitchen, drinking a cup of coffee.

"She's home. Her *dat* said she went up to bed."

He shed his hat and jacket and poured himself another cup of coffee. "You don't usually drink coffee so late."

"I'm not going to get any sleep tonight anyway."

"Is he still arguing with you?"

She closed her eyes and rubbed her forehead tiredly. "*Nee*. I'm just worried about the test tomorrow." She looked at him. "There's cake on the counter there."

"I don't feel much like cake." He dumped sugar in his cup and stirred it. "So Lavina didn't tell you she was leaving?"

"*Nee*. But she prayed with me for your *dat* before she left. Such a sweet *maedel*. Always has been."

"You don't have to tell me that." He sipped his coffee and made a face. Just how much sugar had he dumped into it? "I guess she just had enough of the fuss tonight."

"Maybe she got tired of waiting for you to come inside," his *mudder* said tartly.

He winced. "You're probably right. But she's come out to the barn before."

But she hadn't tonight. Maybe she'd had enough of the fuss as he'd said. He ran a hand through his hair. He didn't know what to think. The cake caught his eye.

Waneta saw him glance at it and laughed. "Have some. Chocolate solves a lot of problems."

"So you women say." He pulled out a knife and two plates.

"Out of the way," she said, getting up. "I'm not having you hack at my cake."

They turned as they heard footsteps on the stairs.

"Amos, I thought you'd gone to sleep."

He grunted. "I smelled cake."

She eyed him sternly. "I'm sure you did."

When she turned her back, David saw she hadn't forgiven him for their argument earlier. "Are you allowed to eat this late?"

"They said no food after midnight. It's only eight."

"So it is."

She sliced the cake, and David carried the plates to the table. Then she went to the refrigerator, brought a quart of milk to the table, and poured Amos a glass.

He looked longingly at the percolator on the stove but he didn't ask for coffee.

They sat eating the cake, not speaking. It was so quiet David could hear the ticking of the clock on the wall.

Finally, David broke the tension. "Would you like me to drive you to the hospital tomorrow?"

Amos shook his head, scattering crumbs from his beard. "No need to miss a day's work."

David looked at his *mudder*. She shook her head. "We'll be fine."

"When will they give you the results?"

"Doc said not for a couple of days."

"Lavina hasn't been here for supper since you came back," Amos said.

And she probably wouldn't come again for a long time, David wanted to snap. But he saw the look in his *mudder's* eyes and he was so tired of the strife, he bit back a retort. "*Nee*."

"Nice *maedel*."

David nearly bobbled his coffee. His *dat* had never anything about her, had barely spoken to her at supper. "*Ya*." He looked him in the eye. "She's the one who found me and talked me into coming back."

He stood and put his dishes in the sink. "*Danki* for supper, *Mamm*. I have to get up early for work so I'm going to bed now."

He turned to his *dat*. "Good luck with the test tomorrow. I'll pray for you."

And he climbed the stairs to bed, leaving them sitting there, not speaking.

"You're the first *dochder* up," her *mudder* said as Lavina sat down at the breakfast table the next morning. She set a cup of coffee in front of her. "David stopped by last night. He looked worried."

"I walked home by myself," she said carefully, glancing at the stairs.

"One or two pancakes?"

"Two please. I didn't eat much at supper." She poured syrup over the pancakes and cut into them.

Her *mudder* served the pancakes to her and then sat down with a cup of coffee. "Why am I thinking something happened?"

"Because you know Amos?"

"Was he rude to you?"

"Not to me. To Waneta, in front of all of us at the supper table. So then he went upstairs to their room and she followed him and they had a big, noisy fight."

"You mean you could hear him yelling at her some more."

"*Nee*, I mean David and I could hear her yelling back at him."

"Waneta?

"*Ya*, Waneta."

Linda sighed. "Amos being so ill has certainly put a strain on the family."

"*Mamm*, it goes back farther than him being sick. He's always been so hard on his *sohns*, especially David."

Lavina forked up a bite of pancake and then set it down. "Their fight wasn't the worst of it." She stared at her plate, then looked up at her *mudder*. "Then David and I had a fight about it. So I walked home."

"That's why David came by. To talk to you."

She nodded. "I don't know, *Mamm*. Things just feel really complicated."

"Maybe it's because you're trying to figure things out instead of being patient and letting God guide you."

She stared at her *mudder* and then she laughed. "Well, of course, I am." Feeling better, she began eating her pancakes again.

"Kate has court on our regular quilt class day, so she asked me if I could come in today. She's coming by in half an hour to pick me up."

"So when is Amos going for this test the family is so worried about?"

"This morning."

"When will they hear the results?"

"I don't know."

"We'll say a prayer for him before you leave."

There was a clatter of footsteps on the stairs leading down from the bedrooms. "Ach, here come my ladylike *dochders,* so delicate and quiet."

Mary Elizabeth grinned as she pushed Rose Anna out of the way. "I smell pancakes."

She looked at Lavina. "You didn't eat all of them, did you?"

"*Schur.*" She slid the last bite into her mouth and smacked her lips. *Mamm, Daed* and I ate them all while you two slept in."

"Now, now, behave," Linda said, laughing and shaking her head. "I've got plenty of batter waiting here for you both."

"So how did supper at David's go?" Mary Elizabeth wanted to know.

Linda turned from the stove and her gaze met Lavina's. "You'd better get a move on if Kate's picking you up."

"Right." She jumped up, taking her plate and coffee cup and putting them in the sink.

"Today's not class day," Rose Anna said.

"Kate changed it. She has court later this week." She went upstairs, using the time to check her appearance and straighten her room, silently thanking her *mudder* for saving her from a discussion of the previous evening.

But she couldn't help remembering her concern at being in the middle of the upsetting scene last night. Often young couples lived with their in-laws after they were married while they saved for their own home or built one. There was no room for her and David here. Her *grossmudder* was expected to move in soon. If they didn't have their own place when they married, it could mean that they'd have to live in the *dawdi haus* at his parents' home.

She shuddered at the thought; in the happy haze that had surrounded her in getting back with David, it had totally slipped her mind until last night.

With a groan she sank down on her bed and found herself biting her fingernails, a habit she'd broken herself of at eight years of age. To distract herself she went into the sewing room and collected her tote, with the quilt she wanted to work on during the class, and set it by the door. Restless, she straightened some fabric on the shelves.

Rose Anna walked in while she was working. "Aren't you the busy bee?"

She shrugged. "You know I like things neat."

"What's wrong?"

"Nothing's wrong."

Rose Anna touched her arm. Lavina had to look at her. Rose Anna was always the most sensitive to the moods of others.

"I'm *allrecht,* really. Just worried about David's *dat* going for a test today." It was the truth even if it wasn't the whole truth.

"It's in God's hands. We hope He isn't calling him home, but if He is what could be more *wunderbaar* than being with Him?"

Leave it to her *schweschder*, the youngest and most innocent, to have just the right words. She hugged her. "You're right. *Danki*."

"Lavina, Kate's here!" her *mudder* called up the stairs.

"Coming!"

She grabbed her tote, stopped in her room for her purse, and ran down the stairs. "See you later!" she said as she ran for the front door.

"I'm glad you were able to change your schedule and come today instead of Thursday," Kate told her when she got into the car.

"Well, I have a pretty flexible schedule working at home every day."

"Still, it was nice." She tapped her fingers on the steering wheel while she waited to pull out onto the road. "So, what's new?"

Lavina hesitated for a moment and then she turned to her. "Do you really think people can change? I mean, really change?"

"Yes," Kate said without hesitation. "If I didn't, I couldn't get up and do my job every day."

"But isn't it true that you arrest the same people sometimes for doing the same thing more than once?"

"Yes, sometimes again and again."

"So then people don't change."

"Many people do. But something tells me we're not talking about criminals, are we?"

Lavina bit her lip but then she shook her head. Her *schweschders* had always been her best friends, but she'd grown close to this *Englisch* woman who seemed to have such good advice.

"I was hoping that David's father would . . . I don't know, mellow because he's been so sick. I mean, if you get as sick as he has, wouldn't you think that he'd want to be nicer to his family in case he—" She gulped. "In case he doesn't make it?"

"Some people would," Kate agreed thoughtfully. "But I've known people who got cancer, and they've had different reactions. Some get angry and stay angry. It's a form of grieving, I guess."

"It's been so hard on Waneta, his wife. And on David since he came back." She fell silent for a long moment. "Then last night . . ."

"What happened last night?"

Kate had become such a good friend. For the second time that day she found herself telling someone about the argument, about her fears of living with her in-laws and being around that tension between them. And maybe having a relationship like they had . . .

Kate pulled into the parking lot of the shelter. She shut off the engine and turned to Lavina. "Why don't we have lunch after the class and talk about this?"

"That would be nice."

They gathered up their purses and totes. "I have to tell you, I like my in-laws but I don't know if I could have handled living with them when we first got married." She looked at Lavina. "Or any other year."

Chuckling, she unlocked the front door and held it so Lavina could step inside.

It felt like the longest day David had ever had.

Every time he glanced at the clock only minutes had passed. He thought about going to see Lavina during his lunch break, but they only got half an hour and he wouldn't make it back to work in time.

Bill noticed his distraction and remarked on it when they went to make deliveries. "Trouble in paradise?" he joked.

He shrugged. "I think Lavina's upset with me."

"You think?"

"Yeah."

"Then she probably is. What did you do?"

Feeling a little irritated, David glanced at him. "What makes you think it's something I did."

"It's usually our fault." Bill leaned back and stretched out his legs as best as he could in the truck. "And if it isn't, it's our fault."

"That doesn't make sense."

"Few things do in relationships between men and women." He flipped open his cell phone, checked for messages, shut it again. "But maybe it's different in your community."

"Things are simpler."

"Yeah?"

Were they really? he asked himself. "Well, I used to think so. We stay in our community all our lives, go to *schul* together, know each other's families. We even have church in each other's homes. So we know each other, date, for a long time."

"So then things should be simpler."

"I thought so."

"Maybe that's part of the problem. You're expecting things to be predictable. Look, you're a farmer. You know raising a crop isn't predictable. You don't just plant seeds, water them, then harvest what comes up, right?"

"Right."

"So you figured you'd come home, get Lavina back, and everything would be okay."

"It was until last night."

"So let's make this delivery, and you can tell me what happened."

David was grateful for Bill's quick work unloading and his willingness to listen to his problems.

"Yeah, you messed up. Bad," Bill told him as they stopped for a cup of coffee on the way back to work.

"So you're taking her side? You think Lavina should have gone home without saying anything to me?"

"It's not about taking sides. But yeah. Don't you see how you messed up?"

"No."

"Did you really think your father was going to behave just because you wanted him to?"

"I—"

"Did you think your mother would stand up to him when he didn't?"

"I—"

"And did you think Lavina should just wait around while you sulked in the barn?" He waited. "Well?"

"You're letting me talk now?" David asked wryly. "Well, the answer to your questions are yes and yes and yes. But I wasn't sulking. I don't sulk. I brood. Lavina told me once I do it really well."

Bill laughed. "Really?" He drained his cup and nodded when a waitress walked over with a coffee pot.

David shook his head at the offer of more coffee and stared at the untasted contents of his cup. "She usually talks to me and helps me feel better about things after a scene with my father."

"Yeah, she's been doing that for years, right?"

"Right." David frowned. "You make that sound like it's bad."

"Not bad. Maybe a little selfish." He stirred sugar into his coffee. "But then women cater more to men in your community. Your mother does with your father. Lavina does with you."

"I listen to her and support her, too."

"Not like what you've said she's done for you all these years."

Bill was right. David shook his head. "No."

"Ready to go?"

They drove back to work.

"So you going to see Lavina tonight?"

"Absolutely."

"Have an apology ready?"

"Don't rub it in."

Bill laughed. "I don't need to. Lavina may do that."

"She's not like that."

"Most women are," Bill said in a dolorous tone.

David stopped at Lavina's house on the way home without going by his own house to clean up and change.

"*Gut-n-owed*, David," her *mudder* said when she opened the door. "I'm sorry, Lavina's not home yet. She's in town with a friend. I'll tell her you came by."

So he went on home, and when he walked in found his *mudder* dozing in a chair in the living room. He tried to tiptoe past, but she woke and blinked at him. "David, you're home already?"

"It's 5:30."

"I should check on your *dat*."

"I'll do it. You stay put. How did it go today?"

"It took hours. They'd overbooked appointments, and then there was some problem with the equipment."

He shed his jacket and hat. "Did you find out when you'll get results?"

"The doctor said a couple of days."

David hung his jacket and hat on pegs in the kitchen and headed upstairs. The door to his parents' bedroom was ajar, so he peeked in. The room was dim, but he could see his *dat* tucked under a quilt, and he could hear the faint sound of snoring.

"He's asleep," he told his *mudder* when he went back downstairs. "You look tired. Why don't I make supper?"

"Grilled cheese sandwiches and soup?"

"My speciality," he said with a grin, mispronouncing the word.

"We have lots of leftovers from last night. No one ate much, remember?"

He nodded.

"Sit for a minute, *sohn*."

He sat in his *dat's* recliner knowing he'd have to get up quickly if he came downstairs. No one was supposed to sit in his *dat's* recliner.

"Did you apologize to Lavina for last night?"

"She wasn't home. Her *mudder* said she was in town with a friend. I'll walk over later."

He thought about his conversation with Bill. "I owe you an apology, too. I shouldn't have said that you should have spoken up to *Daed* earlier."

"Well, I should have," she said quietly. "But I was taught that a *fraa* is supposed to obey her *mann*. He's the head of the home."

"He shouldn't be the dictator."

"*Nee*."

"You surprised me last night when you yelled back at him."

A smile ghosted around her mouth. "I surprised all of us. You should have seen your *dat's* face."

Then she pressed her lips together and frowned. "I shouldn't speak of what happened when we argued. That's between a *fraa* and her *mann*. And I shouldn't have said anything like that where someone outside of the family could hear." She shook her head. "Imagine what Lavina thinks of our family arguing like that."

"I'm *schur* she wasn't surprised by *Daed's* behavior. She's heard enough about the problems he and I have had through the years."

"Well, let's get some supper so you can get over there and talk to her before it gets too late."

She insisted she didn't need any help warming up the leftovers, so he went upstairs to shower and change into clean clothes. When he went downstairs supper was still warming in the oven and his *dat* hadn't come down yet.

"I think I'll go see if Lavina's home yet."

"Tell her I'm sorry about last night, too."

"I will."

When he pulled into her drive another vehicle pulled in after him. Lavina got out of a car and walked up to his side of the truck.

"Hi. I came by earlier but you weren't home yet." His heart sank when she didn't return his smile. "Can we go for a ride? I want to talk to you about last night."

"David, I don't want to talk about last night." She rubbed at her forehead as if she had a headache.

"You mean you want me to come back another time. You're not feeling well?"

"I'm fine. I've just—I've just had enough, David." Tears sprang into her eyes.

"Lavina, please. You're upset. Get in the truck and let's talk."

She rounded the hood. For a moment, when she hesitated, glancing at her house, he was afraid she was going to go on inside. Then she got into the truck.

"I don't want to go for a drive," she said when his hand went to the ignition key.

"*Allrecht*. I'll just start the engine so the heater will keep us warm." He did so, turning the vents toward her. "Is that warm enough?"

She nodded and stared straight ahead.

"I'm sorry I spent so much time cooling off last night that you walked home by yourself."

She shrugged.

"*Mamm* said to tell you she's sorry she argued with my *dat* last night and upset you."

She turned to look at him. "Nothing's ever going to change there, is it?"

Startled by the question, he didn't know what to say for a moment. "Maybe I shouldn't have invited you to supper the night before he had his test. He was anxious."

Her eyes widened. "I never thought I'd hear you make excuses for him."

David shrugged. "I can't believe it, either. But I didn't realize he was so worried about it."

"How is he? Did he have the test today?"

"*Ya*. But they won't have the results for a few days."

She bent her head and looked down at her hands folded in her lap. "This could go on for a long time. Sometimes people have to have chemo over and over."

He hadn't thought about that.

"The thing is, David, even if he gets better and doesn't need more chemo, he's not going to change. The two of you are always going to clash."

"We've gotten better."

She shook her head. "Last night, after I left your house, I got to thinking about what would happen if we got married."

"You're not worried I'm like him?"

"*Nee*. But if we didn't have our own place, we'd have to live at your house until we could afford one of our own. There's no room at my house, remember?"

Tears began to roll down her cheeks. "I can't do it, David. I couldn't bear to be in the middle of the kind of tension you have in your family."

"Lavina, you're getting ahead of things," he said quickly. "We can't even get married until after the harvest next year. We could have our own place by then."

"How?" she asked, pulling a tissue from her purse to mop at her tears. "Neither of us makes enough money to save up for a house with what we earn, let alone the farm you want."

He tried to take her hand in his but she wouldn't let him. "We don't know that. I can get a second job."

"Even that's not going to be enough."

"Have you lost your faith in us?" he asked quietly. "Have you lost your faith that God will provide?"

"Maybe I have," she said in such a low voice that he almost didn't hear her. "I've been waiting for us for a long time, David."

She took a deep breath. "I need some time alone. I think it would be best if we didn't see each other for a while."

With that she opened the door, got out, and ran into her house.

18

David sat there for several minutes, trying to understand what had just happened.

Once, when he'd been a teenager, he'd gone for a ride on a roller coaster at a local amusement park. What Lavina had just said reminded him of the sickening ups and downs he'd felt then.

He didn't blame her for being upset at the scene last night at supper. He'd been upset enough to go out to the barn to cool off. But he felt like she was blowing things all out of proportion. It wasn't like her. She'd always been so calm, so steady. His rock.

Apparently she had a breaking point he'd never been aware of.

Finally, he started his truck and made the short drive back to his house. His conversation with Bill that afternoon came back to him as he parked, locked the truck, and walked slowly into his house. Bill had commented that he'd been a little selfish with Lavina, saying that he'd let her help him through difficult times with his *dat,* but hadn't listened to her or supported her enough. The fact that she was as upset as she was now, when she didn't react impulsively, made him realize he hadn't been sensitive enough to her moods, her feelings sooner . . .

He'd gone over to her house with an apology and now he was returning in utter failure.

Fortunately, his parents had gone upstairs so he didn't have to tell his *mudder* what happened. He went upstairs quietly and threw himself down on his bed.

The thought of a future without Lavina in it was inconceivable.

He rolled over and punched his pillow, trying to get comfortable when his mind whirled and whirled with disturbing thoughts.

Hours later, he got up and got ready for bed, but he knew he wouldn't sleep that night.

He was downstairs before either of his parents the next morning, drinking coffee as the sun came up.

His *mudder* walked into the room and gasped when she saw him. "What are you doing up so early?" She narrowed her eyes. "Or are you just coming in?"

He'd have laughed at the irony of her thinking he'd been out having fun if it hadn't been so sad. "Couldn't sleep." He drained his cup and stood. "Going to take care of chores," he said briefly and headed out before she could ask more questions.

When he returned his *dat* sat drinking coffee at the table, and his *mudder* was transferring fried eggs from a cast iron skillet to a platter that held bacon. She smiled at David. "Just in time."

She set the platter in front of Amos. He immediately transferred two eggs and several strips of bacon to his plate.

David washed his hands at the sink. "*Danki*, but I'm not hungry. I'm going on in to work."

Waneta turned off the gas flame and put the back of her hand against his forehead. "Are you coming down with something?"

"*Nee*." Just a terminal case of heartbreak, he wanted to say. But how melodramatic was that?

"Something's wrong." She studied his face. "Tell me."

"Leave the boy alone. He's said he's *allrecht*." Amos heaped peach preserves on a piece of toast.

"I'm fine," he said again.

"Here, let me pack you a sandwich to take with you."

"You already packed me a lunch," he said, gesturing to the lunch box on the counter.

"This is for breakfast."

Because he didn't have the energy to argue with her and it was faster to give in, he watched her make a breakfast sandwich with a fried egg and several slices of bacon. She wrapped it in aluminum foil and put it in a brown paper bag, adding an apple and a couple of cookies.

"Quit fussing," Amos told her. "Wouldn't be the end of the world if he left without breakfast."

"*Nee*, it wouldn't," he agreed. "That ended last night."

His *mudder* frowned. "What are you talking about?"

"Never mind." He picked up his lunch bucket and started from the room, but his *mudder* grabbed his arm and wouldn't let go.

"Tell me."

"Lavina broke up with me."

"What'd you do now?" Amos asked him. "Have a fight with her?"

"I didn't do anything." He clenched his jaw. "I invited her to supper. You remember what happened?"

Amos had the grace to redden.

"*Ya*," he said. "She told me she didn't think she could handle it if we got married and had to live here and go through something like that."

Waneta burst into tears and fled the room.

Shaking his head, David left. He hadn't meant to upset his *mudder*. Hadn't even meant to upset his *dat*—if such a thing was possible. What *gut* did any of it do anyway? Nothing changed. Lavina had been right about that.

He left and drove to work. The weather suited his mood—heavy, gray clouds hung in the sky.

Bill found him doing inventory when he came into work.

"Boss told me you were in here. What's up?"

"Came in a little early and he put me to work in here."

"Something tells me it didn't go well with Lavina."

"She doesn't want to see me anymore."

"She dumped you?"

David winced. "I'm not sure everyone heard that."

"Sorry. Geez, she was that upset?"

"Seems she can't think about living in my house after we're married."

"But wouldn't you get your own place?"

"How am I going to do that? Most couples live with their parents until they can afford to buy their own home."

Bill sat down heavily on a nearby crate. "I hadn't thought about that."

"Unfortunately, she did."

Their boss stuck his head in the door. "Bill, I'm not paying you to sit around and gossip."

"No sir. What would you like me to do, sir?"

"Vinnie needs some help on the loading dock. Then you and David can make deliveries."

David couldn't help hoping it would take Bill a long time unloading. The last thing he wanted to do was talk about what had happened last night when he talked with Lavina.

Lavina loved her *schweschders,* but she didn't know how she was going to get through the day if they kept asking her how her evening had gone last night at David's house.

So she told them about the meal Waneta had prepared, how Amos looked, about every minor detail she could think of without mentioning the big blowup and without lying, and quickly changed the subject.

She just felt too raw inside to tell them what had happened. And it was so close to Christmas . . . which, when she thought about it, depressed her even more.

Fortunately, they were busy finishing up Christmas orders and no one noticed.

Except their *mudder.* Every time Lavina looked up she saw that her *mudder* was watching her and looking worried.

"Lavina, come help me fix lunch," she said, rising and setting aside her work.

She followed her downstairs into the kitchen.

"*Allrecht*, what happened?" her *mudder* asked gently.

She could have said she didn't want to talk about it and likely her *mudder* would have accepted that. Amish parents usually gave their grown *kinner* privacy about dating matters. But the sympathy in her *mudder's* eyes undid her.

So she told her the story, and as she did she kept a watch on the doorway to the stairs, so they wouldn't be surprised by her *schweschders* entering the kitchen.

"I'm so sorry, *kind.* Are you *schur* you don't want to see David again? It's a long time until next fall. You don't know that you and David wouldn't have your own home when you married."

"*Mamm*, what if I go through another year waiting for David and nothing changes?"

Linda took her hands in hers. "Can you see yourself wanting to marry anyone but David?"

"I think I have to try."

Her *mudder* hugged her. Just then they heard the clatter of footsteps on the stairs. Lavina pulled away and rushed to the refrigerator. Linda went to the stove and turned off the flame under the pot of soup that had been simmering since early morning.

"Oh, we thought lunch was ready already," Rose Anna said.

"Hungry?" Linda asked her. "You can wash your hands and slice the bread."

"Yum, I love soup on a cold day like this," Mary Elizabeth said. "I'll set the table."

Mary Elizabeth and Rose Anna chattered happily about Christmas. Since Mary Elizabeth had nearly finished the quilt begun before the stolen one was returned, she would be getting some extra money when she took it into Leah's. Rose Anna suggested that she could help finish it so they could go into town and do a little Christmas shopping. They always made most of their presents, but it was fun to see what was happening in the shops and say hello to friends like Leah and her *grossdochders* and Elizabeth and Saul.

"Why don't you two finish the quilt and Lavina and I will make some cookies?"

"Oh, I'd rather do that than sew," Rose Anna said, pouting.

"You promised," Mary Elizabeth reminded her.

"We'll bring the first batch up and have a tea party," their *mudder* said.

Rose Anna brightened and followed Mary Elizabeth upstairs.

"*Danki, Mamm.*"

She smiled. "That wasn't just for you. I feel in the mood to do something fun."

They were in the middle of stirring up a batch of gingerbread cookies when they heard a knock on the front door. Lavina went to answer it and was startled to see Waneta. Her thin face looked pale, and her eyes were red and puffy as if she'd been crying.

"Can we talk?"

Lavina held the door open. "Of course. Come in. Please sit down," she said, gesturing at the living room sofa. "Can I get you some tea or coffee?"

Waneta shook her head. "Nothing, *danki*." She pulled a tissue from her purse and dabbed at her nose. "I came to apologize."

"For what?"

"For the scene you witnessed in my home. David said—David said—" she broke off and began sobbing.

Lavina sat next to her on the sofa and patted her back. "What did David say?" She hoped he hadn't been harsh with his *mudder*.

"He said you told him you didn't think you could live in our home because of the way Amos and I got along."

Lavina didn't know what to say. She *had* said that.

"I'm afraid David's going to move out again," Waneta cried. "I can't lose him again. I don't want to lose you." She wiped her eyes with the tissue. "You've been like a *dochder* to me. Please tell me you'll reconsider."

"Waneta, he's not going to move out," Lavina said. "Not now." Surely he wouldn't when his *dat* was still ill. And it was so close to Christmas . . .

But who knew what he'd do? He'd told her he was staying, but that was before she'd told him she didn't want to see him anymore.

"Lavina, who was at the door?" her *mudder* asked as she walked into the room. "Oh, Waneta. Are you *allrecht*?"

Waneta just shook her head and began sobbing again.

Linda sat on the other side of her and put her arm around the woman.

"I'll go get some tissues," Lavina said and hurried from the room. She grabbed the box from the kitchen counter and tried to think what to do. In the end, she walked back toward the living room.

Her *mudder* was murmuring something to Waneta as she returned to the living room. Lavina sat next to Waneta and offered her the box.

"I'm sorry, I shouldn't have come," Waneta said, plucking some tissues out and mopping her face.

Linda patted her hand. "We have to trust God, Waneta. If our *kinner* are meant to be together, they will be."

She sighed. "I know."

Lavina didn't think she sounded like she really believed it.

"I should get back."

But she made no move to get up.

The oven timer buzzed. "Why don't you come in the kitchen and have some coffee and some gingerbread cookies before you leave?" Linda suggested.

"Gingerbread cookies?"

Linda nodded. "Come on. You can take some home to Amos if you want."

"I don't know as I feel nice enough to do that now," Waneta muttered as she followed them into the kitchen. She took off her coat and bonnet, hung them up on pegs near the door, then sat at the table.

Linda pulled two trays of cookies from the oven and set them on racks on the counter to cool while Lavina poured coffee for the three of them.

Lavina used a spatula to move the cooled cookies to a plate and set them on the table before Waneta. She took one for herself and bit in. It tasted spicy and reminded her of all the Christmases she'd made them with her *mudder* and her *schweschders*.

Waneta sipped her coffee and ate three cookies and began to look more cheerful. Linda stirred up some royal icing and set out little bowls of it with raisins, gumdrops, and other candies to decorate the cookies.

Mary Elizabeth and Rose Anna came downstairs and looked surprised to see Waneta.

"We smelled cookies," Mary Elizabeth said after greeting Waneta.

"When were you going to call us?" Rose Anna asked, looking disgruntled as she picked up a cookie.

"We were going to eat them all ourselves," Lavina said with a deadpan expression. She laughed when Rose Anna realized she was being teased.

The kitchen filled with laughter as they sat at the table and tried to outdo each other decorating the cookies. An hour passed before Waneta remembered that she'd said she had to get home.

"Have you gotten the results on the test Amos had?" Lavina asked her.

"Not yet."

"Let's make up a box of cookies for Amos," Linda suggested.

Each of them contributed a couple of cookies they'd decorated. Lavina wondered if the cheerful icing grins on the cookies would make taciturn Amos smile.

"I'll make *schur* he shares some with David," Waneta said.

Lavina felt her smile start to slip, then she forced herself to nod and smile harder.

Her *mudder* packed a basket with a frozen casserole and a fresh loaf of bread, as well as the cookies, and invited Waneta to stop by to help make more Christmas cookies anytime.

Lavina drew on a shawl and walked Waneta out to her buggy.

"Can I give you a hug?" Waneta asked her, looking uncertain.

"*Schur.*" She found herself wrapped in arms that trembled.

"I'll pray for you and David," she said. Then she climbed quickly into the buggy and drove away.

Lavina stood there watching the buggy travel down the road and felt unbearably sad.

David took the long road home.

He'd volunteered for overtime, stopped by to help his former landlady with a few errands, done everything he could think of for the past week to keep from going home right after work.

And he wanted to shut his eyes as he passed by Lavina's house on the way to his, but he didn't dare or he'd run off the road.

It had been one of the the longest days of his life—on a par with the first days he'd left the community last year.

David wondered if there was a worse time to be without the one you loved. Locals and tourists crowded the sidewalks of the shops he passed in town. Everyone looked happy and carried bulging shopping bags.

Englisch homes were decorated with lights and Christmas trees shone in front windows. His *mudder* had even attempted to make their house festive with evergreen boughs on the mantel and pots of bright red poinsettias. But she was quiet and moved like a ghost through the house. His *dat* spent a lot of time in their bedroom the last couple days.

When he pulled in the drive and shut off the truck engine, he sat there staring at the fields that lay barren waiting for spring planting. Who knew what would happen by then?

A buggy pulled in behind him. His *mudder* got out carrying a bag from the pharmacy.

"Why didn't you call me and ask me to pick that up?" he asked her as he waved to his *Aenti* Anna as she drove away.

"She came by and got me out of the house for a while."

They went inside and David set his lunch bucket on the kitchen counter. "I'm going out to the barn." He grabbed up the apple Nellie would expect and headed out.

When he returned his *mudder* met him at the back door. "Was your *dat* in the barn?"

"*Nee*. Why?"

"He's not in our room or the living room. Is the buggy in the barn?"

"*Ya*." David looked at the pegs near the door. "His jacket's here. He has to be in the house."

"I checked every bedroom," she said, her voice rising. "Where could he be?"

Their gazes went to the door of the *dawdi haus*. He was the first to move. "Stay here."

He opened the door and walked into the small apartment where his *grosseldres* had lived when his *dat* and *mudder* had taken over the farm many years ago. It smelled a little musty. The combination kitchen and dining area was empty, as was the tiny living room. He walked toward the bedroom and saw his *dat* stretched out on the bed, his eyes closed. David couldn't tell if he was breathing.

"Amos!" his *mudder* cried behind him.

He held her back with his arm and hurried toward him, fearing the worst. "*Daed*?"

"Amos!"

He jerked awake, pressing his hand to his chest. "*Mein Gott!* What is it? You scared me!"

David sank down on the bed, his knees weak. "What are you doing in here?"

"What, I can't take a nap in my own *haus*?" he demanded.

"Of course. But you've never come in here before," Waneta said, taking a seat in the armchair next to the bed.

He sat up. "I'm trying it out."

"Trying it out?"

Amos swung his legs over the side of the bed. "For when your *mudder* and I move in here."

David wondered if he was hearing things. "Well, that's never going to happen." He got to his feet.

"It will next fall."

Hadn't the man hurt him enough? "I told you, Lavina broke up with me."

"So talk to her."

"Amos, I told you I went to see her," Waneta said. "Nothing's changed."

"Something has. I called the doctor's office today. The PET scan results came back. There's no sign of cancer."

"*Mein Gott*," Waneta whispered, touching her hand to her throat. "Is it true?"

He nodded.

"I'm happy for you," David told him. His words came out sounding funny. It must be because he had trouble getting them past the lump that clogged his throat. "So this means you'll be out there planting your crops again like you said you would. I knew you could beat this."

"God's giving you another chance," Waneta said.

Amos looked at Waneta. "*Ya*. That's what I figure." He turned to David. "You ready to take over the farm?"

David was glad he was sitting. He felt the breath knocked out of him. "You mean that?"

Amos nodded. "Doesn't mean I won't have something to say sometimes."

"I—I'm *schur* you will."

"But it's yours to take on now. You better do a *gut* job."

"I will."

Amos glanced around the room. "This place will need to be fixed up some before your *mamm* and I move in here. It's sat empty since your *grosseldres* passed."

"I know. We can do it. We'll have the time before November next year."

Amos nodded. "Go hitch up the buggy for me, will you?"

"*Schur.* Where do you want me to drive you?"

"I'll drive myself."

His *dat* still looked tired and frail to him, but when he stood it was with a strength of purpose David hadn't seen in a while. He decided not to argue with him.

"Amos, where are you going?" Waneta trailed after him.

"I'll tell you after I see how things go."

David and his *mudder* exchanged baffled looks.

"You going to go hitch the buggy or do I need to do it?" Amos demanded.

"I'm going."

As he left the room he heard Amos asking what was for supper.

His world had shifted, he reflected. But some things never changed.

A short time later David stood at the front door watching his *dat* drive down the road. He stopped breathing when he saw the buggy slow at the driveway of Lavina's house and then park. His *dat* got out and walked up to the front door. David blinked, wondering if he was seeing things. *Nee,* he was seeing clearly. He started breathing again.

His *mudder* was singing a hymn as she moved around the kitchen. David walked in and took a seat at the table. "I don't think *Daed* will be gone long."

"*Nee?*" His *mudder* turned. "Why?"

"He stopped at Lavina's house."

"Really?" She beamed.

"Don't get your hopes up."

"You don't know how persuasive your *dat* can be when he wants to be."

"*Nee*, I've never seen that side of him."

She went to the cupboard, got plates, and began setting the table. David watched her lay four place settings. "Maybe you just need to believe."

He stared at her. "Maybe I do." He looked around. "Do you have a piece of paper and a marker?"

"Lavina, would you come downstairs, please?"

She put down the quilt she'd been sewing and went down to see what her *mudder* wanted. When she walked into the kitchen she got a shock when she saw who was sitting at the table. Amos Stoltzfus sat there looking stern and silent.

"Amos wants to talk to you." Her *mudder* set a cup of coffee before him. "I'll be in the living room if you need me."

"Will you sit?" he asked politely as if it was an everyday thing for him to stop by for coffee.

She nodded and sat. What on earth was he doing here? First Waneta and now him.

"Waneta's been crying ever since David told us what you said."

"I'm sorry."

"*Nee*. You have nothing to be sorry about." He stared into his coffee for a long moment then looked up at her. "A little while ago I told David he'd be taking over the farm starting with the spring planting."

She felt her heart skip a beat. "That's *gut*."

He nodded. "I can't change the past. But I can try to change the way things are in the future."

She didn't know what to say so she stayed silent.

"Do you know what I'm trying to say?" He fidgeted and looked uncomfortable.

He was trying to apologize, she realized. Stunned, she could only stare at him. "I think so," she said slowly.

"If I upset you, well, then you're going to have to speak up," he told her abruptly. "Do you think you can do that?"

His bushy eyebrows drew together in a frown that at one time would have intimidated her. But things seemed different . . .

"*Ya*, I think I can do that." She sat up straighter. "I can do that," she said more positively.

"Then tell your *mudder* you're going to eat supper with us tonight."

She grinned. He was telling, not asking, but she was fine with that. She rose and went into the living room. Her *mudder* was sitting on the sofa looking tense. The minute she saw Lavina she jumped up.

"Is everything *allrecht*?"

Lavina nodded. "Amos wants me to eat supper with them."

Her *mudder's* eyebrows rose. "And what do you want to do?"

"I want to go."

Linda smiled. "Then you should go."

Lavina returned to the kitchen for her jacket and bonnet. Amos sat there with a half-eaten gingerbread man in his hand and crumbs in his beard. He gave her an embarrassed smile. "Got *hungerich* waiting."

She slipped on her coat and tied her bonnet. "Then we should get going."

He was silent on the short drive to his home. It was as if he'd used up all his words.

Lavina didn't say anything, feeling a little apprehensive of what was happening.

And then when he pulled into the drive she saw David standing beside his truck. There was a hand-lettered sign in the rear window. It read *For Sale*.

Then he looked up at her and he smiled. He walked over, opened the door to the buggy, and held out his hand.

19

David stared at Lavina. "I don't know what to say."

His gaze ran over her face. He hadn't thought he'd see her for a very long time. And never here.

"What, you need me to give you the words, too?" Amos barked. "Come in to supper, Lavina."

David grinned. "Come in to supper, Lavina," he repeated.

Amos got out of the buggy. "Put Nellie up, David."

"I will," he said, not taking his eyes off Lavina. "What just happened?" he asked her.

He watched her glance at his *dat* as he walked into the house, then she met his gaze.

"I think he apologized to me. Then he asked me to come to supper. Actually, he told me I was coming to supper."

She slipped out of the buggy but didn't let go of his hand.

"If it was an apology you ought to know. Then again, I don't remember him ever apologizing to anyone."

He squeezed her hand then reluctantly let it go to unhitch Nellie.

"I think it's as close as he ever gets to one. I'll take it."

He walked Nellie to her stall, made sure it was locked, then turned to Lavina and they walked toward the back door of the house. "I know someone else who's going to be very happy here."

When they entered the kitchen David saw his *dat* had already seated himself at the table. His *mudder* turned from the stove and when she saw Lavina, rushed to hug her. The two women embraced for a long moment. When they parted he saw their eyes were damp with tears.

"Now, is there anything I can do to help?" Lavina asked Waneta when they stepped away from their embrace.

"Everything's ready."

David watched Lavina's expression when she turned and saw that four places had been set at the table. Her gaze flew to his, and he smiled and found himself swallowing hard at the lump that formed in his throat. He pulled out her chair and she slid into it.

Prayers of thanks had been said at this big old kitchen table many, many times over the years, but David didn't think any had been as meaningful to him in his life. When it was over he looked at his *mudder,* and he realized he hadn't seen her so happy for a very long time. His *dat*? Well, he didn't wear the same expression but his attitude seemed lighter, and he wasn't glaring and that said a lot. He even joined in the conversation as the platter of fried chicken and bowls of vegetables were passed around.

"How are your *grosseldres* liking Pinecraft?" Waneta asked Lavina as she passed her the basket of rolls.

"They're loving it. I'm glad their friends talked them into trying it for the winter," Lavina told her as she split a roll and buttered it. "We miss them, but it's nice that they're away from the cold weather this winter."

"Next time you come over ask *Mamm* to show you the postcards we've been getting. It looks so pretty in Florida with all the palm trees and the beach with its white sand. *Grossmudder* says the women wear flip-flops, and everyone rides bicycles to get where they want. *Grossdaadi* has been fishing and saw some fish with really big teeth. He wrote that they're called garfish. And one day he saw an alligator."

"People shouldn't be flitting off like that," Amos said bluntly. "Amish don't belong in Florida."

The table got quiet. He looked up from his plate. "Well, just seems strange, that's all," he amended.

"I've always wanted to go."

David stared at her. "I didn't know that."

"*Grossmudder* said she went out and picked an orange from the tree in her front yard. She said it's eighty degrees in Florida right now, and they're enjoying playing shuffleboard and eating ice cream outside afterward."

"I'll bet the warm weather is helping her arthritis," Waneta said. "The cold gets into old bones. The cold and the damp."

"That's what she said before they left. The fried chicken is so good, Waneta."

"She makes the best in Paradise," Amos said, taking a second piece. He bit into it with relish.

"Just in Paradise?" she asked mildly and got a chuckle—an actual chuckle—from his *dat*.

David exchanged a surprised look with Lavina.

"Maybe we could go sometime," Amos said.

"Go where?" Waneta asked him as she poured gravy on her mashed potatoes.

"To Pinecraft."

"*Mamm*, the gravy," David said.

"What?" She stared at him with a blank expression.

He gestured at the gravy boat in her hand. She looked down and saw that gravy was pooling all over her plate, covering the potatoes and the green beans and creamed corn.

She tilted the boat back and replaced it on the table. "Silly me."

"We could spend a week there once I can get away from the farm next year. Leave the young folk to take care of things."

"That would be so *wunderbaar,*" Waneta managed as she stared at him.

She rose to get a small bowl and spent a lot of time scooping up the excess gravy into it, but David could tell she was doing it more because she was emotional than because she had too much on her plate.

"Fishing's *gut*, huh?" Amos asked Lavina.

"*Ya*, that's what *Grossdaadi* says."

"I haven't fished in years. Haven't had the time."

It was happening, David thought, listening to him. It was really happening. Lavina was sitting here with his family, and they were actually acting like a family—one that wasn't stiff and unpleasant and . . . He had to take a sip of water so he could get food past the lump in his throat.

His gaze went to the door that led to the *dawdi haus*. Soon he and his *dat* would be renovating the rooms in it. It was hard to believe. Encouraged, he chose another piece of chicken and began eating it.

The conversation moved on to Lavina's quilting class. Waneta wanted to know how it was going, and that led to her telling them about the presents the women were making for Christmas.

"You should see the cute things they're sewing," Lavina told her. "I got some ideas from Leah's shop. And Mary Elizabeth and Rose Anna are going into town tomorrow to look for some small, inexpensive presents for the *kinner* at the shelter."

"I haven't thought much about Christmas," Waneta said.

"Maybe we could go shopping this week. It's fun to walk around the stores this time of year."

"I'd like that." She looked at her *mann*. "We got the best present this year, didn't we, Amos?"

He looked up and smiled at her. "*Ya*."

David reached under the table and squeezed Lavina's hand. She smiled at him.

So had they, he thought. So had they.

Later, as they took a drive after the dishes were done and goodbyes said for the evening, Lavina thought about what had just happened.

She turned to David. "You know what you need to do?"

"What's that?"

She pulled her hand away from his. "First, keep both hands on the wheel. You don't want an accident before you sell this truck." She paused for a moment. "You need to contact your *bruders* and tell them about your *dat* and his test, and about the farm. About all of it."

"I'm not sure they'll believe me."

"They will," she said. "But don't call them. Go see them."

"You might be right."

A few minutes later they passed through town. Traffic clogged the streets. People packed the sidewalks. Some of the shops and stores had stayed open a little later for holiday shoppers.

"That was nice of you to invite *Mamm* to go shopping."

She shrugged as she watched the shoppers happily lugging their stuffed shopping bags. "You know I like her." She looked at him. "Last time we said something about getting out of the house your *dat* blew up."

He glanced at her briefly. "I remember. That was the night before the test. Life certainly can take a turn, can't it?"

Lavina remembered walking into her kitchen and seeing Amos sitting there. She remembered watching him struggle through an apology.

And then she remembered getting into the buggy with him and seeing David standing in the drive, putting a For Sale sign on this very truck.

She turned and looked at the square white sign in the corner of the rear windshield, as if she needed to see it again to believe it.

When she shifted back to look ahead she saw him glance at her.

"It's true," he said quietly. "Need me to pinch you?"

She laughed. "*Nee, danki.*"

A little later, she reluctantly told him that they needed to head home. "We have work tomorrow."

He nodded and made a U-turn and headed in that direction. As he pulled into her driveway she thought about how this time next year this *haus* wouldn't be the one she'd be walking into. And she wouldn't be walking in by herself.

"Do you think your family will be surprised?" he asked her when she didn't immediately get out.

"I don't think so. After all, at least two of them helped you by playing matchmaker." When he didn't immediately respond she gave him a stern look.

"True," he admitted. He turned off the ignition.

"And *Mamm* was here when your *dat* came earlier today. Then I told her he wanted me to have supper at your *haus*. So I don't think she'll be surprised. So that just leaves my *dat*."

"Should I come in and talk to him?"

"No need. I'll do it. He likes you, and he wants whatever makes me happy."

He leaned over and kissed her. "That's what I want, too. To make you happy."

"I want to make you happy, too."

She glanced at the door. Some of her friends had parents who were overprotective, but she knew hers weren't lurking near the front door wondering why she hadn't come in yet.

And she couldn't wait to share her news with her family. They had loved her and been so supportive for the past year.

She put her hand on the door handle. "Come for supper tomorrow?"

"I will. *Danki*. Love you."

"Love you, too." She glanced around, then leaned over and gave him a quick kiss. "Sweet dreams."

"I'll dream of you," he said, his eyes full of love.

Her entire family was sitting in the living room when she walked in. They looked up.

Most of the time Amish couples kept their plans private until shortly before their wedding. But she couldn't keep it a secret. She didn't want to. All of them wore such expectant expressions. Even her *dat*.

"David and I are together again, and his *dat* is turning the farm over to him," she told them, feeling her heart near to bursting as she said it. "Amos got *gut* news from his test. I think he realized he's been given a second chance. And he realizes he's upset Waneta and me. He's not a hundred percent different, but he seemed to be trying a lot harder to be a considerate person with David and Waneta and me tonight. And he told me I'm to speak up if he upsets me."

She lifted her chin and grinned. "I told him I can do that."

Mary Elizabeth and Rose Anna jumped up and hugged her. Their *mudder* joined them after a moment, wiping her eyes with a tissue.

"We love you," her *mudder* said. "We're so happy for you."

When they all parted Lavina looked over at her *dat*. He stood, this man who was the first man she loved, waiting patiently and simply held out his arms.

Lavina cried as she stepped into his embrace. "I love you, *Daed*."

Lavina was peeking out the front window so she surprised Kate by opening the door before she could knock.

"You're right on time!" Lavina said with a smile. "Everything's ready to go into the car."

"You're taking all that?"

"And more," said Mary Elizabeth as she walked into the living room from the kitchen. She had a shopping bag hung on one arm and carried a big plastic container of baked goods.

"I'm coming too," Rose Anna cried as she followed Mary Elizabeth. Her arms were loaded with more plastic containers. She beamed at Kate. "Thank you for inviting me to the Christmas party at the shelter."

"I'm glad you could come. Maybe you'll come to the quilting class sometime."

Rose Anna nodded. "Maybe."

Lavina piled plastic containers in Kate's waiting arms then picked up two containers and a shopping bag.

"This is too much," Kate told her. "You shouldn't have gone to all this trouble."

"It was no trouble," Lavina told her. "We love to bake. Don't we?" she asked, glancing over her shoulder at her *schweschders*.

"We do," Mary Elizabeth and Rose Anna chimed in together.

They loaded the trunk with plastic containers and shopping bags, and then everyone piled into the car. A light snow was falling when they got to the shelter. They hurried inside with all the goodies.

"I'm already ready for spring," Kate said as she shed her coat, revealing a Christmasy red wool dress.

"Your dress is so pretty," Rose Anna said. "I love red."

She and Lavina wore dark green. Mary Elizabeth wore her favorite dark blue.

"Thank you. It only gets out at Christmastime," Kate said, brushing a piece of lint from the dress. She touched the silly little Santa pin on her shoulder. "My kids gave me this."

Lavina thought Kate always looked so nice whether she wore her police uniform or civilian clothes.

Women and children were already assembling in the big dining room. A Christmas tree stood in the corner decorated with ornaments the members of the quilt class had made. Ellie and some of the children were hanging ornaments they'd made: construction paper chains, stars fashioned of Popsicle sticks dusted with glitter, little clear plastic balls with photos inside that someone had taken of them.

Presents were stacked under the tree, small ones wrapped in fabric or Christmas paper the children had made. Lavina walked over with two shopping bags and began pulling out the presents she and her *schweschders* had brought. The children immediately wanted to help her so she let them. She saw they were looking for their names on the tag and trying not to show that's what they were doing. There was nothing breakable in the packages, and she loved the quick smiles she got when they saw their names.

Mary Elizabeth and Rose Anna opened the plastic containers and began setting out the Christmas cookies and decorated cupcakes, so the children swarmed over and watched their progress with big eyes.

The three of them and their *mudder* had spent days baking for the shelter Christmas party and for their own quiet Christmas celebrations at home. The house smelled of sugar and spice and everything nice.

Lavina joined them and arranged a plate of gingerbread cookies. As she did she found herself wondering if David had talked to his *bruders* yet about their *dat's* test results, the farm, and most important, the invitation to the family party at her *haus* on Christmas Eve. She knew Waneta hoped so very much that Sam and John would come. Amos hadn't said anything but she knew he wouldn't. The two *bruders* were never discussed.

Everyone took a seat and listened to the children sing Christmas carols. Pearl and some of the women had made little sandwiches, and potato and macaroni salads, and a platter of raw vegetables with a dip. Everything was devoured, and then the cookies and cupcakes were passed around and were a big hit.

"You didn't have to bring presents," Kate told Lavina quietly, as Ellie was allowed to read the names on the tags and another little girl passed the presents out.

"I'm so glad you invited me to the class here," Lavina told her. "They're just little sewing kits. Leah gave me a wonderful deal. And Mary Elizabeth and Rose Anna found the books for the children on sale. It wasn't much."

"It's a very big thing for everyone," Pearl said.

Lavina glanced around. She hadn't realized the woman was standing behind her.

"They have so little right now. But they've made presents for each other and everyone's celebrating like a family."

The family celebration the next night was quieter, more spiritual but no less fun.

The family—Lavina and her *schweschders* and *mudder* and *dat* and David and Waneta and Amos—gathered in the living room around a crackling fire.

Snow had begun to fall again, but inside it was so warm and secure.

Evergreens on the mantel scented the air and bayberry, cinnamon, and vanilla candles glowed. Bright red poinsettias were placed around the room. Colorfully wrapped packages were heaped on a table. They'd open them later, not tonight when the celebration was quiet and spiritual.

A big Bible sat on the small table beside her *dat's* chair, waiting for him to read the story of the birth of the Christ child. Lavina found herself wondering why he hadn't started yet. She went into the kitchen to ask her *mudder* and found her checking the ham baking in the oven. The table was loaded with the meal they'd eat after the Bible story and prayers. Her mouth watered at the scents of ham, sweet potatoes, baked corn pudding, and all the sweet baked desserts.

Lavina glanced at the clock. "Shouldn't we start the prayers and story? Everyone's here."

Linda sighed. "I was so hoping—" she trailed off as Waneta walked into the room.

"Anything I can do to help?" Waneta asked, trying to look cheerful.

But Lavina could see her lips trembling. She went to her and put her arm around the woman's waist.

"I'm sorry," she said, blinking back tears. "I'd just hoped . . ."

She jerked when they heard the knock on the front door. The three of them turned, straining to hear who was at the door.

"Merry Christmas!" familiar male voices boomed.

"Sam! John!" Waneta cried and fled the room.

Lavina followed her and watched David's two *bruders* walking into the living room. They carried presents in their arms and shook off the snow dusting their hats and jackets. Their *mudder* threw her arms around them and wept. Amos stood slowly, his expression shocked.

David came to stand beside Lavina. "*Danki* for pushing me to ask them to come. It's only for one night but—"

"But it's a start," she finished, smiling up at him. "Merry Christmas, *Lieb*."

"Merry Christmas," he said. "I love you. And I can't wait for our first Christmas next year."

"Next year," she said, nodding, thinking it'd be their first as a married couple. "It'll be an even more *wunderbaar* Christmas!"

Recipes

Pennsylvania Dutch Baked Corn Pudding

A traditional recipe for the Thanksgiving dinner in the Amish or Mennonite home.

2½ cups of corn, canned, fresh, or frozen
1 tablespoon sugar
1 teaspoon salt
⅛ teaspoon freshly ground pepper (or white pepper)
1½ tablespoons all-purpose flour
2½ tablespoons melted butter
3 eggs, beaten
1 cup whole milk
1 teaspoon vanilla
Dash of cinnamon
Pinch of nutmeg

Directions

Preheat oven to 350 degrees. Drain corn if canned. Thaw corn if frozen. Mix all ingredients in a 1½-quart greased baking dish.

Bake for 35 minutes. Serves 8.

Rice Pudding

2 cups cooked rice (white or brown)
about 3 cups milk
½ cup sugar
⅛ teaspoon salt
1½ teaspoon vanilla
½ cup raisins (regular or golden raisins)
spices to taste . . . like cinnamon, nutmeg, allspice, and so on
½ cup nuts (optional)

Directions

Combine all ingredients, except spices, and bring to a boil. Cook until most of the milk is absorbed. Add spices. Add nuts if desired.

Serve hot or cold. Serves 2 to 4.

Banana Crumb Cake

2 cups all-purpose flour
1 tablespoon baking powder
1 teaspoon salt
3 ripe bananas
½ cup melted butter
2 cups granulated sugar
2 eggs
1 cup sour milk (add 1 tablespoon vinegar to milk and let sit 5 minutes)
1 tablespoon vanilla extract

For the streusel:

¾ cup melted butter
1 ½ cups light brown sugar
1 ½ cups all-purpose flour
1 teaspoon cinnamon

For the glaze:

1 cup powdered sugar
1 teaspoon vanilla extract
2 tablespoons cream

Directions

Preheat oven to 350 degrees. Grease a 9×13-inch baking dish with cooking spray; set aside. In a medium bowl, whisk together flour, baking powder, and salt. In another bowl, mash bananas. Mix in butter until combined and then mix in sugar, eggs, milk, and vanilla. With mixer running on low, carefully add flour mixture and mix until just combined. Prepare streusel by combining all the ingredients in a medium bowl, except melted butter. Blend in the butter with a pastry blender or fork, until coarse crumbs forms. Pour half of the batter into the prepared pan. Top with 1/3 of the crumb mixture. Cover the filling with the remaining batter and top with remaining crumb mixture.

Bake for 50 to 55 minutes until the center is set and a toothpick comes out clean. Cool for at least one hour.

Mix together the glaze ingredients, and drizzle over the cake before serving.

Beef Stew

2 pounds top round steak, cut into bite-size chunks
4 carrots, peeled and sliced
4 potatoes, peeled and sliced
1 package dry onion soup mix
1 can cream of celery or cream of chicken soup
1 can ginger ale
just enough water to cover all ingredients

Directions

Preheat oven to 350 degrees. Mix all ingredients thoroughly. You don't have to brown the meat. Place in an ovenproof casserole dish. Cover tightly with foil. Bake for 3 hours. Do not peek!

Rachel Ann's Gingerbread Cookies

3 cups all-purpose flour
1½ teaspoons baking powder
¾ teaspoon baking soda
¼ teaspoon salt
1 tablespoon ground ginger
1¾ teaspoons ground cinnamon
¼ teaspoon ground cloves
6 tablespoons unsalted butter
¾ cup firmly packed dark brown sugar
1 large egg
½ cup molasses
2 teaspoons vanilla
1 teaspoon finely grated lemon zest (optional)

Directions

Preheat oven to 375 degrees.

Prepare baking sheets by lining with parchment paper, or grease baking sheets with a little shortening.

In a small bowl, whisk together flour, baking powder, baking soda, salt, ginger, cinnamon, and cloves until well blended. In a large bowl beat butter, brown sugar, and egg on medium speed until well blended. Add molasses, vanilla, and lemon zest and continue to mix until well blended. Gradually stir in dry ingredients until blended and smooth. Divide dough in half and wrap each half in plastic and let stand at room temperature for at least 2 hours or up to 8 hours. (Dough can be stored in the refrigerator for up to 4 days. Return to room temp before using.) Place one portion of the dough on a lightly floured surface.

Sprinkle flour over dough and rolling pin. Roll dough to a scant ¼-inch thick. Use additional flour to avoid sticking.

Cut out cookies with gingerbread man cookie cutter. Space cookies 1½ inches apart on the baking sheets. Bake one sheet at a time for 7-10 minutes (the lower time will give you softer cookies—very good!). Remove cookie sheet from oven and allow the cookies to stand until they are firm enough to move to a wire rack to cool.

After cookies are cool you may decorate them any way you like. Rachel Ann likes to decorate them as a gingerbread man, woman, and children.

Glossary

ab im kop—off in the head. Crazy.
allrecht—all right
boppli—baby
bruder—brother
Daed—Dad
danki—thank you
dat—father
Der hochmut kummt vor dem fall. Pride goeth before the fall.
dippy eggs—over-easy eggs
Englischer—what the Amish call us
fraa—wife
grossdaadi—grandfather
grosseldere—grandparents
grossmudder—grandmother
Guder mariye—good morning
Gut-n-Owed—good evening
haus—house
hochmut—pride
kaffe—coffee
kapp—prayer covering or cap worn by girls and women
kind, kinner—child, children
lieb—love
liebschen—dearest or dear one
maedels—young single women
Mamm—Mom
mann—husband
mudder—mother
nee—no
Ordnung—The rules of the Amish, both written and unwritten. Certain behavior has been expected within the Amish community for many, many years. These rules vary from community to

community, but the most common are to have no electricity in the home, to not own or drive an automobile, and to dress a certain way.

Pennsylvania *Deitsch*—Pennsylvania German

roasht—a type of stuffing in chicken, often served at weddings

Rumschpringe—time period when teenagers are allowed to experience the *Englisch* world while deciding if they should join the church

schul—school

schur—sure

schweschder—sister

sohn—son

verdraue—trust

wilkumm—welcome

wunderbaar—wonderful

ya—yes

Group Discussion Questions for Return to Paradise

Spoiler alert! Please don't read before completing the book as the questions contain spoilers!

1. What does home mean to you? Is it the place you live? Your family or friends?
2. Where was your favorite place to live? Why? What would be the perfect place to live? What is your dream home? Dream job?
3. What was your relationship with your parents when you were growing up? Good? Troubled with conflicts? How do you get along with them now as an adult?
4. Have you ever had to walk away from a relationship with a family member or a good friend who felt like family? Why? What happened? How did you handle it?
5. Sometimes family is made up of our mother, father, and siblings. Sometimes it's made of friends who become family. Do you have friends who are family to you? How did this happen?
6. David's friend Bill says you can't go home again. Unlike the story of the prodigal son in the Bible, David's return to his family is not embraced by his father. Why do you think these two men find it so difficult to get along? Did David's mother help or hurt this struggle?
7. Many Amish believe God has set aside a marriage partner for them. Do you believe this? Do you believe in love at first sight?
8. David asks Lavina for a second chance after leaving her and his home in Paradise. Did you think she was too hard on him and should have given him the opportunity to help bring healing to their relationship sooner in the book? Why or why not?

9. Lavina and her sisters are in their twenties and are unmarried. They still live with their parents. Do you think this is a good idea? Would you want your grown child to live with you?
10. When a valuable quilt is stolen Lavina and her sister, Mary Elizabeth, refuse to prosecute the thief. The Amish seldom prosecute those who harm them or steal from them. Do you think they are right or wrong?
11. David returned home to help his mother when his father was diagnosed with cancer. David's brothers refuse to do so. What would you say to his brothers?
12. Sometimes it takes a crisis to make people change. Nearly everyone has had some life-changing event that causes them to reevaluate and change. What were those events for you? How did you change? Were you happy with the change? Why or why not?

The Coming Home Series

Three brothers left the Amish community of Paradise, Pennsylvania two years ago, and became part of the Englisch *community. Now three sisters will try to persuade them to come home, to where they belong . . .*

David, Samuel, and John Stoltzfus—three brothers—left the Amish community a year ago to live in the *Englisch* world for a variety of reasons—some known, some a mystery. Lavina, Mary Elizabeth, and Rose Anna Zook—three sisters—loved them and have never forgotten them. These couples will meet up again and forge a new relationship. Each woman is determined to bring her man back into the Amish fold. Each man thinks that his break with his faith—with his God—and his community is too great. Each woman is convinced that this is not true, that with her love—and God's—faith, love, and happiness will prevail.

In Book 2 of the series, *Seasons in Paradise*, Samuel follows his older brother into the *Englisch* world when he clashes with his father. But there's more to his leaving than what he says. And Mary Elizabeth, the woman he was starting to love before he left the community, is determined to find out the reason so they can be together again.

Here's a sample.

1

Mary Elizabeth always thought there was nothing lovelier than spring in Paradise, Pennsylvania.

Today the sky was a rich blue, not the gray it had been too long this past winter. The clouds that scudded overhead were soft clumps and a pure white, not heavy and dark and spitting snow or rain.

A warm breeze carried the scents of flowers and plants and . . .

Manure and fertilizer.

Her nose wrinkled as she stood on the back porch of her *schweschder* Lavina's big old farmhouse and watched David, Lavina's *mann*, working with his *bruders*, Samuel and John, fertilizing the fields.

Well, to be honest, she watched Samuel, not the other men. Samuel and John came nearly every weekend now that spring planting was taking place in Lancaster County. It took all three of the *bruders* as well as occasional help from their *dat*, Amos, to do the planting, as it would the eventual nurturing of the crop. It would take the four of them and some of the men from the community to harvest come November.

She'd begun to think Amos would never turn the farm over to David. He'd finally despaired at their fighting. Amos had been so difficult he'd driven David, then Samuel and John away.

David had returned to Paradise to help his *mudder* take care of his *dat* when he got the cancer. No one had been more surprised than David and Lavina when Amos had a change of heart after recovering and decided to turn the farm over to his *sohn*.

Mary Elizabeth knew she would never forget this Christmas past, when Samuel and John walked into her *haus* and surprised both families after an absence of almost a year. But that return was brief and temporary.

Both Samuel and John said it was *wunderbaar* that their *dat* had recovered, and they were thrilled that David, the eldest, would take over the family farm. But they refused to return home or to the Amish community the *bruders* had grown up in.

It was a miracle, she'd thought, when they came to celebrate the birth of the Christ child that night. But her hopes that Samuel would stay had been dashed just hours later. The two *bruders* went back to their apartment in town that night.

Mary Elizabeth had thought her heart was broken when Samuel followed David out of the community, but that Christmas night she'd found it was possible for her heart to be broken a second time.

So now she watched Samuel working in the fields she knew he loved but would leave after supper at day's end. And she knew she had to stop yearning and find someone else. She didn't feel like an old maid at twenty-three, but she wanted to make a home with a *mann* she loved, have *kinner*. Be loved and be happy.

"Mary Elizabeth, *kumm* inside and have some iced tea with me."

She turned and smiled at Lavina. Her *schweschder* seemed to glow these days. She'd married David after the harvest in November and now, several months later, she was obviously enjoying being a new *fraa* and making a home.

Mary Elizabeth wondered if there was a reason her *schweschder* glowed besides being a new bride . . . many Amish started their families early. And Lavina and David had lost a year of being together when he had lived away from the community.

So far Lavina hadn't said anything and with a voluminous apron tied over her dress, looked slim as ever.

"See if Waneta would like to come have some iced tea with us," Lavina said as she poured the tea over ice in tall glasses.

Mary Elizabeth knocked on the door of the *dawdi haus* and Waneta opened it. "Would you like to have some iced tea with us?"

"*Danki*, that would be nice." The older woman smiled, walked into the kitchen and took a seat. "It's *gut* to see you, Mary Elizabeth."

"You, too."

Had Waneta noticed how often she came to visit—and so often on the weekends? Mary Elizabeth wondered.

The three of them chatted easily as they drank the tea and ate some chocolate chip cookies Lavina had baked earlier that day. Waneta talked about making some curtains for the *dawdi haus* and seemed happy to be living there, now that Lavina and David had taken over the main part of the *haus*.

"Don't you love the color of the kitchen paint Lavina chose?" she asked Mary Elizabeth. "Yellow is so cheerful. It reminds me of the daffodils that are blooming in front of the *haus* now that it's spring."

Lavina smiled at her. "I'm glad you like it." She looked at Mary Elizabeth. "We painted the kitchen in the *dawdi haus* the same color after Waneta saw how it looked in here."

Waneta took a sip of her tea. "Amos never thought we needed to paint in here, but it had been years since we did it, and it really brightens up the room."

Mary Elizabeth was glad to see how well her *schweschder* and Waneta got along. The two had always been close, and she knew Waneta was grateful that Lavina had talked David into returning when Amos was diagnosed with the cancer more than a year ago.

Amos walked in a few minutes later, hung his wide-brimmed straw hat on a peg near the door, and washed his hands at the kitchen sink. Waneta jumped to her feet and hurried to pour him a glass of iced tea as he took a seat at the table.

"It's warm out there," he said. "Warm but there's a breeze."

"Maybe you should take a little rest. You don't want to overdo."

He frowned as he took a long swallow of tea. "I'll see how I feel after I have this."

"Is the planting going well?" Mary Elizabeth asked him.

He nodded. "After all the arguing about trying new crops and fancy new methods, David's planting exactly what I'd planned." He looked smug.

Mary Elizabeth exchanged glances with Lavina, and her *schweschder* warned her with a shake of the head not to say anything. But Mary Elizabeth knew better. David was planting what his *dat* had planned because the order had been placed months ago and because he was grateful that he'd been given the farm. Without that gift, without Amos softening, David would have had a very hard time buying a farm in Lancaster County.

"Is David coming in for a break?" Lavina asked Amos as she pushed the plate closer to him.

He picked up a cookie and bit into it. "*Nee*, no one wanted to stop yet. Rain's coming later this afternoon, and they want to get as much done as possible."

Lavina looked at Mary Elizabeth. "I think I'll take some cold drinks out to them."

"I'll help," Mary Elizabeth said.

"*Danki*."

"I think I'll take a rest after all," Amos said. "*Danki* for the tea and cookies, Lavina."

"*Ya, danki*." Waneta said. "I think I'll go get supper started. *Gut* to see you again, Mary Elizabeth."

Amos nodded to her and the couple went into the *dawdi haus* and shut the door.

Lavina and Mary Elizabeth filled glasses with ice and tea. "Are you sure you want to do this? Samuel's out there."

Mary Elizabeth sighed. "I know. I want to talk to him."

"I see."

"I'm probably *ab im kop*, but I'm still in love with him."

"I know that feeling. I couldn't forget David after he stayed away for a year."

"Don't tell David what I said."

"You think he can't guess after you and Samuel dated?"

"*Nee*, I guess you're right."

They put the glasses on a tray with a plate of cookies and carried them out to the edge of the field the men were working in. An old table had been placed there so trays could be set on it to serve workers in the field.

Lavina waved to them and the men stopped working and walked over.

David was the first to reach them. He took off his straw hat and wiped his forehead with a bandanna before he accepted a glass of iced tea. Mary Elizabeth saw the love in David's eyes as he gazed at her *schweschder* and looked away, feeling it was a very private moment between the two of them.

Her eyes met Samuel's. He reached for a glass of tea, and he gulped down half of it. She watched the muscles move in the long column of his tanned throat as he swallowed.

"It's warm today," she said as she held out the plate of cookies to him.

"Hey, do I get some tea?" John demanded as he stepped up to the table.

"*Schur*," Mary Elizabeth said, handing him a glass with barely a glance.

"Talk about making a guy feel welcome," he muttered when she continued to look at Samuel.

"What?" Mary Elizabeth turned to John.

"Nothing."

The three *bruders* looked so much alike they could have been triplets—tall, square-jawed, with dark blue eyes so often serious. Samuel and John wore their brown, almost black hair in an *Englisch* cut because they still lived in that world.

"Where's Rose Anna?" John asked.

Mary Elizabeth tore her gaze from Samuel and gave John a chilly glance. "She wasn't feeling well," she said shortly.

He set the empty glass down on the tray. "Well, that was cooling," he said. He picked up one of the cookies and walked over to sit on the back porch.

Mary Elizabeth couldn't help it. The three Zook *schweschders* had always loved the three Stoltzfus *bruders*. So far only one of the *schweschders* had married one of them.

When she glanced back at Samuel, she was surprised by a look of sadness in his eyes before he set the glass down. "*Danki*."

He glanced up at the sky, beginning to cloud over and turned to David. "Ready?"

David nodded. "I'll be in soon," he told Lavina and set his glass on the tray.

Lavina glanced at the sky. "Watch for lightning."

"I will."

Lavina picked up the tray and they walked back to the *haus*. "Do you want to stay for supper? Samuel and John are eating with us before they go home. It's the least I can do when they're helping David."

Mary Elizabeth bit her lip. "It might give me a chance to talk to him for a few minutes afterward." She took a deep breath. "I'm just thinking that it's time we either got back together or . . ." she trailed off.

"Or?"

"Or I need to move on and find someone else. I want what you have, Lavina. Oh, I'm not coveting what you have," she rushed to say. "You know that. I just want to be with a man I love. Make a home, a family."

"I know. And I understand. Maybe we can find a way for the two of you to have a moment alone to talk."

Mary Elizabeth grinned at her. "Playing matchmaker?"

Lavina returned her grin. "Just returning the favor, dear *schweschder*. Just returning the favor."

She set the tray on the kitchen table. "Why don't you help me make supper?"

"*Schur.* What do you need me to do?"

"The men will be hot from working in the field. Let's find something that will be lighter. I already made a pie for dessert. Peach."

"Samuel's favorite."

"David's, too."

Mary Elizabeth walked over to the refrigerator and perused its contents, perfectly at home in her *schweschder's* kitchen.

"We could make a big bowl of potato salad and add cubes of this leftover ham, and maybe some cheddar cheese," she said. "Add some rolls and the pie, and that's a nice meal."

"You're right. Get the potatoes and we'll start boiling them."

The two of them made fast work of chopping celery, onion, ham, and cheese. Lavina swayed when she turned from washing the potatoes at the sink. Mary Elizabeth grasped her shoulders and pushed her down into a chair.

"Are you *allrecht*?"

"Fine, fine." Lavina took a deep breath. "Just moved too quickly."

"Maybe I should get David."

"*Nee*, it's nothing. I mean it, I don't want him to worry."

"You stay put," Mary Elizabeth insisted when Lavina started to rise. "If you don't sit and rest for a few minutes I'll call David."

"*Allrecht, allrecht*. Get the potatoes and let's get them peeled."

They peeled the potatoes and cubed them. Mary Elizabeth put them in a pan filled with water and set it on the stove.

She sat down at the table. "Lavina?"

"*Ya*?"

"Are you—?"

"Am I what?"

"You know."

"*Nee*, I don't know." She looked innocently at Mary Elizabeth.

"Having a *boppli*!" Mary Elizabeth hissed. Honestly, how dense could someone be?

"Sssh," Lavina said, glancing at the door of the *dawdi haus*. She frowned and looked thoughtful. "Oh my, do you think . . . ?" she trailed off.

"I don't know. Do you think?"

A smile bloomed on Lavina's face. "Oh my," she breathed. "Maybe."

They sat there for a long time grinning at each other until they heard the rumble of thunder. Mary Elizabeth jumped up and poked at the potatoes. Done. She drained them, threw some ice in the pan to quickly cool them, then put the cubes in a bowl. Once they were cool enough, she added mayonnaise, the chopped vegetables, ham, and cheese. A quick stir and it went into the refrigerator to chill.

She looked out the kitchen window. The men were making their way in from the fields. She set the table, sliced some bread, and filled glasses with iced tea.

She couldn't wait until supper was finished and she could talk to Samuel.

One way or another, she'd know what to do after this evening.

Want to learn more about author Barbara Cameron?
Check out www.AbingdonFiction.com
for more information on all of Barbara's books
and the other fine fiction from Abingdon.
Be sure to visit Barbara Cameron online!
www.BarbaraCameron.com
www.AmishLiving.com

and on Facebook at

https://www.facebook.com/pages/Barbara-Cameron
-Reader-Page/359763767479635